THE END OF ENDING

A novel about baseball, beer, and love that is stronger than death

Josh Noem

The characters and events portrayed in this book are fictitious. Any similarity to real persons, living or dead, is coincidental and not intended by the author.

ISBN-13: 9798649456685

Cover design by: Josh Noem
Story part illustrations by: Molly Noem Fulton
Library of Congress Control Number: 2018675309
Printed in the United States of America

for Stacey

Praise the name of baseball.
The word will set captives free.
The word will open the eyes of the blind.
The word will raise the dead.
Have you the word of baseball living inside you?
Has the word of baseball become part of you?
Do you live it, play it, digest it, forever?
Let an old man tell you
to make the word of baseball your life.
Walk into the world and speak of baseball.
Let the word flow through you like water,
so that it may quicken the thirst of your fellow man.

W.P. KINSELLA

PROLOGUE

A whisper of breath stirred Martin Taber's chest and he began to awaken. A curtain opened in the dusty attic of his mind and sunlight streamed in. *Rise and shine,* he thought.

He cracked his eyes open but a starchy sheet lay over his face. A memory flashed through his mind: he was six and hunkered inside a fort-tent he constructed by stretching a knitted afghan throw over the lime green couch in his Nebraska home. The secret closeness confined the world to just him and the wind of his breathing.

He tried to lift his arms to wipe free the covers, but they didn't respond. So he bent his wrists to tug weakly at the white sheet that was draped over his face until the quiet hospital room revealed itself. The banked lights overhead were dark, but the new morning was shedding soft light. It was very still. He remembered he was in a hospital, and wrestled with the impossibility that the power had gone off, or that everyone had been evacuated for some threat, leaving him behind.

He focused on turning the crown of his head so that his eyes could locate the plastic panel attached to his bed. He concentrated on lifting his hand and moving it toward the nurse call switch. It obeyed reluctantly, and he furrowed his brow as he dug his forefinger into the raised bump of a button. It failed to glow, though, and he did not hear the corresponding *ding* outside in the hallway. His eyes tightened with alarm and annoyance and he pressed harder. Still nothing — his bed was not plugged in.

He looked up at the darkened lights again and evaluated his condition. His head lolled to the side as he relaxed—someone had taken his pillow. He shifted his arms, but did not feel the drag of IVs or sensors against his gown. The tubes and wires that had streamed from his chest and limbs were all unplugged and looped around the bed, loosely wrapping him in cords and bands and strips of cloth.

He tried to speak: "hhh . . . help. Help me." The most he could muster was a breathy whisper that had no chance of reaching beyond his room. All he could do was wait for someone to visit his body. He decided to focus on the one thing he could control: breathing.

He drew into his lungs an orange and amber alleluia of air warmed by the morning sunlight that was breaking through the window next to him. He let go of trying to manage the situation. The life stirring in his chest felt good.

Martin breathed and waited. He remembered being under his blanket fort and the way the honeycombed gaps in the knitting filtered the world to his eyes. His mother worried he spent so much time in there that he'd suffocate. The compact confinement relieved him of the overwhelming vastness of the plains of the ranch outside his house, where complexity continually confronted him. Every step outside was a trampling of buffalo grass, blue stem, wild rye, prairie clover, ironweed—to say nothing of the insects or the birds that chased them; to not even think of the sandy earth teeming with hidden living things. The density of life everywhere humbled him, and he needed a break from it from time to time—he needed to be just himself with his breathing.

He found that inner silence now in this quiet bed and empty room and waited.

***

Raymundo Villahermosa touched the medallion of St. Joseph the Worker that hung around his neck under his work shirt and made the sign of the cross. He had known that the day would come when they would start to notice him. The two men sitting in the back certainly weren't there for the information he was sharing—they sat through his whole presentation simply staring at him with blank looks.

There were only two questions from the dozen or so workers—all men besides two women—he had called together. He thought it would be safer to meet in small groups in living quarters, but it looked like that strategy had run its course. When he was finished with the session, he packed away the extra copies he had made at the legal aid clinic. He put on his hat, a brown and yellow Sokota seed corn promotional item. The hard plastic in the visor was cracked beneath the fabric of the bill, but the flimsy construction was actually what made it so comfortable.

Half a dozen of the workers lived in the mobile home where they were gathered, and the rest picked up their things and started to file out. The two strangers were last to slowly take their leave. Raymundo's heart was doing jumping jacks in his throat, but he knew fear was a sickness and dared not let anyone else catch it. Speaking from his diaphragm, he firmly and cheerfully thanked the crew who lived there for hosting and let them get back to assembling their meals for the next day's work in the fields.

He stepped out of the mobile home into darkness. The nearest streetlight was a block away and the moon was not yet up. The steps leading to the gravel driveway were rotting and sagged compliantly below his weight. He looked both ways but seemed to be alone. He walked to his truck parked near the front of the home. Should he run, he wondered? Find another way home? Should he even try to go home? What if they followed him?

He decided to just go through with it as though everything was normal. If they were trying to intimidate him, he wasn't going to give them the pleasure of knowing they'd succeeded.

When he reached the front of the mobile home, he noticed a dark black sedan parked behind his blue Toyota Tacoma—it was almost sitting on his back bumper, and it was running. The windows were shaded and he couldn't see into it. He ignored it and walked around the front of his truck.

The moment he put his hand on the door handle, he heard both doors of the sedan open. That's when he knew. They weren't just trying to intimidate him.

He opened his door and placed the folder stuffed with papers and a clipboard on the seat of his truck next to his lunchbox.

"Hey *hombre*," the thin one yelled with a raised his hand pointed at Raymundo. A black snake coiled around his arm in a tattoo. He seemed to be calling out to ensure he was heard by others in the trailer park. "You backed into my *ranfla*. What you gonna do about it?"

Raymundo straightened and turned to them. It was an obvious provocation. He was the first to arrive at this meeting—there were no other cars within a hundred yards when he'd parked. He decided to say nothing. There was no sense in escalating, and there was not going to be talking these guys out of whatever they were here to do.

"I said, you backed into my car, mother*fucker*!" They both were approaching him now. His stomach was a swarm of bees. One carried a tire iron.

***

More than half an hour passed before the door to Martin's room opened. He heard Maureen's voice and opened his eyes. She was affixing her identification lanyard around her neck. Her hair was still wet from her morning shower and it smelled like sliced strawberries and freshly rinsed tomatoes. She was speaking with an unfamiliar woman—tall, with dark hair and small eyes that made her look clever. The tall woman looked like she had just arrived—she was carrying a handbag and keys and a thick, paper-laden metal clipboard.

Maureen stopped short when she saw Martin looking at them. "Martin! Holy shit! We thought you were gone!"

She looked at the other woman with surprise,

then pivoted with a half hop and strode quickly to Martin's bedside to check his vitals. Her eyes darted with concern over his body as she held his arm to take his pulse.

Martin's eyes moved to her face and rested there with recognition. He struggled to pull words from the fathoms of his throat like a full-to-bursting net hoisted from the deep reefs: "You work marvels. . ."

"Martin, it's good to see you here with us. We thought you left us last night," she said urgently as she reached for a clear plastic breathing mask and began strapping it over his head. She called out loud to the nursing station in the hallway: "Can I get another set of eyes in here!?" and clicked on the monitors around his bed. Beeping and whirring started to stir around him.

"Is this . . . Martin Taber?" asked the tall woman. She was looking down at her clipboard and up again at Martin. He heard the hesitancy in her voice.

"Yes, I'm sorry, Isabel, we won't be needing you this morning. Sorry we called you out here. We need to evaluate Martin now—can you please step outside?"

Martin saw a young man in scrubs jog into view, his eyes widening as they met his own. Maureen said, "Steve, we need a read on his oxygenation right away. He was in decline when I left yesterday and at changeover I was told he passed around 4, but I have a weak, steady pulse here."

"All right, now, that's okay, actually," Isabel said, but no one was listening. "This is good news, right here. This is a good thing. The coroner's office doesn't get much good news, so I'm glad this happened. Don't you worry about it. I'm going to leave, then. It looks like you have work to do."

Martin could see Isabel standing on her tiptoes to peer over Maureen and the young man. With a smile in her clever eyes, she said, “Welcome back, Martin Taber.”

PART ONE

The Beginning of the End

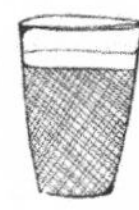

1

She's just a person who drinks beer, Bryant thought as he hastily poured a pilsner for the balding dad in line ahead of her. *Be cool, be cool. She's a person. Who drinks beer. Talk to her like anyone else.*

Fast as a street magician, he snatched the dad's money and shoved a pilsner into his hands; the man sucked in his potbelly to dodge the spilling foam before it clapped against the concrete concourse floor. After a sideways glance and a cautious sip to gain some clearance, the man finally merged into the traffic of families strolling through the ballpark.

Then she stepped forward.

Like a grazing whitetail, this one—those eyes.

"How 'bout an amber before that ump shrinks the strike zone any further," she said.

He saw the words come out of her mouth, and recognized that normal people in a situation like this responded in some way—a reply, maybe? or a nod or something?—but his brain turned into a weather balloon drifting away on the afternoon breeze.

"How, how's it going out there," he managed to say as he reached for a cup. The words manifested precognitively and came out less a question and more like a phrase from someone learning English.

"Dutchman's getting key-holed, but it's not like we're scoring any runs to help."

Reaching for a tap, his brain found purchase. What had she asked for, again?

"Pilsner, right?"

She pointed her chin at him and seemed to consider him from under the well-formed bill of the 'Beaus hat pulled down to her brow. Her eyes felt like an assassin's laser sight dancing on his chest.

"Uh—amber, please. Not hot enough yet for a pilsner."

"Oh, right—hey. You said that."

"Yes I did." Her smile was a bullet shattering his solar plexus. She must have noticed him struggling, and a laugh spilled out of her mouth as though someone had bumped her from behind. Her abundant blonde hair danced a rebellious jig in the ponytail anchoring her hat.

As he filled the cup, his peripheral vision tracked her hand chasing bills from a pocket with a shrug of a shoulder; her other arm mashed an annotated scoring notebook to her rib cage. In her pursuit of cash, her fingers pushed the white lining of her pocket below the edge of her cut-off jeans so it peeked out on her thigh.

Up, up, he told himself. *Keep them eyes up, fella.*

He held out the beer with his good hand, rather than just placing it in front of her, so that she'd have to take it from him directly. When he started to fiddle with the change, she just said, "Thank you," and walked away.

"Come on back when you're ready for that pilsner," he called after her. She kept walking and said nothing, but glanced back with a half smile. He felt his heart flop out of his thorax like a goldfish jumping out of its empty bowl.

Gram's gonna give me the switch when she meets this one, he thought. *She could be trouble.*

***

"So that was interesting," Estelline said as she moved around Vivian to find her seat along the third base line. They'd been sharing tight space in their cramped biology lab for a year and a half, so despite their height differential, at this point she rarely felt unnatural moving around Vivian. Vivian simply tilted her knees to the side and Estelline easily stepped through.

"What—the beer? It all tastes like it was funneled straight from the urinals," Vivian replied. She ran her hand dismissively through the swath of sable hair that tossed above her short-buzzed sides. Sometimes the haircut reminded Estelline of the beachgrass atop the sand dunes at Lake Michigan.

"No—the guy pouring it," Estelline said, taking a deep drink. A sweet, peaty malt crisply washed over her taste buds and left her thinking of citrus. She looked at the cup. "But this isn't bad, either."

"Okay," Vivian said expectantly, sitting up and turning away from the field to face Estelline. "More, please."

"Don't turn your back to the hitter," Estelline muttered.

"Fuck's sake, just tell me what happened!" Vivian exclaimed, standing up and moving to the empty seat on Estelline's left.

"Okay, okay—settle down. He just got stuck trying to talk to me, so there was . . . something there. I don't know."

"Well, what'd he look like?"

When she tried to think how to describe him, Estelline thought first of his eyes. Wide set and bright, they seemed to take her in with a startled expectancy, like he was waiting for her to arrive at a secret he'd just discovered.

"Attractive, but not in a square-jaw way. Earthy skin. Straight, black hair that seemed an afterthought. And he had this perfect mouth—broad, soft lips. I could see every little quiver in them when he talked. He's a little short, I guess."

"Well," Vivian grinned at her, "Lots of guys are short next to you. Didja give him your number?"

Estelline took another drink. "I'm just saying—he was sweet. And nice to look at."

***

When Bryant had lobbied the 'Beaus front office for permission to sell beer on the third-baseline concourse, it wasn't in order to meet women—he was doing fieldwork.

At ten minutes before eight every Monday morning last winter, he planted his lean frame in front of the door to the office of the director of operations for the Andover 'Beaus. Trent was the bleary-eyed, scruffle-faced manager, and Bryant began each week of his off-season with an enthusiastic handshake. He was certain Trent found his withered hand awkward, which served his purposes even better. Bryant never failed to transmit a wide smile, which usually melted whatever resistance he detected in people but didn't seem to be warming up Trent any.

Trent saw so much of him that Bryant imagined him using paint swatches to chart the fading tan line at the sleeve of Bryant's 'Beaus t-shirt as winter wore on—the coffee-stain skin on his sinewy biceps slowly rinsing into the clean khaki of his shoulder.

It went against his nature to grovel, so instead of lowering himself, he built up the organization—he proclaimed that he just wanted to be a part of the great things this ballclub was doing for Andover. He praised the other concessions, he lauded the promotional events on the schedule, he kept up on the hot-stove news of the 'Beaus Major League affiliate. And it worked: Trent was waiting for him the morning of Valentine's Day and seemed happy—relieved?—to tell him he'd been approved.

At the opener in the first week of April, Bryant was thrilled to see people drinking his beer, but he meant business—after brewing in his basement and perfecting a half dozen recipes, he needed feedback from people's faces.

He sold cups of only one size, and though it meant he would struggle to break even, he asked the same as what the concessions charged for their urine-samples. After the first week, he made the price uneven—it encouraged better tipping, but it also allowed him to see faces at the first gulp, which people usually took while waiting for their change. If he needed to buy time, he'd bobble dimes as he searched for a twitch of the nose, a rise in the eyebrow, a rise in both eyebrows, a licking of the lips—all signals revealing an initial impression.

This was why Bryant didn't mind the idea of standing here, four hours a day, for seventy-two afternoons this summer, where he could see only half the diamond (and none of it when the crowd rose for a play). This was a breeze compared to cutting hay with his uncles; even without his bum hand and lazy leg, he would have struggled with that work. He knew that if they saw him, they'd laugh—just like they laughed when he told them he was going to college; just like they laughed when he told them he was coming home with a degree in microbiology to make something that could be bought by the case at the gas station just across the state line. But he wasn't making beer for his uncles to drown in. For all the pain it caused in his life, he knew it could be done well: beer—good beer—could bring people together. So, he decided to make beer for the people of Andover, and he still had a long way to go before everyone knew the name of Black Fox Brewing. Down in his musty-smelling basement, among his steel pots and burners, he had the ambition of a mad scientist distilling rocket fuel.

That single-minded focus also sent Bryant to the library, where he immersed himself in the history of Andover. He wanted to know his town inside and out. Among his lessons was this beauty—the 'Beaus got their name from the gasworks that propelled the town into prosperity in the late 1800s.

He read through a Xeroxed copy of a locally-produced town history compiled for the centennial, and found one of the founding stories particularly interesting. While clearing land in 1889, farmer Emery Canova pulled a large stump out of the ground with his team of mules and heard a strange hissing. At the bottom of the stump hole he saw "a burping cavity about the size of a jar of peaches" emitting air.

Sitting down to contemplate the situation, Canova struck a match to light his pipe. A huge column of fire exploded in front of him, flames rocketing upward in angry, flailing tongues. Bryant read that the plume was thick as a horse and reached high as Canova's two-story farmhouse. Neighboring farmers mistook the sound for a pride of lions bellowing in chorus. The explosion tossed Canova backward with "holes a-sizzling in his hat and shirt."

The history said the burning column smelled of sulfur, and "snarled a thunderous roar." Canova struggled to gather his team, left the stumping gear in the field, and hurried them to the general store that stood at the center of the four-building settlement of Andover half a mile away. He burst in, stammering for help, explaining that he had "cracked the roof of hell" and brimstone was leaking into the township from his farm.

After the town smothered the flame and refilled the hole, they considered it for a winter, many with fervent, nervous prayer. The town elders sent Canova out through Ohio to the east, and Kentucky to the south, to learn what he could about the phenomenon. His travels revealed the discovery to be a breach in a natural gas field. Canova witnessed how other towns in the region harnessed the gas for industry, and within two years, Andover engineered a glassworks and even a small iron foundry.

In four places along each side of main street, gas was funneled into pipes that stood twelve feet off the ground and ignited. Flames danced above the street like flags in a gentle squall—Indiana's poet laureate passed through town and recorded the sound as that of a sheet being tossed and spread over a bed. The giant torches were called flambeaus, and it was a favored pastime to stroll and socialize under the glinting light after the sun went down. A black-and-white photo showed people walking hand in hand below clouds of light: the flames wouldn't stand still long enough to be captured by a field camera.

When Bryant learned this, he set out to locate the cut-off and filled stand-pipes, and found two that remained on the un-renovated side of Main. One had been used to anchor a bike rack and another one stood next to the "cow-to-cone" Dairy Bar—u-bolts had been welded to its side so summer pedestrians could tie their dogs there while they stopped for ice cream.

The centennial account explained that right through the turn of the century, people believed that the gas was simply an inexhaustible natural feature that would flow forever—part of the beauty and mystery of creation, like a waterfall. By the time the town established its first baseball team in 1912, gas production had dwindled significantly thanks to other towns in the region following Andover's example. The iron foundry had to shift to coal for fuel, and the flambeaus burned so inconsistently that the pipes had to be cut off and capped.

The history dedicated two paragraphs to Virgil Hosmer, who brought organized baseball to Andover. He wanted the game to revive the sense of pride and community optimism that had reigned over the founding of the town. He named the team after main street's flambeaus, but the moniker was shortened eight years later when the league required uniforms to bear full team names, not just monograms, and "Flambeaus" proved too many letters for Virgil's aging mother to hand-stitch.

Today, a flaming "A" stands as the logo for the 'Beaus, and though it was emblazoned on every hat in the stadium, to Bryant, one of those characters burned like a bush that was not consumed, calling him by name. He was full of curiosity and wonder when he thought of her—she made him feel cautious and thrilled at the same time. He felt like he should take off his shoes, like he was made of dry tinder.

2

Estelline jabbed her elbow into Vivian's arm with the urgency of a ju-jitsu attack.

"Ow, Jesus!" Vivian whispered forcefully. "What?"

"That's him. Second row on the aisle. Wearing the baseball hat."

"Who?" She sounded a little annoyed and was rubbing the outside of her arm.

"The guy—the beer guy," Estelline hissed. The lecture hall in the biology building was the last place she expected to see him, and the sudden sighting ignited a bubbling feeling of shock or excitement around the corners of her ribcage, she wasn't sure which.

"'Beer guy?' The hell?"

Estelline took a deep breath and turned to face Vivian. The lecturer and her Powerpoint slides had become background noise; she noticed a few nearby students tossing irritated looks their way.

"The beer guy—at the game last week? I said he was . . . interesting?"

"He's here?"

Estelline turned back to those eyes. And lips. He was four or five rows below them in the semi-rounded hall with theater seating and he was listening patiently—his left hand held a pen passively over a blank page in a notebook.

"Second row over there, at the end."

"Oh. Baseball hat," Vivian acknowledged. "Ah, okay. . . Yeah, he's cute."

They both studied him for a moment.

"Look at you," Vivian said.

Estelline suddenly sensed Vivian watching her watching him, and she felt her cheeks flush.

***

Estelline's heart was skipping rope as the lecturer droned on about caloric restriction and its impact on single-cell yeast longevity. It seemed strange to her that she was reacting so strongly to this guy's presence.

The lecture came a grinding halt at last and the crowd offered its obligatory tepid applause. A shuffling noise filled the hall as people began to gather their things and stood to leave. Estelline had already placed her notebook in her backpack and was edging down the middle aisle to get into position to speak with him, but it quickly filled with lollygagging students chatting about weekend plans.

She detoured left through an emptying row and crossed to the far aisle. When she looked toward the front of the room, she could see him still seated in the second row, writing in his notebook. She figured she'd ease into the chair in front of him on the floor level, turn around to launch a conversation, and see where things went. That felt like a safe plan—approach him directly, but leave a comfortable barrier.

Just as she descended to the third row, he stood to leave and stepped right in front of her in the aisle.

His back was toward her and she was now faced with the fact that she'd have to break the ice and navigate the conversation in much closer proximity to him and while they were both moving through the crowd to the exit.

She wasn't one to dally, though, so what the hell.

"So, beer guy—learn anything today?" she said from behind.

He turned and she tracked the widening of his eyes as he took her in—part terror and part roller-coaster joy. She felt a little guilty because she'd had the benefit of twenty minutes to acclimate to his presence and prepare herself. But it was a good sign that he recognized her, for one, and that he seemed to register the same shock and excitement in her presence.

"Hi—hey," he said, fumbling with his words and his notebook. "Yeah—from the game—amber ale, right? Yeah, hi."

"Right on—how's that pilsner coming?" She felt in control and was trying to ease the flow of conversation to let him catch up with her. She turned sideways to face him as they slowly made their way down the few remaining steps to the floor.

"It's ready—*wash-tay*, it's good," he said. "You'll have to drop by next game."

Just then, as they reached the bottom row, she took a step toward the door but the floor disappeared as her foot descended another eight inches. Her reflexes informed her much too late that there was one more step she hadn't accounted for. Her weight had already shifted, though, and her foot swiped through empty air before stomping hard on the floor. She tumbled to her right with her arms flailing upward.

Panic had its tentacles around her brain at the moment, leaving only a sliver of attention to be horrified at the dozens of faces turning toward her sudden movement. She felt like a ballerina having a seizure on stage.

But then, at the last possible moment, her right elbow came down on something firm and soft—beer guy had reached out and caught her arm in a cradle that immediately restored her balance. Suddenly she had both feet on solid ground and all the faces turned away, slightly disappointed at narrowly missing an accident that would have redeemed a boring afternoon with an anecdote.

"Holy hell!" she said. "I just about went down in flames—whoah!"

She was way off script now—this was pure adrenaline speaking. Later, she'd think back at how she approached him as a stalking puma but ended up a Labrador jumping into a lake.

"Haw! You okay? Easy there," he said as she gathered herself.

"I'm good, I'm good," she said, taking a deep breath. "Thanks for the catch—that would've been a mess."

"Sure you're okay?" he asked. "Take a second there."

"Yup—I'm good. Totally good," she said. "Have a good one." In a split-second she'd gone from on top and in control to damsel in distress. She almost would have preferred sprawling out on the floor in front of the whole room to appearing needy. At least she'd be embarrassed on her own terms. *Get me the hell out of here,* was all she could think, and she turned toward the door to make a quick getaway.

"Hold on there, lady. Careful—there might be more stairs out there," he said, stepping past her. "Here, I come from people who know the land, so let me scout it out for you." He got down on all fours and put his ear to the floor. The exiting crowd widened around him, bothered and much less interested in this choreographed charade than the live-action potential of Estelline's stumble. It felt good that he was joining her in making a scene.

He stood up and approached her with serious eyes, still holding character, and gave the report: "I think this one's gonna be okay—there's a little bump in the doorway, but you've crossed rougher terrain. Here —I'll walk you out." He extended his left elbow to her. "I'm Bryant Black Fox."

She tried to contain her smile, but a laugh popped out of her reply—"Estelline Mayfield"—like a cork jumping out of a champagne bottle.

***

"Well, young lady, you ready for me yet?" asked the elderly man. He was smiling and shuffling along with his head bent up, as though he were listening to the floor, or being carried along by the scruff of his neck like a puppy. "I'm not getting any younger."

"I know, Brother Ed, I know," replied Estelline. "You're early, as usual—ready to go."

"Ready to eat, is what I am," he said.

Estelline unpacked a scale and handed it to Vivian; the three-ring binders underneath, thick with ten years' worth of dog-eared and stained data sheets, began to relax and unfurl like time-lapsed flowers in spring. This long-term dietary study had begun before the program could afford laptops, so Estelline and Vivian collected information the old-fashioned way. Besides, pen and paper data collection meant good face-to-face interaction. Undergraduate grunts transferred the notes to an electronic database when they returned.

Estelline first met Vivian Ward two years ago at the orientation for their graduate program in biology and was drawn to the spunk of her intelligence—Vivian was unafraid to ask the obvious questions that everyone else considered below them, and she usually followed them up with a question that took the logic of the answer two leaps ahead. The girl clearly had style: she had tailored her own Levi's with a symmetrical matrix of coffee stains around the thigh that resembled a Moroccan pattern. Estelline appreciated a nerd who knew how to make herself look presentable.

At their usual spot, the folding table at the end of the first-floor hallway, Estelline arranged a blood pressure sleeve, a machine that tested blood samples, and a digital thermometer with a small box of plastic sheathes. She reminded herself of the imposing feeling she had when she first approached the ancient brick building that was home to these brothers. It looked like a cold and imposing institution—worn and birdshit-spattered statues of saints stood guard within alcoves above the building's corners and door mantles. Now she looked forward to her visits—even if some of the brothers could be cantankerous, they exuded stability. Their steadiness in this place was a banked fire in a Gothic fireplace—she warmed herself in their presence.

Over the course of the visits she made with Vivian, she learned that half a century ago the building functioned as headquarters for about 100 men who had given their lives to prayer and service. The brothers who lived there were teachers, carpenters, mechanics, administrators, cooks, engineers, and artists. She didn't understand their promise to live with poverty, chastity, and obedience, but she respected it. These men were not priests—they didn't sign up to lead a parish. They spent their days in prayer and work, sharing life as a community. Somehow, she felt welcomed into their brotherhood whenever she arrived. It felt like visiting a big family that had its own dynamics and spirit.

In recent decades, fewer and fewer men were joining their ranks, though, so the brotherhood has been aging and diminishing. Just under forty men remained, and only a squad was younger than seventy. What was once a barracks for men with thickly-calloused hands had become a nursing home.

For Estelline, the wood floors that creaked in chorus beneath the thin skin of worn carpet had a feeling of home—like a grandparent's house. The smell of sterilizing cleaners was deepened by the stubborn scent of incense and tobacco. The clanking of ceramic bowls in the large dining hall behind them signaled the preparation of lunch.

"Okay, Brother Ed, step right up here. Let's see how you are doing," said Estelline when everything was ready. She fit the blood pressure sleeve on his arm. Other brothers began shuffling down the hallway toward the refectory and the aid station that stood like a road-block checkpoint. "How have you been eating?"

"I'm eating like a teenager if you can believe it. Haven't had an appetite like this since I was in Bangladesh."

"How long were you a missionary, Brother Ed?" asked Vivian as she reached out her hand with an alcohol swab for Estelline.

"Thirty-five years. Helped villagers engineer irrigation for their fields. That makes me sound like a humanitarian, but we were basically digging ditches together. I'd come home and just eat and eat, and I still lost weight. Probably had an intestinal worm. That's what this feels like. I sleep hard these days."

"Brother Ed, where's your walker?" Vivian asked as Estelline stuck his middle finger and drew a few drops of blood.

"I realized this week that I could walk without it, so I gave it to Fulgence. He's finally up and moving." Vivian looked at Estelline to see her response, but she just smiled at him.

"And that's all we need, Brother Ed, thank you," said Estelline. "Enjoy your lunch."

***

"Take a look at this, Stella," said Vivian as they were loading the equipment back into the university sedan they had signed out. She had just tossed a small trash bag into a large dumpster next to the loading bay off the kitchen in the rear of the building, and was holding open the sagging black plastic lid.

When Estelline peered into the dumpster, she saw a stack of half a dozen walkers. Sliced-open tennis balls that had covered the back two legs of each walker were scattered across the rusty bottom of the dumpster; the fuzzy lime-green balls stood out brightly against the swirling mold-black sludge.

The biomedical research department began their long-range longitudinal dietary study a decade ago, and two months ago some peculiarities began to appear in the chemical signature of the brothers' blood samples.

Estelline noticed the first pattern, herself, as she collected blood samples—they had very lush, dense blood. She could see it—it was so richly red. Turns out the brothers' hemoglobin levels were all rising when they should be experiencing a slow decline because of their age.

Then the lab discovered elevated calcium levels. Estelline knew that Brother Ed snuck to the refectory a couple nights a week for a bowl of ice cream, but this was different. She recalled learning in anatomy that the thyroid is the gland that controls metabolism and growth, and that calcium levels are one way to measure activity in the thyroid. Calcium strengthens bones, of course, but it also key to muscle and nerve function. Men of this age should be in the 9-10 milligram range, but all of the brothers were showing levels of 12 and higher—off the charts for any study she'd seen.

Estelline and Vivian had noted these patterns, but there were no apparent conclusions to be drawn yet, and the brothers obviously weren't suffering, so they were directed to continue observations and collecting consistent data. The brothers were an effective control group: they ate religiously, so to speak; they consumed a diet that did not range widely; they took meals at the same times every day; and they did not get other outside food. And they'd been doing it this way for years.

Estelline looked at the vivid green of the tennis balls beginning to soak in the dumpster swill. "This is bigger than just their diet," she said to Vivian. "Something's changing about the brothers themselves —about their bodies."

***

Estelline liked to study in the art building in the afternoons because it was empty and quiet—most art students apparently found inspiration at night—and the rooms had wide tables where she could spread out. The lighting was good, and she could take a five-minute break by walking the hallways and pondering the paintings, drawings, and sculpture produced by students.

She was just finishing her studying and turned her phone on. A short, clipped text from Vivian flashed on her screen: *call me lab results*.

She touched the contact button to call Vivian as she packed up her things.

"Hey, it's me. What's up?"

"Just got the lab results in and there's something new," Vivian said.

"With the brothers?"

"Calcium and hemoglobin still elevated, but there's one more oddity—and all the brothers are showing it. HCS."

"What is that?"

"Human chorionic somato . . . somato-mammotropin—it's just like human growth hormone. It modifies metabolic rate to increase energy production."

"Okay . . . so they're getting it from milk, right? Dairy farmers use growth hormones to increase production—we should check with the cafeteria suppliers." Estelline asked.

"Good guess, but that's impossible —you're thinking of BST, a bovine growth hormone that is cow-specific for increasing lactation."

"So, what, then? . . . They're doping?"

"Yeah, right, Stella—they set out to dominate the city softball league. Human growth hormones are related, but they're artificial, and look different.

"HCS appears naturally in people with only one condition," Vivian explained. "Pregnancy."

3

"Do you wanna sit outside?" Bryant half-shouted toward Estelline. As he bent toward her ear and shoulder, her perfume—he detected lavender, lemon, and juniper—reached inside his nostrils and tickled something below his lungs. She nodded definitively—good call.

He'd picked this place because it seemed nice enough but still casual, and there was live music to set the ambiance. He hadn't anticipated a full band, though, and it was far too loud to be able to talk. He caught the waiter's eye and motioned that they were moving to a picnic table on the patio.

Just after they settled in, the waiter brought out the wood-fired pizza they were sharing.

"Wow—this is good," Estelline said over a sharp intake of air to cool her first bite. "You've been here before?"

"Yeah, and this is my favorite thing to order. You like the goat cheese? With the figs?"

She nodded and said, "And the arugula's a nice touch. Makes you feel like it's healthy."

"Anything that tastes good is healthy," he replied.

"Ooh, say more about that," she said, licking her finger. "What about Twinkies?"

"Once you train your mouth to recognize real

food, Twinkies kinda pale in comparison, right?"

"So where'd you learn to eat real food?" she asked.

"Gram started me out with traditional food—like fire grouse roasted with wild sage and prairie turnips," he said. "This is all back on the reservation in South Dakota. She showed me how to dig up wild potatoes and find chokecherries. Moles would collect groundbeans in their holes and when we'd find a cache, she'd sing a song to them to ask for permission to take them. And we always left a corn cake in trade."

He stopped and gathered himself. That last bit just came out—it was a first date, and he thought he'd just keep things on the surface, but he felt some kind of gravity pulling things out of him. His grandmother and his life before school were fragile and prized possessions that he'd carefully secured in some deep inner room, but here he was taking them out and showing them to her. Why?

"You grew up on a reservation?" she asked. He detected only curiosity in her voice. "What was that like?"

The trepidation he felt was overruled by a faint sense of wonder at what was happening between them. What was he afraid of, anyway?

So he opened the door and let her in. "I'm full-blooded Lakota—Sioux, some say—and grew up in Big Crow, a really small town on the Pine Ridge reservation. It's more like a few trailer homes placed next to each other in the southwestern part of the state. My *unjee*—my gram—she's still back there."

And the more they looked at his story together, the more interested she seemed. He told her about how his mom got pregnant in high school, his dad never part of the picture. He described the accident where a drunk driver took his mother's life and left him disabled on his right side. All of this was pre-history for him—he had no memory of it because it happened before he could even walk—so he could share it as matter of fact, but still, it left him feeling vulnerable.

"Gram raised me. She got me going to a good mission school and kept on me with homework and grades. And then I had a scholarship come my way and got a start on university life at this summer session in the Black Hills—and then dove into science at SDSU."

"So, why are you brewing beer now, instead of working in a lab or something?" she asked.

"I liked studying biology—it was like a new language for me. I had all this life around me growing up. Everywhere there's grasshoppers and snakes and hawks —you can't take a step out on the prairie without crushing something living. People drive through there or fly over and think it's just wasteland, but they're wrong. And biology was this new way to see it and how it all works together."

He described his first job after graduation—testing product at the ethanol plant south of town—and how he arrived at the conclusion that unless he got in with the Game and Fish department or the Forest Service, he'd spend his life in an office cubicle or lab. "That's one place to learn about the world," he acknowledged. "But I'm from hunter-gatherers. I like to get my hands dirty. And I like to use what I know to make people happy—to bring them together."

His college roommate had a beer kit he wasn't using, so, Bryant explained, he started tinkering with it and was surprised to learn that the brewing had enough science under it to answer all of his questions and more. He thought it would remain a hobby, but the more bored he got with his job at the ethanol plant, the more of his paycheck he was spending on brewing equipment. He had a knack for it—he'd just started a year ago with production on a bigger scale and was at the lecture on campus to learn more about yeast.

There was another gear to his drive, deeper down, and he paused to feel its edges, unsure if it would be sharing too much to talk about it right now. Beer had taken his mother from him, it had crippled his body—not to mention what it was doing to friends and wider family back home—but rather than rage at it or flee from it, he found a strange satisfaction in trying to redeem it. It's not what he had set out to do, but every beer that turned out well felt like fixing something that was broken. If so many people used alcohol to dull the world, he was trying to brew something that woke them up, instead.

Not yet, he concluded. He decided to re-direct.

"What about you, though?" he asked. "You like the lab life?"

"I do," she admitted. "I like how you put it—the lab is one place to find truth. I like the idea of taking a slice of life—just a slice—and seeing just how much knowledge you can wring out of it."

He watched her look down at her empty plate to collect her thoughts and suddenly felt a tremendous urge to reach out and brush his finger along the soft, sharp edge of her jawline.

"It's the precision that I like. You can study something and find real answers, but they always lead to something new—usually other questions," she said. She looked up and tucked a tassel of bouncy hair behind an ear that was already full; it fell back along her cheek. "Biology is like seeing chemistry in motion, and it's fascinating to me how it all adds up to work together in a healthy system. Like a body."

He asked about her family and learned they were from Indiana and came from factory work, but always valued schooling. When those jobs dried up, education kept the family moving upward. Her parents lived in Galena, a few towns south of Andover, and she had an older brother who was busy with a big family in Texas.

They finished their pizza and Bryant suggested a frozen custard drive-in for dessert. It was only three blocks away, so they strolled through the early summer evening, enjoying the glow of the fading sun bouncing off the storefronts. He hesitated to remark on the beauty for fear of diminishing it.

They both ordered a mountain of vanilla ice cream stacked atop an overwhelmed cake cone and sat down to race entropy, trying and mostly failing to prevent the rich custard from melting and streaming down their knuckles. Bryant snagged a small bag of dark chocolate-covered coffee beans from the counter as they were checking out and they passed them back and forth when they had a moment between licks. The crackling bitterness danced with the smooth vanilla on the sides of his tongue.

They walked back to the pizza place and he delivered her to her car, a small two-door blue hybrid. He reached out to shake hands as they parted, and she grasped his withered hand with a deliberate firmness and slowly pulled him close enough to kiss his cheek. The halo of lavender, lemon, and juniper scent around her head exploded inside his septum like high octane fuel in a racing engine, his heart valves laboring to keep up with the volume of blood gushing through them. He stood still for a moment filled with wonder, then leaned in and kissed her on the mouth. She leaned in and welcomed him, wrapping her arms around his neck. He tasted the echo of vanilla and coffee on her lips and knew that if he didn't marry this one—this mystery of a woman—he'd never be able to eat ice cream or drink a cup of coffee again.

***

"Bryant introduced me to his grandma Saturday on Skype. They have a word for blond women, apparently: *hinziwin*."

Estelline took a long drink from her beer, watching the pitcher flicking his glove before throwing a warm up fastball. The outfielders were finding their places on three bare spots in the grass like ball bearings in a child's balancing puzzle. It was the end of the summer and Estelline and Vivian were among the faithful who gathered into a core crowd of regulars who resembled a congregation, with pews for seats and scorecards for hymn books.

Estelline had convinced Vivian to commit to season tickets last year primarily for the sunshine, and they had returned for a second season. The rhythm of the game and the occasional dramatic moments of action provided the one consistent break they allowed themselves from the organic chemistry research they were doing over the summer.

"She gets a kick out of Bryant and his beer. Every couple months, she goes to Rapid City, the big town near there, and always checks for his beer at the grocery store. She's sweet. And fiery—she always tells him, 'You show 'em how it's done.'" Estelline raised her plastic cup to her mouth. "Lane's been looking for his curveball all summer—wonder if he'll ever find it."

"Won't matter much if we can't find second base. We need to string a few hits together," Vivian said. A pause, then, continued: "Wonder if Bryant's ever going to find the balls to ask you to marry him."

"He seems nervous to me lately, so I don't know."

"Shut up!" Vivian turned in her seat to look at Estelline. "I was just joking—I didn't know you two were that serious."

"We've talked about it."

She took a drink of beer then asked, "What about you and Grant?"

"It's different with us," Vivian said. She'd been with Grant for the better part of two years, and Estelline sensed they'd arrived at an understanding. "Damn, you two are on fire, though. What about your degree? You'd finish school, right?"

"Yeah, yeah. We're looking at next spring, after graduation."

"Biology and baseball." Vivian turned back to the field. "You two have anything else in common?"

"There's beer," Estelline threw in. "But honestly, the differences are much more interesting."

"Lord almighty, I don't get how you two obsess over that dishwater."

"But I love the biology of it," Estelline said. The leadoff hitter for the Selby County Whitecaps drew a walk—"dammit, Lane! Just watch, this guy will score now.

"The biology's interesting—collaborating with an organism to produce something beautiful. In a garden, you cultivate a bean stalk, you water and weed it, and it grows, and it's delicious. With beer, you introduce an organism to food—yeast to grain—and it transforms into something else entirely. It'd be like planting a tomato sprout and watching it turn the garden soil to cake frosting or something. But even beyond that—"

She paused as the next Whitecap hitter swung and pushed the ball into shallow right with a solid thump. The ball bounced and rolled to the side-wall of the 'Beaus bullpen. The half-dozen relief pitchers grabbed their chairs and leapt up, tap dancing away to make room for the charging right fielder.

The walked leadoff hitter was approaching third with a full head of steam and Estelline saw the third base coach windmill his arm through the air. The runner tilted his head, and rounded the base.

As he approached the bullpen, the right fielder jumped into a slide, grabbing the ball with his bare hand just as his feet hit the wall, which forced his body back up into the air. He landed softly on his right foot and tumbled gracefully into a hurling throw that fired the ball home on a rope. The leadoff hitter was out by a step, and both Vivian and Estelline stood and cheered, whistling loudly.

"Helluva play, Tripp!" Vivian exclaimed as she sat down. "Damn, that was pretty."

"That kid won't be here long," said Estelline. "But he's been fun to watch. He's the one I'll remember most from this summer."

They clapped a moment longer and then sat down.

"I had something to say about beer, I think."

"Magic tomatoes."

"Right . . . all I'm saying is that brewing's interesting biology. And on top of that, it creates something beautiful. We might disagree on how it tastes, but it has a spirit of sorts. It inspires delightful conversations like this, for one."

Bolstered by the play in right, Lane snuck a one-two fastball past the next hitter and struck him out. Vivian and Estelline watched in silence as Lane forced an early-count grounder to second to end the inning.

"Tripp's the one you'll remember most from this summer, huh?" Vivian prodded as the teams exchanged sides.

Estelline just smiled into her beer.

"I can see it working. He's not like anyone else I've ever met, and the guy is all-in with you, Stella."

"I know it."

"Did you guys see that throw?" It was Bryant—he was making his way down the aisle, fighting the stream of people headed up to the concourse during the inning break. His eyes patrolled his lagging right leg as it caught up with his left on each step. He was wearing Wrangler jeans—Estelline had never seen him wear shorts, even on the hottest day; she doubted he owned a pair—and a Black Fox Brewing t-shirt.

"Whatcha doin', brewmaster?" Estelline said. "We haven't even hit the stretch yet."

"I'm tapped out up there, so there's nothing else I can do. By the time I'd go get another few kegs, we'd be into the eighth and they'd shut me down, anyway. I did save one for us, though." He was balancing two cups by pressing one against his ribcage, and slowly sat down next to Estelline. "And I have a hard cider for you, Viv."

"Thanks, Bryant—that's thoughtful," Vivian said.

"What is this? It looks different," asked Estelline.

"Try it," was all Bryant said, observing her. Estelline lifted the opaque, tawny yellow beer to her lips and let the frothy cold pool into her mouth the way she let water from the garden hose fill her cheeks when she was a kid. It was like drinking a lightly toasted piece of sourdough bread, brightly layered with melting salted butter and honey. To Estelline, it rhymed with the inning: hustle-sweet like Tripp's pop-up slide, sharp and direct like the cannon throw home, and fully decisive like the umpire gathering his weight to punch his arm in the air. She turned her cheeks to the sun, closed her eyes, and allowed a half smile to settle over her face.

"Damn, B," Estelline said, eyes still closed. "*This* is what I'll remember most from this summer."

Bryant let out a sigh. "That," he said, "is the honey-wheat I've been crafting since the third inning of the April 21st home game."

With a startle of recognition, Estelline turned in her seat toward Bryant. He smiled.

"I call it 'Last Stand Blonde.'"

She gently pulled him closer and attached her eyes to his. "Well, then," she whispered, putting her arm around his thin shoulders. Her fingertips followed the ridge of the seam on his shirt to where his neck sprouted, and rubbed against the stubbly black hair on the back of his head. "In that case, I surrender."

4

"Hey, good lookin'! How'd your study go?"

Bryant was bent over the large basin of the basement work sink, his elbows peeking over the sudsy giant pot he was rinsing. He carefully lifted one arm, then shook off the bubbles and reached over to his portable speaker to turn down the country music he was listening to. He heard the familiar creak of the bottom step of the unfinished basement stairs as Estelline gently lowered herself to sit down.

"Good," she said. Bryant waited for more. "The academic part's coming slowly, but the lab. . . It looks like we're on the edge of something new."

"That's cool—with those brothers, right?" His back was to her as he worked, and he called over his shoulder over the sound of running water. "What's happening?"

"It's strange—their bloodwork indicates that they're all pregnant."

"Pregnant?"

"Yeah. . . something weird's going on over there," Estelline said.

"Well, don't you go catching whatever it is they have." He turned from the sink to give her a wink. "Ready for dinner?"

"Yes—I'm hungry." There was a long pause. He thought he detected sadness in her tone—a hint of caution and reluctance in how that came out. He waited—was a storm brewing? Finally, she said, "I missed you for lunch."

He took a deep breath—*shit*. Earlier in the day, he finished boiling the wort just before they were to meet for lunch, but had to text her to make it a dinner date so it could cool before he pitched it.

"Sorry 'bout that. Things got away from me here," he said, scrubbing harder. "Did you grab a bite with Vivian?"

"I can understand that things come up," she said. "It' just that things always seem to come up."

He stopped working, turned off the water and grabbed a towel. He turned to her and said, "Aye-ee, Stella—we both have work to do, but mine will spoil if the timing isn't right. I can't help it if I can't leave a boiling pot here. What should I have done?"

"You should've made sure you could follow through with your plans," she said forcefully, sitting up straight. "This isn't new to you—you know how long all of this takes, right? You've been doing this for a year now, and still it consumes you. I keep waiting for some consideration—I keep waiting for the moment when you prioritize me enough to get your shit together to be on time."

He turned back to the sink and said in a low voice, "I think I have my shit together. I didn't realize how essential lunch was to you."

"It is not the lunch, B—I got something to eat with Viv and it was fine," she said, standing up. "It's just getting old—you're always texting or calling to change plans because you didn't account for something or got behind. And that disrespects my time, which disrespects me. It makes me feel like this"—she swept her hand around the basement at his pots and burners and tanks—"has become more important than this"—she waved her hand between them.

"I'm trying to make this my career, Stella," he said, turning quickly and stepping back toward her. "And I'm on the edge—if I let a batch go bad, I'm in the hole. Things have changed since we started dating, you know. If we're going to build a life together, we can't live on student loans—someone's going to have to pay for—" he stopped short and lowered his head.

"For what?!" she demanded. "Pay for what, Bryant?"

"Aw, hell," he muttered. He threw his towel into the sink and walked past her up the stairs.

"See! You would never walk out on a boiling pot of wort!"

He opened the screen door at the top of the stairs and walked outside, letting it slam back on its hinges. He stood on the back stoop for a moment, then glanced back inside. Estelline was still sitting at the bottom of the basement stairs, holding her head in her hands. He took a deep breath, then stepped toward the driveway, got in the car, and backed away from the house.

***

"Stella?" The screen door smacked again as he stepped into the kitchen. She walked in from the living room and sat down at the table. From a noisy plastic bag he pulled a box of fried chicken from the grocery store—its sides were staining with grease—and opened the fridge to grab two plain bottles with no labels and white caps.

"Listen, I'm sorry things got off track down there," he said, sitting down. He opened the beers and rolled his sleeves up.

"Thanks for coming back," she said. He almost couldn't hear her.

He stopped and looked at her. "Did you think I left-left?"

"You did leave." He could see her tears welling up.

"Stella, I'll never leave you." He got up, pulled her chair away from the table, and knelt in front of her. "Look, I might need some space, but I'll always come back. This is the most important thing to me—you are the most important thing."

"I'm sorry—I came in charging for a fight, I guess. I just got tired of hearing another excuse. I'm coming to expect it, and I know we're better than that."

"Yeah, you're right—we *are* better than that. Can be, anyways," he said. "I was thinking it over at the store, and I can be better organized when it comes to plans. It makes sense you'd feel the way you do."

He sat back in his own seat. "I really love my work with the beer and I want to make it mean something here—you know I'm committed to that. There's no getting around the long hours I have to put in to make this fly."

"I never doubted your commitment," she said. "I know you want to make a living out of this. And I don't mind the hours—I'm putting in long hours, too. That's just what it takes to leave a mark. But I need to know that when we're together, I can count on us being together."

Bryant nodded his head. "Yeah, I see that. Time's

scarce for both of us, so it has to count. . . Stella, I'm sorry. I was just squeezing us in."

"Right. . . Our slots of time together are like the hops you order in from wherever—"

"Willamette Valley."

"—and you have to protect it and use it well. I've seen you with those boxes—you don't just leave them laying around out on the back deck."

They both took a long drink. Bryant fished around the box on the table for a drumstick and handed it to Estelline. He picked out a thickly-crusted breast for himself and they both slowly picked at their food in silence.

"I meant what I said about building a life together," he said. Her smile broke over him and he felt the warmth that came from standing under a sultry shower with the water streaming over his crown and chest. He took a deep breath. "We'd make a happy couple."

"Happy . . . probably. Crazy—definitely," she said. "I kind of think all that's beside the point, actually. At the end of the day, I know we'd make each other better."

This was nowhere near how Bryant envisioned it, but he believed life—or some spirit behind it—spoke to him with hints and clues. Following those signs made him feel like things are meant. He smiled at her broadly and asked, "What are you doing this New Year's?"

5

"*Bonjorno*, this is Bishop Thomas Newell speaking from the United States. I'm calling to initiate a report with the Promoter of Justice." He took a sip of coffee. "Yes, I'll hold."

Newell's clerical's suit hung on him as though he were a thin, hard-surfaced mannequin; thin, wiry glasses balanced on a peaked nose. Most bishops had size and girth—"episcopal corpulence" he remembers calling it in seminary—because they ate everywhere they went.

He knew now that the weight came with the job because of the food—it was all luxuriant and unavoidable because people wanted to honor the dignity of the office. He learned to stay on his feet during dinners when he visited parishes and charity balls. He focused on visiting tables and connecting with his people, which served two purposes: he only consumed what he could carry and eat while speaking, which was usually wholesome; and he knew that once he sat down and let everything come to him, the only people and food he received would be the rich kind. He preferred the discipline of hunger.

Newell turned in his hand the frayed business card with the number he'd just dialed. He remembered receiving it during his first *ad limina* visit to the Vatican last June. Every five years, bishops are required to travel "to the threshold" of the tombs of the apostles, and to visit the pope to give an accounting of their diocese. It was largely a symbolic visit—as though the Holy Father would be interested in what is happening in Andover, Indiana—but in this line of work, symbols are important.

He recalled worming through the courtyard in the Vatican, squeezing through bulking, sweaty bodies of other bishops and curia officials who looked down at him with surprise, wondering what urgent matter could be calling such a puny aide somewhere. A bony claw had seemingly dropped from the sky to grab his shoulder from behind—it belonged to a tall, thin priest who also seemed to be a supporting character in the room. The two of them were small tugs in a harbor full of tankers.

The priest was old—with grey curls rebelling in his hair—and Newell remembered casting him as Ugandan, based on his accent. It was a very short conversation because the priest did not cease scouting the room with his eyes. He didn't introduce himself, either—he just said he was from the Congregation of the Causes of the Saints, and encouraged Newell to let him know if he saw anything he couldn't explain.

Newell recalled being unable to command his eyebrows to conceal his confusion. *Hell, I couldn't explain the health insurance plan for employees of my diocese,* he thought. "You'll know it when you see it," old man said, handing him a card. "We're getting rumblings and are trying to paint a picture." Then he just stepped away to catch another bishop who was passing.

Newell dismissed the encounter, but couldn't forget it. He couldn't shake the man's distant purposefulness—as though his house was burning a thousand miles away somewhere and he was recruiting firefighters. He looked down at the card—it contained only a phone number.

An unhurried voice came on the line—male, and accented Italian: "'Allo, Bishop Newell. 'Ow I can help you?"

"Someone from your congregation spoke with me last summer when I was in for a visit. He told me to let you know if—when—I saw something I can't explain. Something out of the ordinary."

"Is a canonization *causa*?"

"No . . . I mean, there seems to be something miraculous involving a Holy Cross brother by the name of Martin Taber, but there is no apparent saintly intercession. And it is bigger than just him—there appear to be similarities with what other brothers in his community are experiencing."

A slight pause, then the voice lowered and spoke directly into the receiver. "*Incinto*?"

"I don't understand."

"*Ormone*—for woman with child? *Ormone*?"

Newell was silent for a moment, wondering about the significance of this statement. "Yes, exactly."

The voice clipped, "Please hold." The line was silent for only half a moment before a gravelly German voice came on the line. "Bishop Newell, *ja*?"

"Yes. I'm calling from Indiana, the United States. What's going on with this pregnancy hormone?"

"Do you have documentation?"

"Yes, extensive—these brothers had been part of a dietary study for several years. We can see exactly when things started to shift."

"Kindly fax that to us, then we have independent scientist to your diocese as Devil's Advocate within a few weeks for further study. His name is Monsignor Wagner Groton."

"What does all of this mean—what is going on?" asked Newell.

"We can say more when we see your case, but until then, send along what you have, and keep it out of *dee* news. Groton will make arrangements to be there soon."

"Who else is involved with this? Where else is this happening?"

Silence—he had hung up.

6

"The snow's disappearing," Bryant said, looking out the window as they headed south on I-75, somewhere south of Knoxville.

"This is good," Estelline said as she drove. "This is what we wanted."

He turned off the music, shifted in his seat, and turned to her. "What will you remember the most?"

"What do you mean?"

"At our ten-year anniversary, what'll stick out about yesterday to you?"

"Hmmm . . ." She drove for a while. "I'll remember all the kissing."

"Not last night," Bryant laughed. "About the day."

"No, no," she chuckled, too. "No, I meant all the kissing at midnight. When we counted down at the reception."

"Oh, hey—that was good, wasn't it? I've never seen uncle Henry kiss Claire before. Not like that, anyway—like he meant it."

"And Vivian and Grant had fun," Estelline said.

"Yeah they did—did they break two glasses?"

"Yeah and then when we were leaving I heard another hit the floor and I didn't even have to look."

"I think I'll remember holding your hands during our vows," Bryant said. "That's what I want to remember, anyway. The way your hands felt."

"How'd they feel?"

"Trembling and strong."

Estelline gave him that look, the one that told him *I'm completely serious* and *I'm having a ball* at the same time. Two short boxes, one full of blooming gardenias and the other flowering white hyacinths, sat in the backseat. They had stood as table centerpieces, and someone from the wedding party collected them and packed them in the car last night for their getaway this morning. Bryant filled his lungs with the inebriating fragrance.

"Did you see Maddie?" he finally asked. "I can't believe she stayed awake that late. When everyone started kissing each other, she toddled over to where Leo was tucked in and tried to kiss him."

"I saw that, too. It made me think . . . I can't imagine having kids," Estelline said. Then, after a beat: "I suppose we will, though? Some day?"

"I think we're going to want to," he said.

"But why? Just because it's how things go?" Estelline said. "They just come to occupy your whole life. I mean, I love Maddie, but Quinn and Mitchell just *disappeared* after they had her."

"They're happy, though. Have you heard from them? Mitch told me he already knows raising Maddie will be the most difficult and most rewarding thing they've ever done."

"Come on," Estelline said. "Maybe for Mitchell that's true. But Quinn's teaching human rights lawyers, for Chrissake."

The melting snow spilled intermittently across the asphalt and their tires whipped through the wet patches to make a cold, uneven rhythm that sounded like a sparse echo in the silence.

"Anyway, I'll certainly remember the kissing last night, too" she said quietly. "We're starting to get pretty good at that."

"Well, you know what they say—practice makes perfect." Feigning nonchalance, Bryant looked out the window and said, "We could pull over and work on it some more. . ."

"B! We've only been driving for six hours! Do you know how long it takes to get to Key West?"

"Are we in a hurry?"

She looked at him with smiling surprise. "Hm," she said in a fake pout, calling his bluff.

She turned on the blinker and turned onto the approaching exit ramp.

7

"Isabel—body found out on Hurley Road. Can you take it?"

Isabel Dupree had been a Marion County deputy coroner for exactly two years and not once had Gary entered her office, yet here he was standing in front of her desk with the suddenness of a fire alarm. Her heart tripped and blood momentarily drained from her head—this would be her first solo assignment in the field, one that would involve an investigation.

"Absolutely." It came out of her mouth without a command from her brain.

"Called in about half an hour ago—Britt's out today, and Bruce is investigating in Avon. I'm in court. That leaves you."

Gary disappeared for a moment and then returned to drop a thin file folder on her desk. "I could be there by noon, but it's located out by those worker camps, so your Spanish might be handy." He walked out the door.

"Holy shit," she whispered. She lifted her cell phone and tapped the top name listed in her favorites list: Roslyn.

"Forget something?" Roslyn answered. Isabel could hear the clatter of small voices from the daycare in the background.

"Nothing—just calling to say I won't be by today

to see Parker for lunch like normal. Should be able to pick him up at regular time, though."

"Okay—no problem. We'll bundle him up for some outside time."

"Thanks—see you this afternoon." She set the phone down and looked at her investigation kit—it sat beneath her desk unopened since she put it together after she completed her certification. She took a deep breath.

Listen to the body; hear the story, she thought.

***

In about twenty-five minutes, Isabel had passed through the city of Andover and into the undulating, fertile hills east of town. She glanced out the window—rows of dark, naked pear and cherry trees flapped by in a stable pattern resembling the slow shuffling of a giant deck of cards. What must have been fuzzy new buds hinted mint green mist among the branches.

She slowed after cresting a hill when the flaring lights of three law enforcement cruisers came to view in the shallow valley below her. She recognized two as sheriff's department vehicles—one unmarked—and the other a state trooper sedan. Their right tires sat on the road's thin gravel margin and 50 yards beyond them sat a rusty red pickup truck. Past that, the road rose again and disappeared over a slightly shorter hill than the one she just came over. They were clustered in a small glen, damp and darkly nestled within the surrounding sleeping orchards.

A middle-aged man wearing a jean jacket dangled his legs where the tailgate should have been on the dented truck—he slouched and stared at the lights as he talked to two officers whose backs faced Isabel. As she pulled behind the rear-most cruiser and slowed to a stop, she felt like a caboose latching to a train—an afterthought tacked on to the engines and freight cars that did the real work. A clutch of officers huddled at the front of the lead car, talking with their faces pointed at their boots.

Isabel opened her door and took a deep breath. The morning was still new and she could smell the dense cold air pooled in the valley. Small fingers of melting snow were still in the process of disappearing in the very bottom of ditches. The calls of birds reached into the valley like tendrils of sunlight filtering to the ocean floor, but the branches around her held no flitting bodies—all was still.

Long strides from her nearly six-foot frame carried Isabel purposefully toward the huddle of officers who turned silent. She found that people usually snapped to attention when she walked like that—even men, and even when it registered that she was Latina. She doubled down on her professional disposition and called out, "Morning all."

"Morning, ma'am," one of the state troopers said, turning and ushering her to the scene at the edge of the ditch. He was a large, solid man — his body armor vest looked like it was strapped around a barrel — but his voice sounded gentle to her, almost like he knew she was new to this. The sharp lines of his four-cornered campaign hat contrasted with the soft features of his broad face. "You from the coroner's office?"

"I'm Isabel Dupree, deputy coroner."

"Thought we'd see Gary out here—been a while

since we had a homicide."

"He's in court this morning. When was the body discovered?"

"'Bout an hour ago. You can see it over here—looks like it was stuffed in this culvert sometime this winter, but washed out with that rain we had this week. Ground's still part frozen, so lots of runoff came through here.

"The two detectives are speaking to a man up there who hit a deer this morning—knocked his rear-view mirror clean off then stumbled into the ditch. He stopped and got out to check it and that's when he saw the remains.

"I'm off, but this crew from the Sheriff's office will see you through. Have a good day, Isabel."

The huddle of officers remained silent as she stood on the graveled edge of the road and looked into the ditch. She furrowed her brow to appear diligent, but she was wrestling with her nerves. She studied bodies in her training; she was used to seeing bodies in the morgue; she had even worked alone with the bodies of people who had died in hospitals or nursing homes. Somehow, this was different—this was a place where a dead person was not supposed to be.

As she stood there taking in the scene, she felt like she could sense some kind of power—a sort of negative charge or aura—active in the ditch. She could feel it palpably—it seemed to dictate everyone's postures and dispositions. Her eyes took in the decaying body. She knew it was only half-buried organic material—not much different in essence than the fence posts marking the edge of the orchard—but she felt some kind of authority attached to it.

She recognized that feeling as the authority of death. Even in her line of work, she could push its reign out of mind most of the time, but moments like this reminded her that every living thing shared the same destiny—a return to the earth—even if this was a violent example. A heavy, empty feeling of dread wrapped around her trachea.

She inhaled deeply, wiped it all from her mind and began double-checking the process from her training that she had hastily reviewed before setting out. Her mind used a kind of self-talk to put what she saw into words as a way to note what she'd write down in the investigation report.

No clothing, no impressions around the body. Okay—listen to the body, hear the story, she thought. *Decomposition is in the dry stage. Too cold, too wet for insects. Likely frozen, but for how long? Months? Weeks? Skeleton showing through at elbow, shoulder, skull. . .*

The body lay in a near fetal position parallel to the road, deposited in dead grass and twig debris that had swept up to and around it. The way it lay reminded her of when she was a girl and built dams of sticks and mud in the gutter of her street to capture water running out of the driveway as her dad washed the car. She gently stepped down the ditch and approached the body.

The figure could have been a mummy sleeping on its side, half dug in to the earth for warmth, except for the disposition of his head, which was turned down at an impossible angle, face completely buried in mud. Bone in the back of the skull was exposed around a large crater where it had been crushed, and Isabel could see a small pool of partly frozen water within. It looked like a shell some dark, winged creature left behind after it hatched in the cold and flew away hungry.

She felt no revulsion toward the remains because she knew there was a story that made sense of whom the body belonged to and how it arrived in this ditch. She squatted down to open her investigation kit, politely circumventing that authoritative negative charge that lingered in the valley in the same way she would step around people to pass through a crowded room. The officers looking at her from the roadside began to talk again.

I'm listening, she thought.

8

"Well, young ladies, are you ready for me yet?" asked Brother Ed as he approached Estelline and Vivian's table. Estelline heard the floor creak in time beneath his firm strides.

"You bet, Brother Ed, step right up," Vivian said. "We've been waiting for you. Let's get you in that dining room."

Other brothers began to emerge from the staircase that opened in the middle of the hall, and settled into a line. Estelline fell right into her regular rhythm with Vivian, collecting blood samples, taking blood pressure, recording data.

Estelline inflated the blood pressure sleeve on a brother who smelled of roses. He was closely watching her work, and she sensed curiosity from him. "Have you been working in the garden, brother?" she asked. "Your flowers must be blooming early—their fragrance has followed you in."

The man simply smiled and said, "I was out there early, burying the banana peels I steal from the garbage —don't tell anyone. Buds are just starting to show."

"Well, you smell good, brother."

As the sleeve inflated, Estelline noticed two men —priests it looked like—standing at the back of the line. They were both wearing black suits with the distinctive white patch at the throat, and they were silently observing the set up.

"Vivian—we have some supervision today," she said quietly as she reached behind her for more thermometer sleeves. Vivian looked up and Estelline saw a puzzled look on her face. Then, with a raise of her eyebrows, Vivian said, "Oh right—I forgot to tell you that we'd have visitors. There was some interest in the study and Dr. Bowdle invited them to have a closer look. . . She didn't say anything about them being priests, but she told us we could talk about anything. They're kind of in charge around here, and we need their support to continue the study."

The line of brothers dwindled. Estelline could hear the conversation from the dining hall behind her swell as more and more brothers finished at the research station and found a table. She was beginning to pack up supplies when she heard the conversation hush and she knew that Vivian had finished with the last brother, that he had walked in to the dining hall, and that the community was beginning their prayer before the meal. The dense, starchy bouquet of bread just out of the oven filled the quiet with warmth.

"Excuse me, ladies—may we have a word?" It was the smaller of the two priests—the one whose body belonged to a poor accountant from a Christmas play, but whose eyes belonged to a battleship crew chief. A bulky suit struggled to corral the frame of the other priest —his shoulders looked like distant plateaus or buttes, and his thoroughly greyed hair, still full on his head, looked like a peak on the horizon laden with snow.

The two introduced themselves: Bishop Newell spoke with a clipped and light rhythm to match his stature; Monsignor Groton's English was staccatoed with a Spanish accent, but turned mellifluous when he named his hometown of Santiago, Chile. They explained their conversation with Dr. Bowdle and that they wanted to observe the data collection.

Estelline had never spoken with a priest before, but guessed that a bishop ranked higher; she wondered where a monsignor landed in the hierarchy. Vivian explained their research protocol, that the department had been coming here for years.

"And recently you began to found a strange hormone in the blood of these brothers, correct?" asked Groton with his heavy accent. "Something only is found in pregnant woman?"

"Yes, that is correct," Vivian said. Estelline could hear Vivian easing into a frank and candid professional demeanor.

"It is impossible these men to be pregnant, so how do you explain this? What are your theories?"

"You might be better speaking to the director of this study about that," Vivian said. "Dr. Bowdle is the one connecting the dots."

"We did, but she refuses to connect dots until data is conclusive. She is a good scientist," Groton smiled. "I'm asking what you think."

Estelline saw Vivian turn to her, and recalled the long conversations they shared about what they were observing. Estelline felt genuinely confused and curious, and sensed that something mysterious was at work in this hall. Vivian had mocked her sense of wonder, but Estelline pushed back—she was just reserving judgment.

She didn't share Vivian's conclusion, but gave her a small nod now as the bishop and monsignor waited.

They are asking, she thought. *Might as well put everything on the table.*

"The bigger picture here is that these brothers are changing—we're tracing their diet and blood data, but these are indicators of a substantial change to their physiologies," Vivian said. Estelline saw her floodgates open, and the professional frankness spilling into unreserved excitement. "If you spend enough time around here, you can see that these brothers are getting younger."

"How does one see this?" Groton asked. He seemed unfazed by the idea.

"It's been months since the fire department has had to cart someone away from here—it was getting to be a weekly occurrence. And these brothers literally have a bounce in their step—they're tossing out their walkers and canes.

"You know the evolution chart that shows an ape progressing to a walking man? I think we're seeing the man's next step." Vivian was leaning toward the men now. "There's no fundamental law of nature that says that we *have* to get old and die—the aging process is a trait acquired through evolution. Some types of cells can be kept alive indefinitely under the right conditions. I think these men—at least their bodies—are evolving past disease and aging."

"So you are saying that these men will live forever?" Groton asked. The question sat between the four of them for a moment and Estelline winced inside as she sensed the shaky ground beneath this statement. But she had no safer place to stand.

He redirected: "So why these men? Why here and now? To take your hypothesis—obviously these men are not reproducing, so what is evolutionary advantage to developing this trait?"

"This is all hypothesis, of course," Vivian said. Estelline could hear her coming down now, finding her footing. "We continue the study because we don't know. But it's possible that it is precisely because these men are not reproducing that these signs are showing up with them first."

"I see," said Groton.

"What about Brother Martin Taber?" Newell said. "Has he been part of your study?"

Estelline recalled the name from their data sheet —she had received a message about his absence. But an alarm rang in her gut about confidentiality—they'd been trained on protocols for these medical records.

"I have the full cooperation of the Holy Cross superior to explore this study and health histories," Newell said—he was reading her hesitation. "We have permission to discuss specific cases."

"Brother Martin was in our data sets until he was taken to the hospital," Estelline said. "We missed him for a few cycles, and then heard that he made a surprising recovery. The other brothers have this tone when that comes up—like they're in on some joke and are waiting for us to hear the punchline.

"I forgot to tell you this, Viv," Estelline looked to Vivian quickly, then turned back to the men. "Last cycle, I took him to the side to get him re-evaluated—we have a process to re-establish baseline data for anyone who misses one of our dates. Everything was right on track from when he left, but I had trouble drawing blood."

"What do you mean?" asked Vivian.

Estelline turned back to Vivian and explained: "I stuck his finger, but I just couldn't draw anything. I could see the stick, I could see the blood, but when I placed the slide tube on it, nothing. . . I stuck him three times in three different fingers, but couldn't get a drop."

She turned back to the men. "I felt bad—he was nice about it and was actually chuckling whenever I stuck him, but I didn't want to keep putting him through that. I figured the slides had something wrong with them. I didn't see him today, though."

"We should probably ask the superior about him so we can get him back in the study," Vivian said.

"I'll make a note," Estelline replied.

"This has been helpful—thank you," Newell said. "Monsignor, do you have any other questions?"

"No. Thank you both. It was nice to meet you and to see your good work. Thank you."

9

Riding their bikes was a cunning plan, Bryant thought, chucking a grateful thought up to his *unjee*, wherever she was—he could feel her defiance pumping through his veins with his elevated heart rate. He was feeling warm enough to unzip his jacket, though he was glad he had insisted that they wear gloves.

"What's the worst can happen?" he asked as he set his bike down in a cluster of dead branches. He liked riding his bike—it was the one activity that left him at no disadvantage in mobility.

"If you're going to jail, I'm going to jail," Estelline said, nesting her bike on top of his.

"Haw—we're not going to jail," Bryant said. "We're just taking a look."

Bryant's wayward foot shuffling over crumbled cement created the only disturbance around the deserted Tyndall Glass Factory. Cars rarely passed through Webster Road on a weekday, he knew, and he embraced the stillness of this Sunday morning that stretched itself over them like a silent yawn, even from the town's modest business district a quarter mile to the west. It was a quiet morning, just as he had anticipated.

He looked across Webster Road at the old Sherman Iron Works, which anchored the other side of this neighborhood that was founded by industry, then forgotten by globalization. Back in the library, Bryant lingered over the old black-and-white photos of draft horses pulling away thickly-timbered wagons loaded with axels and enormous boilers and other industrial parts produced here. He had read that when the gas field diminished after the turn of the century, the two manufacturers hung on for a time and then finally closed in the 1920s. The small businesses that had sprouted around them—lunch counters, secondary parts shops, a bakery—melted away. In Andover's post-war expansion, residential neighborhoods on the city's east side developed around the block. The two factories were like ancient trees in a neighborhood—too big to tear down, so the city just paved sidewalks around them and waited for time and entropy to do their thing.

"Would they tell you anything about the property?" Estelline asked, following Bryant. He led the way stepping carefully—eyes doing double duty evaluating the factory and picking a path over the pavement through dead weeds and debris. He stepped over a hubcap and a length of PVC pipe. Raccoons had torn open a black trash bag and sorted the garbage across a pile of rotting wood beams.

"Sonsabitches wouldn't even show me the listing," he said as he charged forward. With his lagging leg, he kicked aside a plastic five-gallon bucket with the bottom broken out of it and its clatter jangled between the brick walls that lined the road.

"I tried to tell them I was approved for a loan and just wanted to look at it. The guy looked like he wanted to tussle my hair and tell me to go back to my lemonade stand," he said. "Figured the perfect time to break in is when the hypocrites are all at church."

"That's ridiculous, B. I'm sure they don't see many young people like you coming through ready to buy a factory," Estelline said.

"I could see it in their eyes—a crippled Indian talking about beer. . ." he said. "Fuck 'em, hey. It's not like I'm afraid to fight."

When he had been in the library doing his research last winter, Bryant read about how the first owner of the factory, Daniel Tyndall, left Pennsylvania in 1880 as a teenager. For generations, his family blew glass bottles and jars around a growling, glowing oven built by their Dutch ancestors there. The Tyndalls fed it an unending stream of Pennsylvania coal, and Daniel did not want to spend his adulthood covered in soot, so he struck out for the clean air of the west. He worked as a farm hand, a river porter, even a teacher until his wandering, enterprising mind staked a claim in Andover by establishing a dry goods store there.

Tyndall came up in Bryant's research because his was the shop into which Emery Canova scampered in the spring of 1889, the smoke still steaming off his overalls. Tyndall was young, but part of the council of town leaders who sent Canova out to learn more about what had happened in his pasture.

When it became clear that Canova had not breached the roof of hell, but had discovered a natural gas field, Bryant could see that it was no leap of the imagination for Tyndall to understand the industrial advantages of an ample source of relatively clean-burning fuel. The store was sold soon afterward and he sank everything into a kiln he rigged to a gas well near Canova's farm. Bryant read lore about the glassworks that told of Tyndall promising his momma she could have clean white sheets, and clean white tablecloths, and a clean white Sunday dress—so the whole Tyndall clan became flatlanders to join their youngest boy in 1891.

With no cost or effort to produce fuel, the family honed their craft and grew their business. Paging through archived accounting books, Bryant could see the jump in production that came from the time Daniel expanded the business by opening this factory in 1897. Soon this building was supplying bottles and jars for the region, and Tyndall shades for kerosene lamps were fast becoming a symbol of grace and elegance in parlors across the Midwest. Their light shades became more and more elaborate through the early years of the 1900s with the arrival of electric lighting because the enclosed bulb did not produce soot that needed to be cleaned from its surface.

***

"This place—" Estelline said, "—it's really big."

She stopped their careful creeping and surveyed the factory, which stretched for 100 yards along Webster Road, golden-ochred bricks framing tall archways every ten feet. Within each arch, she saw thick, opaque glass capping an iron double door. The factory did not rise above a single story, but the roof on the end nearest town rose to a single, dominant smoke stack. The chimney was fat on the bottom—Estelline thought it looked like a giant, yellowed traffic pylon. She could still make out "Tyndall Glass" in square lettering around the base.

She heard Bryant testing a few of the iron doors

—each set was latched and locked together with rusty chains. The padlocks looked like they wouldn't work even if they had a key. They bowed and bellowed as Bryant tugged on them, but she could tell they were not close to opening. "They used these doors for ventilation—can you imagine working around a furnace in July around here?" he said.

They walked to the end of the building without the smokestack. The pattern of arched doorways did not extend around the corner—she saw instead a row of boarded-over windows. She imagined offices lining this wall on the inside.

Bryant approached the window on the far corner and tested the plywood—it peeled away with a dry, rotten gasp that sounded like Velcro. "Help me up," he said. Estelline made a cup with her hands and he hobbled over the window frame; her long legs allowed her to hop on to the sill with her knees and step in.

The small, dark room appeared completely empty aside from the dust that had snowed on the ground over the decades. Through the open doorway, Estelline could just make out the factory floor beyond, which was dimly lit through the opaque panels of glass that floated above the formation of iron doorways.

As they walked into the factory, she heard small birds flapping in the rafters of the open beams below the roof. Aside from a few scavenger-pillaged sacks with Sokota Seed Corn labels, she could see straight through the whole length of the building to the foundation of the smokestack, which widened into a wide, round furnace.

"They made glass here, but what else was this building used for?" Estelline asked.

"Not much—a seed corn supply store set up shop in here in the '60s and '70s, but all that disappeared with Reaganomics," Bryant said. "This is in good shape. I'm glad they kept the furnace—probably would've brought the whole building down to take it out."

Estelline was drawn to the furnace—it was clearly the object around which the entire building was designed. A large loop of ductwork, scaffolded from roofbeams above, lassoed the furnace and smokestack. The base of the furnace was ringed with square brick openings at chest level—each entry the size of a dumbwaiter door—and in the center of each was an iron porthole.

"These are called glory holes," Bryant explained. Estelline snickered.

"Oh, it gets better," he said. "The gas would come in through these vents and feed into the furnace, and the glass blowers each had a trough of material they kept full and molten below their window. There's no other way to put this: they'd dip their rod in, and then turn it and blow. They'd push it in and pull it out of the furnace to keep it hot as they shaped the glass."

"Yeah, that sounds R-rated," Estelline said.

She approached one of the square openings and touched an iron lever. Rust was eating below its chipping, black shellacked paint—it was cold as death. It seemed to open the whole square window on a pair of hinges.

Her eyes traced iron rods from the window downward, and where they met on the floor she saw a flat treadle, the size of the gas pedal in a bus. She stepped on it, and the rods articulated to split sliding metal partitions behind the porthole with a scream.

The hole that opened was just big enough for her face —she looked in. Wide, orange-glazed bricks lined the inside of the furnace like pavers; they turned to black as they ascended to the curved ceiling and the five-foot round chimney cavity in the center of it. It smelled like salt.

She heard a squeal of metal as Bryant opened the whole window next to hers. He apparently couldn't get the treadle to work and so he swung open the whole frame. He leaned in from his hips and they quietly gazed around the interior, imagining the work that had taken place here. "Those spouts above the glory holes —that's where the gas flowed in and fired the oven," Bryant said.

"How'd you learn so much about glass blowing?"

"Did my homework on this building," Bryant said. "What'dya think I was doing all that time in the library?

"Thought it'd be fitting to fill bottles in a place where they coulda been made. When I get big enough, it'd be cool to fire this thing up and start making my own bottles here for special releases."

"I thought they emptied the gas field a long time ago," Estelline said.

"Well, they ran out of what they needed for industrial use—they couldn't keep this furnace going 24-7 like they needed to. But there might be enough for what I need here and there—sterilizing and keeping a few burners going."

He backed away and approached a raft of pipework against the wall. Estelline heard him jangle the locked chains that were looped through the valve wheels to test them. "Something must be able to flow through that if it's locked up," she said.

She froze as she heard the low rumble of a large vehicle approaching outside. When she heard the crunch of its tires on the crumbling cement in front of the factory, she looked at Bryant with intense concern.

"Just relax—let me see who it is," he said.

Estelline heard the slam of two thick doors, and guessed it was an SUV. She heard voices, but couldn't make out the words. She stood still watching Bryant peeking through a small gap between one of the iron doors and the brick frame of its archway. Her heart began heaving blood through her body—it made a rushing sound in her ears as she strained to tune into the sounds outside.

Bryant quickly turned with hasty, silent strides —like he was walking on something hot—and moved toward the furnace, grabbing her wrist. "What?!" she whispered. "What is it?"

"FBI," he said, looking down. "They're after us."

"Bullshit," she said, but she could summon no confidence to place behind it. Bryant began to climb into the furnace through the creaky square window he opened. "What are you doing?!" she whispered loudly.

"We have to hide—they don't know we're in here," he said. "Climb in."

After he lowered himself into the furnace, she stretched a leg over the side of the window, ducked her head and eased her way in. The cradle that used to hold molten glass provided a landing below the window, and with a long stride, she had taken a second step down and was in the center of the furnace. She sat down next to Bryant, their backs to the cradles.

"What did you see?" she asked. Bryant didn't

move. He was silent for a moment with an ear cocked. Then he turned to her and whispered, "Two agents. Guns. They had a picture of us."

She looked at him blankly, not understanding.

He coughed, and turned his face away. He said weakly, "They had a search dog, too."

She began to spice her stare with accusation.

"A small little Scottie terrier," he chuckled, "but it looked mean."

Estelline cranked her elbow into his shoulder. He was laughing as he tipped over. "You're the sonofabitch," she said. "I can't believe you."

"Oh man, I had you," he said. "I had you going." His giggles were making a crackling echo inside the furnace.

"I hate you," she wheezed with half of a smile. "... FBI...

"Seriously, though, who is it?"

"They look like volunteers setting something up. Maybe a race or something. They had banners and were wearing matching t-shirts. Probably have a 5k that goes through here today."

"What do we do?" she asked.

"I don't know—what do you think?" he turned to her with a serious look. "Should we go out, guns blazing? I'm not going back to prison—they won't take me alive."

"Shut up!" she chortled at him. "I'm serious!"

"They'll see us if we leave now. If we wait for another hour or so, we'll be able to blend in with more people."

"So we just wait?"

"It'll be part of our story about this place: 'Remember when the FBI had us holed us up in here?' we'll say."

It was like sitting in a small, quiet, stone hut, and Estelline found the curved surfaces easy to recline against. Bryant stretched out and laid his head on her thigh.

"How's work?" he asked. "Any news on those pregnant brothers?"

"Not really—still gathering data," Estelline said. "It's odd, that's for sure, but not in a weird way. Just mysterious, I guess. Kinda cool to be around, not knowing what's really going on yet."

Silence settled over them, and she could hear an ATV pull up and idle as another voice joined the organizers outside. It sped away.

"What do the brothers think of it?" Bryant asked.

"Hard to say—they don't talk about it much. It just fits with who they are and what they believe, I guess, but they're not throwing their hands up and flashing it around," she said. "They're changing, but they're still the same in a way—they are who they were when we started, only more so."

"What do you mean?" Bryant asked.

"Well, take this one brother—Martin. He was part of our study, then he got sick and ended up in the hospital. It was bad—looked like he died—but then he came back. No one really knows what happened. We haven't been able to get him back into the study, so he's just kind of around—he's real quiet. The other brothers talk about him with this sincere respect. It's not like they worship him—it's just . . . he brings life to them, he enlivens the place.

"So, for example, he's always pushing Brother

Harrold in his wheelchair. Brother Harrold lost a leg to diabetes, and the staff nurse helps him get along. I started to notice that Harrold's been looking better—not just getting stronger, like the rest, but sitting up straight, looking us in the eye. Well, Martin's been helping him shower every morning. He used to get a sponge bath twice a week from the nurse, who's a guy, but still—humiliating, you can imagine. Here's Martin, taking half an hour every morning to help Harrold into and out of the shower. And then, after that, Martin goes out and works with migrant families for the day, teaching English and all."

They listened to the rustling of the birds that had made this spacious building their home. Estelline wondered if a chick could hatch here, grow up, mate, and die without ever having to leave the factory.

"It makes me think about our conversation about kids," she said. "These guys are happy, but in a really deep way. Actually, a number can be flat out assholes, but even then you can see they're tapped into something. They're not scavenging around, digging for anything. And the ones like Martin, they pour themselves out, and they seem to get fuller."

Bryant sat up and seemed to study her closely. "So that makes you think about having kids—because they'll make us happy?" Bryant asked. "What about all the independence we have? You were pouting about your friends who disappeared after having kids..."

"I guess it looks like disappearing from the outside. But with these brothers I'm starting to see things from the inside... I can see how it makes a kind of sense, I guess."

"I figured you'd come around," Bryant said, looking away.

"You did, huh?" She looked at him until he looked back, and then held his eyes.

"Yeah, I did," he said, turning his gaze up toward the chimney. "It's like investing in this building. Probably doesn't make sense to most people, but I want to make great beer for a great city—I want to be a part of this place, you know?—so I gotta go all-in. I can't fill the space right now, but once I get it, I'll grow. Starting a family is the same thing. We have a lot of room in our marriage right now—sooner or later I knew we'd wanna start using that space productively."

"I'm deciding how I feel about you applying business strategy to our marriage."

"Well, I don't mean we have to be 'productive.' I just mean we'd start to get serious about what we're about, and I think what we have going is bigger than just you and me."

Estelline leaned her head to the side for a moment to effect a thoughtful pose. "All right," she finally said. "I can dig it."

She leaned down and kissed him.

10

Isabel walked across the street in brilliant sunshine. For the first time in months, she could feel its warmth. She walked through the shaded glass doors of the grey-bricked municipal building, took an immediate right to a stairwell tucked in a corner, and descended two flights to enter the only office on the bottom floor. The receptionist, with a phone tucked into his shoulder, greeted Isabel with his eyebrows and nodded her down the hall.

After a half-dozen strides, she knocked on the doorframe of a windowless office as she peered in. "You ever notice the light in here never changes? It's gonna be a glorious day out there today."

"Bah—sunshine don't pay bills, sweetheart," Chelsea said, aiming her bifocals at her computer screen by raising her wrinkled chin. She turned to Isabel and pointed her nose down to readjust her vision. "Medical examinations under constant, unchanging fluorescent lights do, though."

"What do you have for me," Isabel said.

"On the victim out on Hurley Road?"

"Right—anything I don't know?"

"Not likely," Chelsea said, getting up and handing her a file. "Autopsy yesterday showed the obvious—death by blunt force trauma to the back of the head. I'd guess a tire iron. A few other injuries consistent with rough handling before death, but that's going to be a bugger to prove, given the state of decomposition."

"Could you tell when it happened?"

"Hard to say—lots of conflicting conditions. Coulda been frozen for weeks. Best guess is a month." Chelsea sat back down and lifted her chin to the computer screen once more. Isabel flipped open the file and scanned the summary page that sat atop a dozen freshly-printed reports.

"Where do I start?" Isabel asked.

"Well, he's Latino, for one. Mid-50s."

"That could explain why there hasn't been a missing persons report to match this description," Isabel said, turning to leave. "I figured this would point toward the camps."

"Enjoy the sunshine, dear," Chelsea said.

***

Isabel slowed her tan, county-issued Ford Focus as she approached the hill that sat above the valley where she examined the victim earlier that week. She pulled over to the side of the road and recalled the chill she felt when she first took in the scene.

She wished she could have taken it all in like this —alone, without a crowd of sworn-in men observing. She narrowed her eyes—this time it was diligence, not nerves—and held up the small, digital voice recorder Gary gave her to record observations during the investigation. She'd never used it before this case, and it still felt weird to address it out loud.

"Valley is secluded from sight on the road—maybe the only place in three or four miles that's hidden. Still, victim must have already been incapacitated —risky to struggle with someone, a car could pass by any time. Someone made a quick stop to stuff the body. . ."

She sat still, considering the scene. Her engine idled until that negative power returned as a shadow in her mind. Knowing the story was waiting for her elsewhere, she disregarded it as before, slipped the car into gear, and moved on.

***

It was noon when Isabel snapped her left blinker on as she approached County Road 40, a stream of gravel flowing southward from the orchards east of Andover. Though it was marked only by a small black-and-white sign, she couldn't miss the turn. Produce trucks and worker buses leaving the gravel on their orbits between camp and area farms deposited a permanent but ever-shifting delta of mud at the intersection.

She rumbled seven miles to Wilmot—more a center of commerce than anything resembling a town. Her eyes scrutinized a few supply stores, two gas stations, and an oversized mechanic shop for farm rigs—she was looking for a place to begin a useful conversation with someone. She pulled to a stop next to a white-bricked general store.

There were no houses or places for people to live in Wilmot—this was a place that facilitated labor. Extending southward beyond the general store sat a grid of dozens of trailer homes where workers lived during the summer picking season. A quarter mile beyond that was a compound enclosed with a fence that held a series of long barracks and cinder-block homes. Gary told her that ten or more workers shared rent for a roof to sleep under, but he also mentioned that going there now would not help her investigation because it would be mostly empty—workers were still south. Like a band of hummingbirds, they would move north in stages as the migrating sun spread its warmth and life. As the sun waned in the fall, they'd trickle back southward.

She turned down the AM station broadcasting Spanish-language talk radio and switched the ignition off. She hoped listening would help her brush up on her Spanish, but she was surprised at the trouble she had keeping up with the flow. Maybe the rhythms would help her get up to speed once she started a conversation, she thought.

She entered the store with a clank from the cowbell hanging on the door handle. She stood for a moment taking in the visual flood of food and articles that crammed the space, floor to ceiling. Piñatas and streamers hung from the rafters; baskets of toiletry items and toys grew like mushrooms in any available corner. Tall shelves displayed everything from tortillas to devotional candles to bags of charcoal.

Two check-out counters helped orient her—one to her right, in the store's front corner, appeared to be for purchasing goods and groceries. It was decorated with cell phones wrapped in hard plastic display-cases and cartons of cigarettes and tabloid magazines. A woman with a tight, short-sleeved yellow shirt stood behind the counter, watching her blankly.

Isabel could see a second counter to her left; it

was buffered by a single row of three Formica-topped tables, each set with four white, hard-plastic patio chairs. Below that counter, a glass case presented fresh food of some kind behind a thin film of condensation. A dry-erase board hung above it with a menu. She could hear something sizzling back there, but saw nobody attending to it.

She turned to the woman behind the counter, smiled, and greeted her in Spanish.

"*Cómo puedo ayudarte*?" the woman replied. Her hair was pulled glisteningly tight across the scalp to a long spout of a ponytail. The woman scrunched her cheeks to the left as she spoke but Isabel spotted the missing teeth she was trying to conceal—her right canines, top and bottom.

"*I am looking for someone.*" she replied in Spanish.

"*Who are you looking for?*"

"*That's what I'm trying to discover—I'm looking for family or friends of an older man, in his 50s, who has been missing for a few months.*"

"*Missing? Let me call Siego.*"

"*Who is Siego?*"

"*Siego will know who you are looking for. One moment.*" She picked up a dingy, white receiver and tapped the numbers by memory with long nails.

Isabel heard her explain into the phone that she was talking to someone who was asking about a missing man. She stopped speaking midway through her second sentence and hung up. "*He said he's near and will come to see if he can help you.*"

"*Thank you,*" Isabel said. She walked over to the middle of the three orange tables, pulled out a chair, and sat down. She did not like the idea of someone else deciding whom she should speak with, but decided to see where this went. She could always continue digging on her own after.

In a moment, she heard a car pull up outside. A man stepped out—she could see snatches of him through the parts of the store windows not covered in signs and flyers. He appeared to be a full step past mid-life; his gut gathered around a thick torso instead of wandering over his belt. He had the kind of thinning hair that seemed to disappear in bright sunlight—tightly curled with an auburn tinge.

He walked in and looked at the woman behind the counter. She nodded toward Isabel without saying anything. He turned to Isabel and smiled.

"*Hola*—Carlos Siego," he said in English. "Sorry you had to wait."

Isabel stayed seated to shake his hand—she was taller than he was and did not want to put him on edge. His hands felt thin and meek in her palm; his fingers felt like a lawyer's. "It's no problem. Isabel Dupree—I'm a county investigator." She handed him a card. "I'm looking for a missing person."

"I know a lot of people in this community. I hope I can help you," he said, smiling at her. He looked at her card, paused, then asked, "Have you had lunch? I'm starving. I just came from a long meeting and didn't have breakfast."

Without waiting for a reply, he turned to the other woman. "*Al pastor, por dos. Y Coca-Colas.*" The counter-woman immediately moved to the other counter and began assembling the order. The sizzling intensified.

"Your card shows that you are from the coroner's

office. I hope it is not that serious," he said.

"I'm afraid it is," she said. "But the investigation is simply to identify the deceased person. It's not criminal." She almost added *yet*, but held back. This statement sat on the table between them for a moment and it did not feel right jumping in without some context and introduction. She pulled out a small writing pad. "You said your name is Carlos? Can you spell your last name?"

"S-i-e-g-o. *See-ay-go*. Carlos Siego. I manage a labor contracting service here in town, so I work very closely with our laborers. They're good people. I know their families, if they have them here, and help them find good jobs so they can move on from the fields. They deserve more. I've been in Wilmot for almost ten years now.

"I have to say I haven't heard of anyone missing. But it would be easy to be mistaken with so many working the harvest down south. Perhaps it will become clear when they return in another month or so.

"But, take a moment to relax. You're on government, time, no? And this is my brother's store, so lunch is on us. We will work together, but first let me hear what it's like working in a coroner's office."

Isabel decidedly kept things on the surface. She told him the abbreviated story of her criminal justice studies at the local community branch of Indiana University. She steered clear of telling him anything about her recent hiring and training and explained again that her job is just to identify the deceased, hoping that he would fix on that instead of her responsibility to make a recommendation to law enforcement about the circumstances of death.

The counter woman brought out two red plastic baskets, each nestling two pairs of palm-sized corn tortillas topped with soggy stringy pork, wilting cilantro, and clumpy crumbled white cheese. A small plastic bowl held red rice on the side. The smell reminded Isabel of the 24-hour cafeteria at the community college where she studied late some nights. The counter woman opened thickly-glassed bottles of Coke, *psht*, and set them on the table. Carlos never looked at her.

A nagging worry about the meat gnawed at Isabel, so she tussled the tacos to make them look half-consumed. She stuck to the rice and asked about the farming around Wilmot—the crops and the seasons that brought the workers. Carlos volunteered a description of the camp, confirming the information that Gary gave her about it being empty now. He told her that some workers had been given greater responsibility by some of the farms as foremen—*capataces*, he called them—and lived near Wilmot year-round to help with maintenance and the lighter off-season work. Carlos offered to take her around to some of those men to ask them about her missing person.

They finished eating and got up to leave. Carlos left his empty bottle on the table and walked out of the store—Isabel followed him, offering "*gracias*" to the woman behind the counter. She only skewed her cheek—the flat eyes tracking her as she exited.

After Carlos lit a cigarette, he led her around a small loop from the store to a gas station, two supply warehouses, and the cavernous metal-sided barn that maintained farm rigs. In each place they entered, Carlos was recognized and greeted. Isabel noticed that whenever he entered a space, people knew he was there—he did not have to go looking for anyone. She thought he was doing a poor job of putting on a show for her when he waved at nearly every truck that growled slowly through the town's intersection. He hailed anyone who was walking in or out of a store with a yelp and knowing gesture. There were lots of ostentatious smiles.

He introduced Isabel and let her explain whom she was looking for. The men she spoke with all listened politely and pondered her query before responding that they didn't know of anyone who could be missing.

They crossed the street back to the general store. "I am sorry that we have not been able to help you, Isabel," Carlos said. "Are you sure he was from Wilmot? Where was this person found? Was it nearby?"

"I can't disclose anything about the circumstances—you understand" Isabel said. "I came here because he was Latino and there has not been a missing persons report to match his description."

"And so you think he is undocumented, I see. Well, maybe you could try some of the towns to the south and east. Near Ohio, there are several meat-packing plants that employ people from El Salvador and Honduras, places like these."

"Thank you, Carlos, I'll keep looking," Isabel said. "I appreciate your hospitality. Thank you for your help."

She climbed into her car, and as she set down her notebook, decided that she wanted to see the camp, anyway. She started the car and began backing out to drive through town southward. She turned the wheel right and let the tires begin moving, but Carlos was standing just outside of her door within the arc that the front wheels would make. He didn't move. She stopped.

"You came from this way," Carlos said through her closed door and window, pointing across the hood of her car toward the north-bound CR40. "That is the way out."

"I know," she said, making an effort to roll down her window to buy a moment to collect a lie in her mind. "I have a meeting in Hamlin County this afternoon."

Carlos just nodded and smiled and slowly stepped backward. As she drove away, she could see him standing still, watching her.

***

The next morning, as Isabel was returning to her car after dropping Parker off at the daycare center, her phone rang. The number was not familiar.

"This is Isabel Dupree."

"Isabel, this is Brother Martin Taber. We met yesterday when you dropped by the center."

"Yes, Brother Martin. Thanks for speaking with me yesterday."

"I told you I would speak with some of the families that come through the center, and I found some leads for you."

"Oh? What did you learn?"

"We always conclude our tutoring sessions with prayer, and after praying, I told the students I was looking for a missing person so that I could help their family, who wants to find them. These were middle-elementary school kids—I asked them if anyone knew of someone missing a grandfather or uncle.

"Six hands went up."

"Six?" Isabela asked.

"I spent the evening visiting the homes of these kids to hear the stories. None of the kids has an immediate family member who is missing—thank goodness—but when I tracked it all down, I found three missing people—three men."

"Do any of them fit my description?" Isabel asked.

"All of them do, roughly," Martin said. "They were all established in the farmworker community, been around for years, living near Wilmot, or between Andover and Wilmot. All were between forty and sixty, which means that they were no longer working in the fields, but supervising and coordinating.

"I'm having trouble getting stories beyond the fact that they're missing. The families are really tight—I can get kids to talk at the center, but rarely a parent. They are all afraid."

"Of deportation?"

"Yes, that's a constant anxiety, of course, for many of them, but there was something more intense behind it. It was more panicky.

"I asked when each was last seen, and they all clammed up. On my way out of one house, I was able to ask a young man, a teenager, son maybe, if he knew if his father might be in trouble. He skirted the issue, but I knew this kid, see, so I could press a little. He said that his dad was speaking with other crew leaders about something.

"I asked if it was about organizing workers, but he wouldn't say. He clearly had something wrapped around his axel, though.

"There's a story here, Isabel."

11

The first home game for the 'Beaus that featured an evening warm enough to be outside without anything more than a t-shirt took place four hours after graduation. Vivian promised Estelline she would meet her in their seats just off third base to resume their summer tradition. Estelline wondered if she detected a bit of a test in Vivian's invitation—as though she wondered if things had completely changed after the wedding.

They hadn't, of course. Bryant was to be vending at the game, anyway, and there was no longer any studying to do, so Estelline felt ready to relax. Graduation, dinner out—it was all a big fuss, and she was glad to be able to sit and watch someone else doing work for a while.

As they sat down after the national anthem, Estelline asked Vivian about her new position as associate director of biomedical research for the university.

"They have big plans for this study," Vivian said. "It's funny how we started with this when it was just a little pet project, more to give students exposure to lab work and data analysis, and now it's getting major attention. The NIH is in on this."

"That's huge," Estelline said. "Where will the study go from here?"

"Well, first we need someone to comb through

our data to confirm it, and then we're expanding to Dimock Woods—the assisted living home on the north side of town. One of the professors has a parent there and has been noticing the same thing we're seeing at Columba Hall."

"Maybe it's contagious."

"Dunno. . . I start on Monday, which makes for a seamless transition, I guess. I'm a little nervous it'll feel like nothing's changing."

"At least you won't have to deal with Dr. Thomas and biochem."

The 'Beaus battled the Lake Norden Lakers to an even tie through six, then busted the game open with three consecutive doubles in the seventh. At the change in the eighth, Estelline looked up to see Bryant at the end of the aisle holding three cups.

"That's my husband." Estelline said. "Still getting used to that."

"Last call," he said, handing Vivian a cup—a thin lip of foam was sliding down one side as he held it with two fingers.

"Thanks, Bryant—what is it?" she asked.

"I know you're not a fan of the brew, but this is mead—honey-wine. With a touch of hops," he said. "I'm trying to meet you part-way."

She took a sip, set it down, and said, "Hunh."

"Yeah, that seems to be the consensus," he said. "I have two kegs left up there. Can't win 'em all, I guess."

He handed Estelline her cup and sat down and took a long drink from his own, letting the mead sit in his mouth for a moment before swallowing. "Oh well. Damn shame—I'm paying out the nose for honey from that orchard east on Hurley."

"Maybe you should just call it honey-wine," Estelline offered. "People probably don't know what to expect with 'mead.'"

"I'm planning to unload this at the Celtic festival in two weeks," he said. "It'll have that antiquated, old-world feel to it there."

"What did you think, Stella?" Vivian asked.

"Oh, I've had it before," Estelline said, placing her hand over her cup.

"Well, what'd he bring you, then?"

Estelline looked at Bryant, but he wasn't giving her anything. Then she looked back at Vivian. "Water."

"Water. Like, plain water?"

Estelline turned her eyes to the field and waited for it. Bryant did the same, with half a smile. Vivian kept looking at her, then her eyes widened.

"Fuckers! You're pregnant, aren't you!"

12

Bishop Newell entered Leola's and greeted Alex. As she turned to tell her brother in the kitchen to put together a pita sampler, Newell shouted a greeting to either Haakon or Jerauld behind the grill—he couldn't see. He recognized their mother, Leola, in all of them —tall and thin; rich, black curly hair; and strong hands with ropy veins.

Newell had been coming here ever since he was installed in Andover. The Lebanese restaurant was one of the only establishments where a person could get a decent, healthy meal late on a weeknight in town, and it was four blocks from the cathedral and his office at the chancery. The family escaped Beirut in 2006, and every once in a while, he saw them worshiping at the cathedral, though he suspected they were Eastern rite. He took special care to patronize their small diner whenever he could—he knew it was a rare restaurant in the Midwest where a vegetarian could eat so well.

He'd just sat down in the corner booth when Alex came by with the platter and a tall glass of water with no ice. He pulled out the Devil's Advocate report and set it on the table. He had been studying it intensely over the past week. Its conclusions about the brothers and their returning youthfulness seemed incredible, and struggling to understand it reminded him of laboring to translate a passage in his high school Latin class.

He could only advance a sentence at a time, and frequently had to backtrack for comprehension.

"Thank you, Alexandria," he said. "I'm expecting someone else, so I'll wait to order."

"You're welcome, bishop," she said. Like her mother and brothers, she had a small mouth, so her smile made her look shy. "I'll bring another setting for your guest."

A laundromat and a tax service bracketed Leola's in a shopping plaza that was nestled around a single lamppost on the corner of Bison and Lyman. Half a dozen square tables checkered the front of the diner and three more two-person tables trailed toward the single restroom in the back. Everything was wrapped around the kitchen, which was obscured by stacks of cans and baskets of vegetables and hanging nets of onions. Newell sat in the front corner, next to the large window on the opposite side of the room from the door. A young man and woman—they looked like they could be in college, Newell thought—were the only other customers. They had finished their meal and were lingering in conversation while holding hands across the table.

He only had to wait a few moments before the door opened, and was glad to see it was Martin Taber. He was looking forward to maybe gaining some clarity —his gut told him that he needed to figure out a response plan, that this situation called for some leadership, but until he had a measure of certainty, he lacked vision. It was paralyzing—a feeling he was unaccustomed to, and disliked.

"Brother Martin, good to see you again," Newell said, standing and shaking his hand. "Sit down, sit down. Help yourself—this is hummus, this is baba ghanoush, and this is garlic paste. All very good, but we can order something more substantial in a moment. . . Thanks for driving over to meet me this evening."

Martin settled in to his seat. "It's no problem, bishop—I'm a night owl, anyway."

Newell offered some formalities and small talk to help pave the way for the point of the meeting. What he needed from Martin was rather personal, and he knew he needed to warm up to it. "How're things at the center?"

"Going well. We're gaining some tutors from St. Gregory's and they're a big help."

"When'll the workers return?" Newell asked.

"Some are already back. The bulk will be here next week, though. The kids are excited—they'll be seeing cousins and siblings and uncles for the first time in months. Hard for them to focus."

"Do you have any concerns?" At this, Newell detected a hesitation in Martin's face, but decided to let him decide whether or not to tell him what he was thinking.

"Not just yet, bishop," Martin said after a moment's pause. "We have some missing men, but it's possible they'll be returning. I'll let you know if there's a problem. We're looking in to it. Nothing definite yet."

Alex greeted Martin with her timid-looking smile and asked for their order. Martin hadn't even cracked the menu, Newell knew, so, after confirming with him, he ordered rice wrapped in grape leaves and falafel.

"If it's okay, we can just share a few small plates," Newell said. He was impatient to get to the point of their conversation. "I asked you to meet me to talk more about the investigation that involved you recently."

"With the Devil's Advocate, yes—Monsignor Groton."

"I received his report and I find it . . . confusing. The whole situation is confusing, frankly, so I'm looking for some insight from someone who's in the middle of it.

"As you know, Groton's job as Devil's Advocate is to find scientific, logical objections to alleged miracles. His investigation is aimed at raising any possible reasonable explanations so that, if indeed we're looking at a miracle, we can be sure it's supernatural, and not a natural phenomenon. The problem is, I'm having trouble believing his conclusion that this is the result of some natural process. I can wrap my mind around the concept, I think, but it just doesn't ring true—seems like a huge leap."

"What's he saying?" Martin asked.

Newell sat up straight and leaned in across the table. He studied Martin; the only sound was the thrum of a kitchen vent and the knocking of metal pans as Haakon or Jerauld cleaned up. "He said it's an unprecedented, but not unimaginably natural step beyond entropy."

"What's that mean?" Martin asked. Newell identified with the twisting exclamation in his brow, but noted that his voice remained a steady keel in the rapids. That's what he liked about this brother, he remembered.

"Entropy is the tendency of everything to fall apart, basically," Newell said. "Things get old and break. Happens with everything—it's a universal law that everything moves toward disorder. Groton argues that we're seeing the start of a new stage in evolution where humans have cracked some mechanism to transcend entropy. Or, at least, he says it's possible."

"A new stage of evolution. . ." Martin pondered. He seemed to be cradling the concept gingerly, as though it might break apart if he tightened his grasp. Whenever Newell tried to pick it up, his imagination skittered around—he had trouble getting a good grip. "How does that make sense?"

"The advocate admits that the evidence is just emerging, but that there are enough lily pads to jump from where we are, A, to you and the brothers, B, and land with dry feet," Newell said slowly, dragging the salt and pepper shakers across the table. He was keeping his eyes on Martin to make sure that he was following. "The bottom line is that you and your brothers"—he lifted the salt shaker—"are separating from the normal course of development. The advocate mentioned other examples without being specific—I think their office is getting claims like this in other parts of the world."

They both reached in and gathered small scoops from the platter to arrange on their plates. They pasted their pita with knives like masons mudding bricks with trowels. Newell considered the brother as he chewed. He was staring at a point above Martin's left shoulder as he thought and ate. Newell recognized that he was taking this at face value and examining it without pretense. He was glad to be at the point where they could get down to business—this is why he asked for the meeting, and he was ready to dive in.

"Fantastical as that sounds, the alternative is almost beyond imagination," Newell said. He was trying to modulate his voice so that he wasn't speaking loudly or too fast. He knew this was Martin's first pass at these ideas, and he was introducing another leap. "Say this evolution theory doesn't stick—what then? If this is a supernatural phenomenon, what does that mean? My mind has been going to some strange places. Could it be a sign of the end-times?"

"The resurrection of the dead?" Martin interjected with his mouth full. A spinning speck of cilantro stumbled to his plate, and he reached for his glass of water to quell a choking cough. Newell could see the whites of his eyes as he gazed intently at him over the glass as he gulped.

"Look, we've never before seen miracles on this scale before—involving dozens of people all at the same time. This phenomenon isn't just a rescue from an individual experience of suffering—like a child terminally ill with a tumor who's suddenly healed. We're used to those kinds of miracles—it's rare, but we've seen it. Whatever's going on is bending a fundamental law of nature for a group of people—and out of the blue. It's not like you guys all had cancer. You were just getting old, and now you're not. This is something untold before. We don't have anything to go on."

"But the final resurrection is a part of the apocalypse. Wouldn't we know about it—the second coming?"

"Well, no one noticed when he came the first time," Newell said, leaning back. "Why should it be any different now?

"Look, I'm not saying it is, and I'm not saying it

isn't," Newell said. "I think it stretches belief to think that Andover, Indiana would be the place that ushers in the end of time, but that's what they said about Bethlehem, too. Either way—if it's the end of entropy or the inception of the eschaton—it won't make sense that it's happening here. But sure as Sheol, something *is* happening" and here he smacked the salt shaker against the formica table top, *whack*—"and it'll turn things upside down. It's just that I can't lead until I can see what's behind it."

Alex brought out the grape leaves and steaming falafel, and both men sat back and took the break to breathe. Martin's gears were turning, it was obvious. Newell tamped down the emotion rising in him—was it fear? He'd need to examine that later. This was the moment he'd been steering toward all night, though, and he was glad to be at the point where he could finally ask his question.

"So, let's keep it small. Let's just look at our experience, here at this table. If we only consider what happened to you at the hospital—was it . . . resurrection?"

"Well, why not? I was dead and now I live," he said. Newell sat back in shock, and raised his brow. He wasn't expecting such a clear, straightforward response.

"But you know, it's nothing we haven't seen before," Martin continued. "I've been thinking of it more as a change in degree, not kind."

"What do you mean?"

"You're looking for a tsunami, but what happened to me on that table was more like a high tide. We tend to only think of dying and rising in final terms, but it happens every day, like the tides. We're immersed in that pattern, and this was my high-water mark, I guess. I don't know how else to explain it. It was new, but not different."

Newell wanted something real—he needed something he could touch and dig his fingers into. "Okay, fine—but did you really *die*? Was your body *dead*?" He became aware that his hands were tightly gripping the table top.

Martin looked down and Newell caught the hairline fracture of a suppressed grin. After a long pause, Martin said, "I don't know, bishop. I've wondered about it, and that's about as far as I get—wonder. I don't have an answer. Besides, what would it change? Here I am."

Newell set his knife down with a loud clack, but he knew it wasn't Martin's fault—if he knew more, he'd tell. He wasn't being obstinate. They ate in silence as Newell took a breath and set aside his emotions. He was sitting across from a human being, not an issue or problem. It was a fundamental lesson he had learned about ministry, and remembering it shifted his keen craving for clarity to compassion. "How are you feeling now?" he asked.

"I feel very, very well," Martin said, visibly relaxing. "My heart feels strong. I have plenty of energy—an abundance, actually. I feel like I can walk through walls, if that makes sense."

Newell didn't know where else to take this. The disturbance in his judgment and emotions required time and prayer. There was a lot riding on this, and he had to find a place to stand to find balance.

As they finished eating they talked about the community. Brother Martin thanked Newell for the meal and departed as Newell paid Alexandria. Newell was putting the receipt into his wallet as he exited, and looked up to say a parting word to Martin before walking back to the chancery. He swung around and saw no car, and no sign of Martin. He couldn't recall hearing Martin arrive or depart in a vehicle—no doors clunking closed, no ignition starting, no tires on the cracked asphalt. He just disappeared.

***

Newell walked through the chancery to a short hallway that connected it to the cathedral. The church was dark and empty—the only light that shone was the red candle above the tabernacle behind the altar. Newell sat in the front pew and waited for the echoes of his movements to die in the cavernous obscurity shrouding him. He took a deep breath.

He always found it easiest to pray in an empty church. It was somehow restful to sit still in a space that was normally so active and lively, so purposeful. He could smell traces of incense, and he thought that this is what sailors must feel like when they smell the sea from land. The emptiness never failed to exude the mystery of a new world to him. More often than not, he ended his days sitting right here in this front pew.

Tonight, his mind bounced between his conversation with Martin and the homily he had to prepare for tomorrow's evening prayer for the elderly. *There's always something,* he thought. Once a year, he gathered the aged of the diocese in the cathedral to honor and pray for them—it was a way to recognize and elevate their dignity. He doubted anyone who wasn't an octogenarian noticed the event, but was convinced it was important. He didn't realize the service would be competing with the extraordinary phenomenon he was discerning, but it wasn't going away and he had to prepare something to say.

He breathed deeply several times, trying to clear his mind and open his heart. Usually, he could find the presence within a few moments, but he was having trouble tonight. He felt something knocking to get in, so he abandoned his usual approach to prayer and meditated on the Scripture reading and on Martin's words. He lowered his chin to his chest and relaxed and waited.

The text for the prayer service came from Paul's letter to the Philippians, chapter three. One line from that reading swirled in his head: "*He will form this humbled body of ours anew, molding it into the image of his glorified body...*"

He breathed deeply again. He did not know what to think about the brothers and Martin, and his confusion there was blocking any conclusions about his preaching. He didn't know how to make sense of Paul's words in the light of what was happening. He didn't know how to explain why the Church had clung to Paul's words for generations. He didn't know if he believed that this hope that anchored billions against the swells of time and annihilation could be sprouting new fruit here—in a yellow-brick building in Andover, Indiana. For the first time as a bishop, he was at a loss for words.

He looked up and took in another deep breath through his nose. He distinctly caught the fragrance of flowers—lilies. *Odd,* he thought. *We haven't had lilies for weeks.*

Now that the cathedral was in ordinary time, the altar and sanctuary were decorated with simple green ferns and palms. There were no flowers. He sniffed again, and the scent of blooming lilies was unmistakable. He turned his head—it seemed to be emanating from behind him.

He stood up and sucked air through his nose and began slowly walking toward the rear of the cathedral. Near the door, the scent faded. He walked to the aisle along the east wall and resumed his search.

Three side altars faced the pews on each side of the cathedral, and the middle altar on the east side held a display case full of relics. As he approached this alcove, the redolence of lilies seemed to pulse at him—it made his eyes water, it was so fragrant.

The cathedral had always kept and displayed relics of the saints—either pieces of cloth that had touched the body of a saint, or parts of the bodies of the saints themselves, such as a bit of hair or a tooth or bone. When he gave tours of the cathedral to high schoolers preparing for confirmation, Newell used this side chapel and its relics to remind the teens that real people with real bodies had found holiness. It always seemed like they were more interested in each other's shoes or the windows—he usually doubted if they had heard him, but unfailingly afterward, three or four lingered at the kneelers in front of this display case.

Bishop Newell reached around the corner and flicked on the switch that governed the single spotlight in the alcove to illuminate the reliquary. No flowers were placed around the case, or even around the small, marble altar on which it rested.

When Newell focused on the display case itself, he squinted, thinking that the sudden transition from darkness to light was playing tricks on his eyes. He wiped his eyelids to make sure he was seeing correctly. The display case was full of condensation—he couldn't see through the glass.

He reached out to touch the glass and wiped his finger across the surface several times with incredulity. The condensation was formed on the inside. And the glass felt warm. It was as if he was looking at a small, velvet-lined greenhouse.

13

"B? What are you doing?"

Bryant looked up and saw Estelline standing in the hallway between their bedroom and the guest room, slowly shuffling on the wood floor, rubbing her eye.

"Oh, you're up—have a good nap?"

"Fitful—I was hot," she said with a pout. "Did you turn on the furnace?"

"Stella, it's sixty-five degrees in here—you're the furnace," he said. He smiled and raised an obvious eyebrow: "But I'd be glad to turn you on."

"How's it going?" Estelline asked. His blood was moving from clearing the guest room out to prepare a nursery, but he realized she wasn't ready for banter yet. He had cleared a stack of boxes full of books, three old Gatorade coolers he used to experiment with fruit ales, a small cubby fridge converted to a keg cooler, plastic bins full of winter clothes and boots. He wheeled their bikes into the small garden shed across the back yard. She probably woke with the bumping of the leather recliner he was moving around to get at the other sundries.

"Making room for baby, baby," he said, unable to help it. "This recliner rocks, you know—should be perfect for getting the little peanut to sleep at night. Holy hell, I watched a lot of movies in this chair—the things it's seen! Never thought I'd sit here with a baby in my arms."

"Bryant Pennington Black Fox. That chair will not be a focal point of this nursery."

He knew right then the game was up—she was employing a middle name. Early on, they made a game of withholding their middle names from one another, and, when the situation called for it, threw out a new one, hoping to strike it rich. He always had to think of one ahead of time—he could never make a name appear on the spot. But Estelline could, and he noticed that the more insistent or frustrated she felt, the longer the name got. He used it as a barometer, and "Pennington" told him that she wasn't budging on this.

"Stella. I love you. And I love our baby. I'm not getting rid of this chair. But I will move it into the basement."

"Fair enough," she said. "I'm hungry."

"Think you can keep something down?" he asked. "I'm 'bout ready for some dinner. Happy to go get us something."

"That'd be fine, but it can't be greasy. Or spicy," she said. "I feel like cucumbers for some reason."

"How's about a sammich?"

"Yes. Ham. With honey-mustard. And something crunchy. But not crunchy pickles—oh! that's why cucumbers, I guess" she said. "I'll look through some of these old textbooks to see if we can donate them or something."

Before he stepped out, Bryant looked back in to the room, just to admire Estelline, now sitting cross-legged and leaning over a box. The way her torso twisted, he thought he could make out the slightest pudge in her belly. He cast his mind into the future and pictured a toddler walking to her and falling into her lap right where she was sitting. He knew in his mind that it was going to be a lot of work; that it was going to change everything about the way they live, including her body, probably permanently; that it would cost money they didn't have. But damned if it wasn't exciting. Anxiety-producing, uncertain, confusing, unfamiliar, disorienting—it was these things, too, but those feelings all floated on a growing, throbbing ocean of enthusiastic anticipation and devotion. That reverent burning sensation was back in his belly. It felt like he was falling in love all over again.

We're turning into a family, he thought. He knew the transformation would be a sea-change, but he also understood that the sea changed without changing—it was ever the sea, just in different shape or tone or color. He had the instinct that they'd always be who they were together, only more so. Gazing at the horizon of their marriage, their family, he was overcome with gratitude—he was drowning in it.

14

After dinner together in their single bedroom apartment, Isabel sent Parker to play with his Star Wars action figures while she cleared the table. Her feet were tired, and she recalled that she needed to take their trash downstairs tonight. The plastic shell that encased the pot pie they had shared balanced on top of the garbage filling the tall, thin bin next to the coffee maker.

After the dishes were put away, she continued straightening things in the kitchen, and made her way into the living room. She saw a trail of goldfish crackers across the couch and she stopped, stood up straight, and looked at Parker.

"What? What, momma?"

"Parker, do you see what I see?"

"Yes."

"What do I see?"

"I dunno."

"I see goldfish on the couch."

"I see goldfish, too."

"What are they doing there?"

"They are a trap for my tauntaun. He ranned away."

"Parker, will you please pick up those goldfish and put them in a bucket for your tauntaun?"

"Yes, momma."

"Thank you, Parks."

She worked alongside him, straightening pillows and checking the cushions. Down the crevice around the center cushion, her hand bumped into hard plastic. She reached deeper and felt a collection of figurines stuffed down there. Lifting the cushion, she saw Han Solo in his Hoth parka, Greedo, two fat Ewoks, a stormtrooper with a missing leg, Luke in his Jedi blacks, Lando in the disguise he wore in Jabba's palace. Even that bald guy from Cloud City with the toaster wrapped around his head.

"Parker, honey, who did this, now?"

"*Capataces*, momma."

"No, Parks, who put these guys here?"

"I was playing that the *capataces* made those guys distappeared."

"Parks, this is a mess. . ." she reached a full stop. She sat down on top of the cushion she was just raising and reached out for Parker, who had his hands full of goldfish. The crackers were spilling out because his little fingers couldn't hold them all and he was dropping one for every one he picked up.

"Come here, Parks," she said. She picked him up and placed him on her lap. "Tell me what happened to these guys. When you were playing with them."

"I was playing and they were distappeared."

"Who made them disappear?"

"The *capataces*."

"Who are the *capataces*, honey?"

"They are the ones who distappeared them."

"Who plays *capataces* at daycare with you?"

"Marcos. And Reynaldo, sometimes. I like to be Boba Fett because of his jetpack. . ."

Parker kept talking, but Isabela was not listening. Her mind was in Wilmot: the sizzling taco meat she feared rancid, the cigarette smoke curling around Carlos as they walked through town, the counter woman's missing canines. Hadn't he used that word?

15

"Bryant, wake up."

Bryant's eyes struggled to open. He leaned over to see the time. It was just after three in the morning. "You okay?" he asked, squinting. "What's going on?"

Estelline was sitting up, and leaning over her legs. Her arms were around her waist. She breathed deeply. Adrenaline shot into Bryant's heart and he quickly sat up and put his arm around her curved back.

"Stella, what is going on? How are you doing?"

"It hurts. Something's wrong," she said. "I'm cramping."

He got out of bed and clicked on the light.

"I'll call the midwife," he said. "Do you want anything—a hot water bottle or something?"

"No, just call," she said.

He went into the kitchen and opened the stand-alone cabinet in the corner where they kept all their bills and records. He pulled out the folder where they had been keeping the printouts and brochures from their prenatal visits. As he opened it, two, small, flimsy sonogram pictures fluttered—one wafted to the floor. He paged through to the back pages, and found the after-hours number to call.

The on-call nurse answered, and after getting his address and phone number and insurance carrier and Estelline's date of birth, she finally asked, "What is going on tonight, Mr. Black Fox?"

"Estelline is having cramps. They woke her up."

"How far along is she in the pregnancy?"

Bryant recalled their sonogram last week was done at eighteen weeks. "She's at nineteen weeks," he said. He walked back into the bedroom. Estelline was in the bathroom, sitting on the toilet, hunched over.

"Is she bleeding?"

"Are you bleeding?"

"Yes, I'm starting," she said in a strained monotone.

"She's starting to," he said.

"What color's the blood?" the nurse asked. "Is it dark red, or pinkish?"

He looked at her, and she had her legs spread open on the toilet seat, looking down. A thin, viscous black sludge slowly stretched down into bowl. "It's dark," he said. He felt alarm growing within him, but he didn't know what to do with it.

"Okay, that indicates something serious with the placenta and the baby," the nurse said. "You should bring her in to the emergency room right away. Do you know where to go?"

"Yes, we'll bring her right in."

"Just place a towel on her seat and bring her in. I'll let them know you are coming."

He hung up and immediately began moving Estelline gingerly to the car. She walked with small steps with one hand on the wall. He sprinted back to the bathroom to grab a towel.

***

He left the car running as he parked in front of the large, brightly lit "Emergency" sign. He helped her out and heard a sticky wet sound as she stood—he looked at the seat and saw the towel has filled with blood. He closed the door—he'd deal with that later—and held her as she continued to walk with small, bent-over steps. The wide revolving door began to slowly rotate like a giant windmill as they stepped into it. When they entered, the nurse behind the counter got up from around her desk and helped them into the first waiting room. She called for another nurse to cover the front desk and entered with them. She left the door open, pulled the curtain closed, and handed Bryant a thick, plastic-backed pad. He helped Estelline onto the hospital bed. The nurse took down Estelline's information on a notepad and then left.

Bryant stood next to Estelline, and held her hand. It was quiet, but he could hear people walking with long, quick strides outside their room. Two or three people were communicating sparsely and quietly, using short phrases and acronyms he didn't understand.

He didn't know what to say. Estelline's eyes were closed and she was looking pale.

"They are on it, Stella. We're getting help—it's going to be okay," he said. "Just rest."

He looked over her body and noticed that the pad he had placed below her was darkening.

"Estelline, you are bleeding a lot—can you hear me?"

She opened her eyes. "I'm worried about Tally," she said. "I'm worried that we're losing her."

A pang went through Bryant's heart. Just two nights ago, they had agreed on the name. The sonogram showed a girl, and Bryant wanted to honor their grandmothers. Courtney was the middle name, from Estelline's grandmother. Talithakoum was the name given to his Sioux grandmother at the reservation mission school—they had agreed on Talitha for their daughter's first name, or Tally.

Estelline closed her eyes. "It hurts," she said. She looked at him. There was a dark crevice between her eye brows and her lips were the same pallor as her stone-grey cheeks.

Two nurses came in with a doctor. Bryant hastily assumed she was from India—she had ashen skin and spoke in a British accent. They examined Estelline and asked Bryant a few questions to confirm the length of the pregnancy. Nurses attached sensors to Estelline's fingers and chest. The doctor explained that miscarriage is not uncommon, but that it usually does not involve so much bleeding for how far along they were. She said they would have to perform a "D and C."

"What's a DNC?" Bryant asked.

"Dilation and curettage—it is a scraping of the uterine wall," the doctor said. "She is having a miscarriage and we need to evacuate the uterus, make sure everything passes. We need to stop this bleeding—it is a good thing you brought her in."

"Doctor—her pulse," one of the nurses said.

"We need to go," the doctor said. They started to adjust the sensor cables and lowered the bed so that it could be pushed to the surgical unit.

"Can I come?" Bryant asked.

"Sorry, no—we will tell you when she is out of

surgery and can be seen," the doctor said. "It will be an hour or two."

They started to wheel her out the door.

"Stella, I love you," Bryant said, walking next to her as far as he could. "Everything will be okay. I'll see you after. I love you."

She began to open her eyes as two solid doors opened. He could see her mouth move, slowly forming the words, "I love you." A nurse stayed behind and put her hand on one of his shoulder blades. She directed him toward the waiting room. He watched Estelline's head move down the hall until the doors closed.

***

Bryant stood in the corner of the waiting room, his head propped against the wall. He waited. He had long ago turned off the babbling television. He waited. He could not sit, and he could not sleep, and he was exhausted. He waited. There was nothing for him to do. He waited.

***

The British or Indian doctor knocked on the wall on which Bryant's head rested. He had closed his eyes, but snapped them open and stepped toward the doctor. He noticed that there was another woman with her, but she was not dressed in scrubs. She was watching the doctor, who had a serious look on her face.

"How is she?" Bryant asked.

"Mr. Black Fox, I'm sorry, but we could not save her," the doctor said.

"I knew . . . I knew we'd lose the baby," he said. "Can I see Estelline?"

"Mr. Black Fox. I'm sorry. I'm not talking about your baby. I'm so sorry—this is not easy for you to hear. I'm talking about your wife," she said. "She has died."

PART TWO

The End

16

Aurora Villahermosa couldn't remember the last time she saw sunlight through her widow when she woke up. Without Ray's heavy body next to her in the bed, the covers rested on her in an unnatural way. At every turn, she felt imbalance in the mattress. Lying there only made her aware of the cavity where his body should be, so as soon as she was awake, she got up and started preparations for the day. While the kids were still sleeping, with the world still and quiet, she dwelled and worked in darkness, waiting for dawn.

This morning, as she heated up the pans on the stove, she heard the rumble of a heavy vehicle approaching their house on the gravel road that connected it to Wilmot. Trucks often passed by, but it was unusual for one to be out at this hour. She cocked her ear: it was not passing by—the engine slowed to a rumbling idle and lingered in front of their home.

A harsh bang rattled the screen door on the front of the house, and then the engine revved. She heard the truck's door slam and dirt spit under the tires as it sprinted away.

She cautiously moved to the front door and opened it. Through the screen door, she saw a small, square, hard-plastic cooler—blue with a white top, the kind that could hold a six-pack and some ice. The bottom was gunked with mud; dried clots had flecked off on her front step. As she swung the creaking screen door open to pick it up, she heard footsteps behind her. She turned back to look into the house and saw her eldest son—her gaze fell on his ankles, which were sprouting ever further below his pajamas.

She tried to hide any body language that would broadcast the Klaxon horn sounding between her temples. She tried to casually sling the cooler under one arm.

"Miggy, it's too early for you to be up—go back to sleep," she said with a forced smile.

"What was that, Ma?"

"Just a delivery—UPS or something. Go to bed."

He didn't move. She closed the door, and turned to walk back into the kitchen with the cooler and he followed her.

"Mama? Is that Dad's lunchbox?"

"It's nothing, Miguel," she said, deepening her voice with authority. "Go to your room until it is time to get up."

He turned toward the hallway and stopped again to look at her. She noticed how his body was changing—the light from the hall rested softly on his shoulders and she could see the striations of muscle in his firming flesh. She watched the anxiety turn to suspicion in his eyes before he slowly turned and returned to his room.

When she heard his bedroom door close, she placed the cooler on the kitchen table and opened it. It only held a few things in the bottom, but on the underside of the lid, one word was written in black marker: Raymundo. She lifted out her husband's flimsy brown and yellow Sokota hat; the medallion of St. Joseph the Worker he always wore was tangled beneath it.

An avalanche of sorrow began to tumble within her, turning to anger as it gathered momentum. They were salting the wound, and the feeling of powerlessness doubled her frustration. Drops of wet vexation fell from her cheeks and pattered on the countertop.

She felt two long arms warmly wrap around her from her back. Miguel's skinny body embraced hers from behind. She turned and pulled him close. They both breathed deeply together for several long moments.

Aurora pulled back and wiped her eyes. "We need to take these things to Hermano Martin," she said.

***

When her shift at the recycling center ended at five o'clock, Aurora clocked out and hurried to Ray's blue Toyota Tacoma truck, hoping she wouldn't have trouble starting it. It snarled to life and she drove to the Andre Center.

She got out of the truck and grabbed the empty box she had thrown in the bed on her way out of the recycling facility. She carried it around to the passenger side, where she opened the door. Wrapping the sleeve of her shirt around her hand, she lifted the cooler and placed it in the empty box. As she approached the building, Martin opened the door for her—she wondered if Miguel told him she'd be coming.

"*Hermano*, they were back again."

"What'd they break?"

"Someone threw his lunchbox at our door early this morning and drove off," she said, lifting the lid to the paper box. "Inside are a few things that belonged to Raymundo. I want to give these to the investigators."

She saw Martin glance sideways around the dozen or so tables filled with children working on homework or crafts. Six adult tutors—mostly older, retired folks—orbited the tables. He pointed her to the kitchen, and she placed the box on a stainless-steel countertop and set the box top next to it.

"You didn't see who it was? Or what they were driving?"

"It was still dark and they were gone by the time I got to the door."

"Okay. I'll pass this along and will let you know what they say. Maybe there are fingerprints," he said. "I'll make sure it gets back to you, though."

She felt grateful that he understood the importance of these items to her, so she smiled and nodded at him.

"Must have been a shock to receive this."

"It was a hard day. Every day he's gone is hard," she said, looking down. "The worst part is that no one talks about him. Normally, when someone dies, people gather around. Everyone's keeping their heads down, though, picking in their own row, you know? No one talks about him, even though he was . . ."

She kept her head lowered, and wiped her cheek with one hand. She was surprised that Brother Martin was handing her a tissue—did he keep some on him at all times? She was grateful that he did not fill the quiet space between them—this was the one place where the silence was not oppressive.

Gathering herself, she said, "I worry for the kids."

"Miguel's a real leader," he said. "He watches out for Gabriel, who works hard, and especially Rafa—he doesn't let anyone tease Rafa. Little Maria doesn't need anyone to help her, though—she's going to be mayor one day. I think they're all doing very well, considering."

Aurora smiled at that, but only to show him that she received his encouragement. Below the surface, her heart was crumbling into a dark sinkhole.

***

"Isabel—someone here to see you," rang the receptionist's voice through the phone. "A Martin Taber."

"Be right there," she said. She pressed the disconnect button on the phone and paused, wondering what brought him here.

She left her office and turned down the hallway, where she saw him standing next to the front desk holding a box of printer paper. She shook his hand warmly and welcomed him back to her office, where she closed the door.

"*Hola*, brother — what can I do for you?"

"This was tossed at Aurora Villahermosa's house early yesterday morning," he said, opening the paper box. She stepped closer to look inside and saw a dirty, hand-sized blue and white cooler. "It's a lunchbox, and inside are a hat and a medallion. Aurora recognizes them as Raymundo's. She thought it might help the investigation—maybe there are fingerprints."

"These people aren't stupid," Isabel said as she put on some purple latex gloves and picked up the box. "They wouldn't be giving the victim's family something that could point back at them. Did she notice anything about who delivered it?"

"It was too early—still dark, she said."

"It's an odd thing to do out of the blue..."

Martin sat down and leaned his long elbows on his bony knees. "The randomness is part of it—they're reminding her who's in charge, that they're always watching."

Isabel filled her cheeks and let out a burst of air as she considered this. She leaned back in her chair and said, "Martin, I gotta be honest with you. I've handed this case on to detectives, with a strong recommendation to investigate these *cabrones*—sorry, 'bullies'—but it isn't going anywhere. Unless they were sloppy with this, we don't have any hard evidence. And no one who witnessed anything will talk."

She looked in his face pleadingly, but he looked down.

"The other two families aren't even here anymore—they're gone..." She didn't want to send Martin away empty-handed—he had done a lot for her in making the identifications and tracking down the families.

"Tell you what, I'll take these to forensics, just to see if we can find anything of interest here at all—fingerprints, hair fibers, whatever. I'm not hopeful, but I'll let you know if we find something."

"Thank you," he said, standing up. "Can we be sure to get the items back—they mean a lot to Aurora."

17

Vivian directed Grant to Bryant's house and when he pulled into the driveway and turned off the car, she took a deep breath.

"You okay?" Grant asked.

"Yeah, it's just not going to be easy. I have no idea what he'll be like."

"Want me to come in?"

"Nah, I think more people will overwhelm him. Thanks though."

"Okay. Just let me know when you're done and I'll zip on back. I can pick up some food if you think it'd help."

"Thanks, babe. You're the best." She leaned over and gave him a quick kiss, then got out and walked up the few small steps to the front door, suppressing her own grief and distress. She didn't think Bryant would be hysterical—he didn't seem the type to lose his head like that—but she wasn't sure. This was uncharted territory.

She knocked before turning the knob and entering. "Hello? Bryant? Are you here?"

"In the bedroom," she heard him state flatly. The sound came from the end of the hallway that extended out to the right from the living room she had just stepped into. For all the time she had spent in that house, she had never seen the bedroom.

Knowing that she'd find immense grief at the end of that hallway made it difficult to move her body there—she might have been walking underwater. When she reached the end and looked through the bedroom door, she saw Bryant, half sitting, half leaning on the bed, surrounded by Estelline's clothes, some folded in stacks, some strewn about. A single reading lamp was on in the corner. He turned his head to her, and his eyes looked like empty wells full of dark, still water.

She felt grief fall upon her and turned in to the doorframe, leaning her face into it, and covered her eyes with her hands. From the moment she received Bryant's call, Estelline's death wrenched her, but now she felt most keenly the finality of the loss—this is where Stella belonged: here, in this room, with him. Her death was like a conviction, an unfair punishment from an implacable judge, and Vivian felt its irrevocability. Estelline was gone and she wasn't coming back.

When the wave of sorrow passed, Vivian looked to Bryant. He was still in his half-slouch against the bed, ashen-faced. His emotions were already spent—she could see that he had been wrestling with anguish and had lost; he had nothing left. She saw his chest moving with slow huffs—a full two seconds passed between each breath, and she could hear the air tumbling out of his body when he exhaled. He looked tired.

She got up and cleared a spot next to him. They both sat there for a long moment, looking at the open, gutted closet. She simply shared the room with him.

Finally, she straightened and started folding the strewn clothes and adding them to the piles on the bed. "What did you see?" she asked quietly.

Bryant looked at his hands. "When they told

me in the waiting room, I had trouble understanding. I could hear the words coming out of their mouths—and I knew what the words meant individually—it just didn't make sense. It was like they were speaking a language I was just learning: I knew the vocabulary but not the grammar. Something went wrong with Estelline, but all the doctor said was that she was gone. Gone where? I kept wondering. How could she be gone? Why would she leave without me?"

He was talking in a low, deliberate tone, as though he had told this story to her a hundred times already.

"Then the doctor told me that she had died—'Estelline has died,' she said. I suppose I should've seen it coming, at least to fear it, but honest to God it just dropped me. I felt like one of those boxers getting knocked out cold—I was fighting, searching, struggling, then the punch connected and it was lights-out."

Twenty seconds of silence passed between them.

"I didn't believe her. I demanded to see her. They said that the coroner needed to inspect the body, so I could look at her but not touch her. Protocol for anytime there is the possibility of a 'self-induced abortion,' which is in-*fucking*-sane. The whole goddamned thing's insane.

"They took me to the operating room. Big light above a table that was covered with a green paper sheet. All the machines had been cleared to the walls. It was really quiet.

"The social worker pulled back the sheet, and there she was. Still as can be. IVs still attached to her arms, but all the tubes and wires just dangled to the floor. That's when this fear clenched me by the throat—

like a wicked wolf. I said her name and she didn't even twitch. Like I was talking to a stone."

Vivian put her arm through his and clasped his hand. She had never touched his right hand before—he always led with his left because of his disability. Even though it was small and bent, it felt soft and warm.

"They said that after the inspection, she'd be taken to a funeral home and that I could work with the mortician to spend time with her. They said I should bring clothes for her funer . . ." He broke off. Rivulets fell from his eyes, but his face remained still. He wiped his cheeks and took a breath and continued: "funeral. So I am picking out the clothes she's to be buried in."

"I can't believe how much it hurts," Vivian said. Again, they sat in silence, staring at the closet, eviscerated.

***

The parking lot for the Monroe Funeral Home was empty when Bryant pulled in with Vivian. It was a long, one-story building, and when they entered the enormous doors under the porte-cochere, the first thing Bryant noticed about the funeral home was the scent. It reminded him of the clean, sanitary smell of the hospital, only more antiseptic. Large ferns greened every corner he could see and it seemed a paradox that they were growing in such a sterile setting. It felt like a lab-grown jungle.

The funeral home director was ready for them—Bryant guessed him to be in his late 50s. He had a full mane of neatly-cut white hair and offered a firm hand; he looked into their eyes and spoke very clearly. They confirmed that they were carrying Estelline's clothes, and he thanked them for coming.

Bryant let Vivian step behind the director first as he showed them past the viewing halls to the preparation room. Before he opened the door, he explained that when they entered, they would find "the body" on a table. Bryant bristled at the phrase—it seemed to put Estelline in a jar of formaldehyde. The remains had been embalmed, the director said, and they could spend as much time as they needed to prepare it for the services tomorrow.

He opened the door and motioned with his arm inside, letting them pass. He closed the door behind them.

A harsh, blue light met Bryant's eyes as they adjusted from the soft, subdued lighting in the viewing areas they just passed through. They were standing at the end of a long work area that was divided into two halves by a low countertop. In the center of each workspace stood a stainless-steel table surrounded by white cabinets.

He sensed Estelline's figure before he saw her face—he recognized the outline of her form below the white sheet that covered it. His own body filled with longing—he knew that this was one of the last times he would see her body, and yet it was so diminished. It was a husk, a shell.

"I'm really grateful for your help," Bryant said to Vivian as they approached the table. "I wouldn't have been able to do this alone—for a number of reasons."

"It is an honor. I really feel that way," Vivian said. "Didn't her mom want to do this?"

"She's just overwhelmed," Bryant said. "She'll

spend some time with her after we've gotten her ready. You're the only one who knows how she would've wanted her hair, how she would've wanted her makeup."

They looked at her for a moment. "She looks good," Vivian said with a trailing whine—Bryant saw that her chin was trembling. She sniffled loudly and sighed. "She was such a beautiful person."

Bryant approached Estelline's body and leaned down to place his head near hers. He stroked her hair—it had been washed, and fell back from her face sharply, giving her a severe look. How he wanted her to open her eyes, for a smile to color her countenance. He kissed her in the corner where her cheek met her mouth, and her skin felt cold on his lips, as though he had set his mouth on the seam of a leather couch.

All of the chaos that entered his life that night at the hospital—the phone calls to tell family, the report from the coroner, insurance companies calling, funeral arrangements—it all made him tremble. Everything depended upon him, and yet nothing mattered. He was a child lost in a blizzard, disoriented and afraid.

But here, with her body, he felt a calm seeping in. Her body anchored him—if he was no longer able to love and honor her in life, he was resolved to love and honor her body. He'd figure out the rest later.

Vivian went back and forth on a few different outfits, but when Bryant thought of her wedding dress, it was the only thing that made any sense to him.

They pulled the sheet back slowly, revealing Estelline's naked body. It was so white, Bryant thought. Vivian was not crying or sobbing, but Bryant felt pity when he saw the tears falling from her eyes. He remembered that she had lost a dear friend.

Perhaps it was his *unjee's* influence that gave him tranquility here. She had opened his eyes to the cycles of the natural world. Every year, she purchased a hunting license to stock venison for stew throughout the winter. He remembered visiting once and seeing the carcass of a deer hanging in the tree outside of her house. She called him over and he marveled at the size of the body cavity—as a boy, he could have fit inside. He remembers her explaining that it was simply flesh and bone, and that the spirit of the animal—what it was that made it real and alive—was gone. We respect and honor the body as a way to give thanks, she told him. It was a mystery that never left him.

They dressed Estelline's body with the simple wool skirt and long white sweater she wore for their wedding. Bryant cradled her limp neck and head so that it didn't roll too sharply. As they placed each layer of clothing over her sagging limbs, they restored her joints to a natural, resting position before proceeding. To get the skirt beneath her torso, Bryant wrapped Estelline's arms around his neck, embraced her, and lifted. It reminded him of their dance at the reception, but his grasp on her now was one-sided. He was holding her flesh and bones, and that was all.

He pointed out to Vivian the pale champagne stain in the lower left hem of the sweater, and held Estelline's cool hand as she dressed her hair and applied makeup. Vivian told him that they had talked about his pickup truck while she helped Estelline with these cosmetics on their wedding day. Estelline said that she had never imagined being with a man who owned a pickup truck.

***

Vivian held on to Grant's bulky arm at the funeral, three rows back from Bryant's slender, slumped frame in the front row. Estelline's parents sat on the other side of the room, and a clan of thirty or forty of the extended Mayfield family members clustered around them. People on Bryant's side of the aisle were widely spaced and scattered—mostly local friends and colleagues.

The service itself was brief, and though Vivian knew this was the last time she would see Estelline, she was trying not to make the image of her in the casket an indelible memory. She was trying to grasp and hold the living impressions she could call to mind: Estelline bracing her arms on the passenger-side dashboard as she laughed too hard; Estelline flashing a "can you believe this shit" look at her during class; Estelline studying Bryant as he told a story.

It was a short ride from the funeral home to the cemetery on a bright, sunny, Wednesday morning. The cars they passed slowed and pulled to the side out of respect, and Vivian felt grateful for the gesture.

Grant was driving slowly through a red light as part of the funeral procession, and asked, "Do you have a sense of how Bryant's doing with all this? Doesn't look like he has much family." It was the first time Vivian had seen Grant in a suit, and it didn't fit him well; his coat stretched tightly across the shoulders and seemed to oppress the arm that reached to the steering wheel.

"Bryant's family is mostly out West, but looks like some of them made it," Vivian said. "He's pretty quiet, so it's hard to say how he'll come through this."

"I feel for the guy. I hope he's okay. There's a lot of living ahead of him," Grant said. "Time heals."

"Sometimes it just pushes things into the past, but that doesn't always make them less painful," Vivian replied. "Sometimes you just grow accustomed to how much it hurts."

The cemetery came into view.

"I'm going to have to check in on him from time to time, I think," Vivian said. "I owe her that."

***

Standing in front of the huddle of darkly-clad mourners at the gravesite, Bryant wondered if this is what it felt like to have a threatening disease—people exuding pity and concern, but keeping a sterile distance. Maybe some of his ancestors felt this way standing in line at the agency with the blistered rash of small pox beginning to appear on their faces.

The minister's voice was matched by songbirds darting in the large blue spruce standing behind him. Bryant could hear the dim hum of traffic around him and felt offended that people would be going about their Wednesday as though nothing extraordinary was happening—as though it was a perfectly fine day to shop for shoes or pick up a prescription or drop off mail.

At the conclusion, people slowly dispersed with their heads down. The men gravitated toward other men and shook hands as they walked back to their cars. Bryant glimpsed Vivian stepping through the departing crowd toward the grave, where he remained.

She wrapped him in a hug, and he was thankful for the touch, but he did not feel like reciprocating. She remained silent and watched Estelline's parents set a bouquet of flowers on the closed casket. They turned to leave with the minister.

"C'mon, Bryant—I'll stand with you at the reception."

"I'm not hungry, and I don't want to talk to anyone," he said. They stood silently together for a moment. "I don't want to leave her."

"There's nothing left, Bryant—she's gone," she said, reaching out to touch his arm. "I'll help you get through this."

He looked up and saw two workmen near the spruce tree, waiting for everyone to leave. "This is what I feared the most when I understood she was dead," he said. "This is where I finally leave her."

He called to the workmen, "Can I help you?"

They seemed slightly panicked at this question. One busied himself extinguishing his cigarette with great care; the other swayed unsteadily on his feet. Bryant continued to apply his gaze at them until the shifty one took a few steps toward him. He was wearing blue coveralls and Bryant noticed two stains from oil that had dripped down the right leg.

"Can I help you?" Bryant said again to the man as he approached.

"Sorry, sir, we're here to fill the grave."

"I know. I want to help you. Can I help fill it in?"

"Never done it that way before, but, sure, you can help. Grab a spade—careful around the backhoe."

Bryant took off his suit coat and handed it to Vivian. "I have to do this," he said.

18

An expletive startled Bishop Newell out of the reverie that had come over him from the rhythm of his steps: "Ho-lee shit, it's hot out here. Sweatin' like a pig passin' a peach pit."

He recognized the voice and looked up to see that he was overtaking Father Howard Brown, who was clearly tired of lugging his rotund waist in this march. He looked like an ambling black sack of apples. Newell extended a plastic water bottle toward him, and stopped when he paused to open it and drink. He listened with concern to the wheeze underneath Howard's chugging breath as people streamed quietly around them. Newell wondered if it would be hard to flag down a first-aid responder if it came to that. Howard finished the bottle off.

"This's a lot farther than I thought it'd be," Howard finally said, looking at him. He appeared unrepentant about the fact that Newell overheard his audible curse. "I think hell might be like this. A little cooler, maybe."

"It's a hike," Newell replied. He remembered that Howard rarely showed any concern for the formalities that others carefully cultivated around him. In and of itself, that didn't concern him—he didn't need to be coddled—but he worried about where the cynicism was coming from and where else it was sprouting. "But it's good to be out here with everyone. Nearly there, big fella. Walk with me." He was looking forward to getting out of his blacks and taking a cool shower.

They continued walking, and Newell slowed his pace to accommodate Howard. Before long, they entered the final staging area on the Colfax Bridge. Newell maneuvered to the edge, where they could lean against a barricade and listen to the speakers with the sun behind them.

Howard greeted several sweaty parents who walked past them with red-faced children. "How many do you have here from St. Pat's?" Newell asked.

"Oh, twenty or thirty, I'd say," Howard replied. "There is a core group of young families who hang together—they're pretty active on this issue. Lotsa kids.

"Hey Max—lookin' good there, fella," Howard said, stepping away from the barricade and stooping down to talk to a boy walking behind a stroller. "Give me a ride back to the rectory? No? Please?"

They both made eye contact with Max's parents and smiled as they passed. The father had a floppy assemblage of limbs dangling from the harness around his torso: a small child whose head was concealed under a wide-brimmed cloth sun hat.

"Little Quinn—that baby was the last baptism we've had," Howard said after they had passed. "Been rather slow, in fact."

"When was that?" asked Newell.

"Oh, maybe two months ago."

"And you haven't had any other baptisms since then? At all?"

"Nope. But it's all evened out, I guess—haven't been any funerals, either. They're probably all waiting for me to go on vacation. . . Reminds me I should save some Jameson for Langford when I leave."

Newell stood silently in the heat and pondered this. "That's odd—has anyone else noticed this kind of thing?"

"My drinking? Hell, I hope not!"

Newell chuckled and just looked at the man. He saw Howard give an exaggerated look of comprehension.

"Oh, you meant have other pastors in Andover had it slow?" Howard asked, wiping his forehead with a soaked handkerchief. "Ah . . . Kevin Wallace over at St. Agnes mentioned he's had some extra time. He's always asking me to golf with him. I keep tellin' him I drink my beer sitting down, preferably at a 'Beaus game. It's much more fun to watch other people chasing balls around the grass than do it myself."

Newell had tuned out—his mind was casting back to the conversation with Monsignor Groton before he returned to Santiago. Two other speakers addressed the crowd, but Newell only passively joined the applause. He was reaching to connect two disparate things in his mind—the abstract principles from Groton and the concrete realities from Howard.

He shook hands with Howard when the crowd dispersed at the close of the event and parted without any of the conventional salutations. When Newell returned to his residence, he went straight to his desk and pulled out the advocate's report—the one Groton sent him after returning to Santiago.

As he skimmed, his eyes fell on a fragment he had underlined on his first read; he had flagged it with a question mark in the margin: ". . . if phenomena are supernatural, authenticity will be evidenced in the ontology of the people of God. . ." He remembered the confusion that originally struck him with this phrase, but now it sparked in him with acute curiosity.

He would have to wait until Monday to call the county coroner's office. In the meantime, though, he could do his own research—he started placing calls to the pastors with whom he could speak plainly.

***

Isabel settled in to her desk chair and gingerly removed the plastic cover from her large mocha, so as not to get any stray drips on her yellow blouse. The whipped cream had melted into the coffee already, but that made it easier to drink. It floated above the warm chocolate flavor as she poured it into her mouth. She swallowed slowly, caught her breath, and waited for the caffeine to engage.

Gary leaned in her door, but kept his feet in the hallway. "Mornin'," he said. "I need you to follow up on something for me. Got an inquiry from a Catholic bishop—you're Catholic, right?—can you look into it and call him back? He's called twice already this morning."

"Sure," Isabel said, reaching for a pen. She wondered what other assumptions were lurking behind Gary's broad, flat forehead. "What's he want?"

"He's wondering about death rates for the county so far this year and how it compares to yearly averages. We usually have to submit an interim report this time of year to County Health and the BMV and the Sheriff, anyway, so might as well start crunching those numbers. Ava tracks all of that in our system—all the documentation feeds into a database—so you can ask her to help you run a report. Here's his number." Gary stepped in with one long stride and handed her a small pink slip of paper.

"Got it—I'll get on this today."

"This morning, please. I don't need this guy hounding me all day."

"Alright—I hear you."

"Thanks."

***

An hour later, Isabel picked up the phone and carefully dialed the number from the pink slip. She heard the phone ring once when a crisp baritone voice answered. She was expecting an administrative assistant, but the man identified himself as Bishop Newell.

"Hello, this is Isabel DuPree. I'm calling from the coroner's office to respond to an inquiry."

"Yes, of course. Thank you. I was wondering if you have current data on death rates in the county."

"I've just been looking into that. Your request came right on time because we have to compose a mid-year update, so this is gonna give me a jump on that. Here's what I got for you:

"The average death rate in the U.S. is eight per thousand. Marion County has 345,000 people, and historically we've been right in that range—2,500 to 3,000 deaths per year, on average. This includes all deaths now—we only investigate maybe a fifth of those. Here at midpoint in the year, you'd expect us to be at 1,300 to 1,500 deaths in the county, and it looks like we're below 1,000, so we're a little lower than normal, but I guess that's good news."

"Thank you, Isabel—just the kind of thing I was hoping to learn," the bishop said. "Can you tell me if we are below average in any particular area—is there a cause of death that has a different rate thus far?"

"Lemme see. . . Our interim report only has detailed information for the cases we investigate. So if someone dies a natural death in hospice, for example, we don't investigate and that death is recorded in our system automatically—we don't even review the numbers that come from the general population until partway through the year, like this. So I only have specifics for the cases we investigate."

She was scrolling through the Excel spreadsheet trying to make sense of the fields she was seeing as she talked. "Something like 550 cases come through our office for investigation every year, and it looks like about half of those are accidents. Most of the rest are resolved as natural deaths, but some are either inflicted deaths by homicide or suicide. That's the average. Okay, now, hold on. I'm gonna see what year-to-date looks like in comparison. . ."

She paused as she scrolled down, searching. "Alright, so we're halfway through the year and of the investigations we've conducted, 131 deaths were accidental and 44 inflicted—about on track." She scanned the natural deaths field, but had to pause to try to make sense of what she was seeing. "Sorry, I'm trying to understand this. . . It shows only six were resolved as natural deaths. That has to be a mistake—."

"Isabel, let me tell you something," the bishop jumped in. She heard in his voice a low-vibrating energy—he sounded like he was reaching out to her. "This fits with what I've been hearing from our pastors—they've had very few funerals in the past two months or so. I think there's something happening, but I'm not sure what. I have a theory that it's related to baptism."

"Baptism? We're talking about deaths here, father. I mean, bishop." She winced. The silence lengthened, and she feared she'd offended him. Then she heard him doing math beneath his breath.

"You said we should be around thirteen-hundred deaths in the county so far," he said, "and we're at what?"

"Ah, 883," Isabel said. Her forehead was starting to ache—she had been thrusting her eyebrows downward in confusion.

"Well below average—down by a third at least. And among the cases you investigate, you're also below average, but only in one category."

"Natural deaths."

"And I'm telling you that I've been talking with a dozen pastors across the diocese—now this includes the whole northwest corner of the state—and the only funerals they've presided over this summer have been for accidental deaths. Natural death among people in our parishes have crawled to a stop."

Then, as if he was talking to himself, he said quietly, "It has to be something with baptism."

Isabel took a deep breath. She was not understanding whatever significance the bishop was attaching to baptism, and it was getting annoying that he was driving so hard at it—what would it matter to her, anyway? She set that aside for now, though, as the reality sunk in that this was going to be her whole day. Which meant that she would have to compress the rest of her workweek into four days.

"Okay, bishop, alright now. I have to thank you for this inquiry. This needs more research, no doubt. I gotta look into this, and I'll get back to you when I get it figured out. Maybe later this week."

19

Bryant was in and out of the real estate office so quickly that he could have left his truck running in the parking lot. He had finished the negotiations in a haze over the past two months—as though the trajectory of his enthusiasm had carried him to the brink of the deal, and then, when Estelline died (was it a month ago already?), simple momentum carried him through it. He signed the paperwork and agreed to terms perfunctorily, mechanically. Picking up the keys to the old glass factory was just the last formality—in fact, he forgot to come in yesterday when they were ready.

He drove to the factory, parked, and unwrapped a sandwich, eating in silence. He assumed that there would come a time when he would be able to resume the energy it took to push the brewing forward, but he couldn't see it anywhere on the horizon. Since she died, his life was moving forward in a heavy fog—he could only see a few feet ahead of him.

He got out and approached a set of large iron doors in one of the bays along the factory's exterior. He twisted the key in the padlock—it gave a reluctant click. He pulled back on the iron latch that extended across the frame and pushed the heavy door. It opened with a grinding, rusty stutter; a bird zipped past his head, liberated.

He stepped inside—he was facing the large furnace—and a car passed by on Webster Road. The sound of tires rolling on crumbled concrete reminded him of leaping into the furnace with Estelline. Something dense and dark and cold pooled in the bottom of his abdomen. He walked slowly to a glory hole and looked inside. Light was pouring through the portals on his side of the furnace, casting a shadow over the cradle inside—the one they crouched behind to avoid the "FBI." Whatever was amassing inside of him filled his body cavity and was rising up his throat.

What the hell am I supposed to do with this? he wondered with a deep sigh. He was going through the motions with his business and had no desire to spend the sweaty hours it would take to move his equipment here from his basement. All of his brews were in a holding pattern—he was recycling old recipes, clocking the hours it took to crank out the gallons he sold in the concourse of 'Beaus games. He couldn't remember having the energy and initiative it took to innovate and try new combinations. And now he was deeply committed to the enterprise in order to pay for this building and grow his operation big enough to fill it.

"Fucking hell," he said with a resigned exhale. The words slowly rambled around the furnace and mingled with the fine dust settling in the open air of the empty factory.

***

At the ballpark that night, Bryant packed away the last of his empty kegs from the beer stand and looked up to see that the game was in the bottom of the eighth, 'Beaus trailing the Monarchs by two. He decided to take a seat in the nearly empty section above third base, a few rows above where Estelline would have sat with Vivian. The night air was just turning cool. He was grateful for the distraction of something to watch, and decided to sit here for the rest of the game—it was better than returning to the quiet, empty house that used to be their home.

As he sat, he noticed a large man to his right, four seats over and a row up. He was leaning back and his left arm was draped around the seat next to him, as though he was sharing the game with an imaginary spouse, and both were at ease enough to take it in without needing to talk. The 'Beaus shortstop struck out looking to end the inning, and he leaned forward and yelled, "C'mon, Dallas, that's a goddamn sin—game's on the line, guy! You can't go down without at least swinging!"

Bryant looked over his right shoulder to see the man compose himself and settle back in. He looked at Bryant and shook his head. "They're just kids, but hell, it's not a hard game to understand. They'll be seeing ninety-five next inning from the closer."

Bryant nodded and turned back to the field, putting his foot up on the cup holder in front of him. He looked up and could make out two stars gleaming through the glow of the city and the halo of stadium lights.

"Where's your girl been? Haven't seen you for a while—she and her friend were good for conversation on nights like this. Stands get pretty empty..."

Bryant looked at him and then turned back to the field. He didn't want to get in to it with a half-drunk loner.

"Figured you two were nearly matrimonial, the

way she lit up when she saw you."

Bryant looked up again and the man was leaning forward and returning his gaze. He apparently wasn't going anywhere.

"She left me," Bryant said, tossing it out with hope it would shut him up.

The man huffed with incredulity and Bryant saw a fragment of peanut arc from his mouth toward the field. "Pffft! Horse manure. I don't buy that." He rocked forward and levered his rotund girth out of his seat. Bryant watched him teeter for a moment on his feet, stretch his back, then carefully reach down and lean on the seat in front of him as he swung his right leg over.

He's gonna sit that fat ass right next to me, Bryant thought. The man had a death grip on the seat back—Bryant saw the knuckles on his pudgy fingers whiten, and heard a grunting wheeze as the man carefully and with great effort swung his other foot around. In his free hand he held a half-full plastic cup—swill from the concession stand, Bryant noticed—and glanced at it several times to make sure it wasn't spilling.

Bryant stared at the man in disbelief—he was now standing in his row and stretching out his back again. He took a waddling step nearer Bryant and hovered his rump over a seat uncertainly. As he rocked back, Bryant could hear the plastic chair squeak in surprise as it struggled to accept his girth.

"No way she left you," he said, turning his gaze to the field. He resumed his posture with his invisible, silent wife, who was now sitting in the empty seat between them. "Relationships like yours don't end that way. At least at this point. They dry up later sometimes, but you two were all-in, anyone could see.

C'mon, now. What happened."

Bryant considered the pitcher throwing his last warm up pitch, the catcher slinging the ball to second, the shortstop gathering the ball on the hop with a sweeping motion. The routine and rhythm made speaking feel less dangerous—as though it were patter, secondary to the important work they were observing. This guy was a stranger he'd never see again. It couldn't last past this inning.

"She didn't leave me for someone else," he said, looking at the man. "She died. I buried her a month ago."

The man had the cup to his mouth and immediately hunched forward and coughed, the beer splattering between his legs. *Fitting*, Bryant thought.

"Holy Mary, mother of God," the man whispered when he regained control of his esophagus. "I'm sorry, guy. That's . . . that's . . ." He looked at the field in silence with his mouth open. Bryant waited for the man to recover—he had gotten used to introducing this news to people and watching the terror wash over them before they made their apologies and fled, leaving him alone. *Swing and a miss sends the fat man packing*, Bryant thought.

But he didn't leave, and they watched the inning begin without speaking. The leadoff hitter for the Monarchs sat on a late-count arcing curve, applied force, and pounded the ball through the night air. It traveled over the left-field fence with a mutter from the crowd who realized that the night was over. Bryant saw the remaining stragglers begin to shuffle from their seats around the stadium, and hoped that his interlocutor would be one of them now that he had introduced the impossible.

The big man wiped his mouth, took a shallow breath, then sat up straight with his chin lowered to let a shallow belch escape. Recovered, he took a deep drink to finish what was left of his beer and sat back, staring at the field without seeing the game. "Well that sucks," he said. He blew out through his cheeks and Bryant smelled stale alcohol. "Holy shibblets, that sucks."

Bryant cracked a smile. It was a response he had not heard yet. The fat man seemed to share his lament —he didn't sense the pity that so many others slathered on him.

"How'd it happen?" the man asked with his eyes on the next batter who was digging in.

"We were expecting a daughter. She woke up one night bleeding—miscarriage. They couldn't stop the blood, and then she was gone."

"It happens like that sometimes," the man said, shaking his head. "Like someone comes along and rips out a buncha pages from the book you're reading. You're walking along with a story, and suddenly the only thing left is jagged edges. Makes you wonder what's the use of reading this story at all, even?"

"That's exactly right," Bryant said, staring at the grass on the field. "Things make no sense now that she's gone. It's just . . . over. I buried her—I put her in the ground. There's nothing left. It just all feels like a waste."

"What've you been doing with yourself?"

"I dunno. Trying to get back to level, I guess, but I don't know why. I'm going through the motions, honestly. Even with my beer. Especially with my beer."

The top of the inning ended on a pop fly to shallow left. Bryant watched the 'Beaus third baseman leisurely lope backward with his face to the vacuous darkness beyond the ring of stadium lights. He caught the ball, then trotted across the field to the dugout for the bottom of the ninth.

"I can't wrap my mind around the fact that I won't see her again," Bryant said softly.

"Shit, you don't know that," the man said. Bryant looked at him, but he was keeping his eyes on the field, even though the Monarch closer hadn't started his warm-ups. Bryant continued to apply his gaze, and said, "What's that mean?"

"You don't know that you won't see her again. You don't know what happens after death," he said. "No one does."

"Now *that's* horse manure," Bryant said, turning away. He leaned forward to stand up.

"Well, guy, where I come from, it's not."

Bryant turned to face him—he wanted to see the man contradict him in this matter to his face. "I may be a reprehensible drunk," the man continued, "which is what my sister keeps tellin' me, and I keep tellin' her that I drink, and may be representable . . . reprehentable. Damn. Rep. Ee. Hense. Able."

He took a deep breath. He looked up, lost, and Bryant noticed sadness in his eyes at his inability to call his thoughts back from where they had wandered. "Okay, well, all I know is where I come from, people don't give up on each other just because they died."

Bryant leaned back into his seat with a thump and raised his chin. This was a good opportunity to confront a line of thinking that had been raising its head ever since Estelline's death. "And where's that?" he asked. This was raising his hackles, he knew, but he decided to see it through.

Without waiting for a reply, he said, "Oh I see —you believe in heaven and that I'll see her there if I'm good, don't you? You believe all this fits into some grand plan, that it'll all be okay in the end? 'Cause I've heard all of that already, and I can assure you: it's *bull*-shit." He heard his own voice rising, and looked around to see if he had drawn any attention. The stands around them were empty. The man stayed silent.

They watched the action happening on the field, but they were not attending to the game. Bryant could hear the ball hissing to the plate from the hand of the Monarch closer—he felt the same way: edgy, aggressive, and dangerous.

After the leadoff man struck out, the man broke the silence. "Look, your love had a power to it. Has a power to it," he said. "It moved you. It changed you. Anyone could see it—I could see it, even, and I'm usually blasted here.

"That kind of power doesn't just decay and disappear. It's stronger than that."

Bryant fought the familiar anger back down his neck, thinking that the man had no basis at all for that statement. Somehow, however, his lack of pity helped, because he clearly wasn't saying it to mollify him. Bryant recognized in the man someone who wasn't terrified in the face of his pain, someone capable of plain conversation. He wanted to hear more, but it was like lighting a candle in a gale.

"What are you saying about my dead wife?" Bryant asked the question clearly and pointedly. On the field, the closer brushed back the first 'Beaus hitter with a high fastball, sending him to the dirt. Bryant turned to the man and said, "You think that when I die, I'll see her in heaven."

"You can call it heaven, but it's a little childish to picture it as white robes and harps in the clouds." Bryant felt the man charging forward, unfazed by his warnings. "It's more like an ending to the story.

"All you can see now are the jagged edges, right, and you think the rest of the story's been ripped out. I'm telling you the middle chapters are gone, but there's still an ending. You gotta skip the what's been ripped out—no choice, they're gone, which sucks, guy, it sucks donkey balls, I know—but the last few chapters are there. If you can get to them, things'll make sense again."

Under his breath, Bryant heard the man mutter into his cup: "It's the only thing keeping me from drowning."

Bryant's mind was chasing its tail, but the flame had taken to the candle and he felt the glimmer of a glow inside his gut.

"How do I get to the end of the story, then?"

"Well, being a Bible-thumper won't help much here. There's precious little in the good book about what exactly we have to do to get to heaven. Only once is it spelled out for us—it's in Matthew, chapter twenty-five."

The 'Beaus batter grounded weakly to the Monarch's second baseman, who cradled it up off the dirt, inspected it for a half-second, and flipped it to first.

"There it says that we'll get to heaven if we take care of the least among us—if we feed the hungry, give drink to the thirsty, welcome the stranger, clothe

the naked, care for the sick, visit the imprisoned. The works of mercy—and they're not only a ticket to heaven, they're a little window into heaven.

"And that's it. Take care of people in need and you'll see heaven. It doesn't say a blessed word about if or where you go to church—nothing, even, about what you believe. Pretty simple. And I'll tell you what: I never met someone who took care of the poor who didn't deserve to be in heaven."

Bryant heard a change in the tone of the public address announcer's droning chatter—he was wrapping up the game with relief evident in his voice, giving final statistics. They had missed the final out and the game was over—'Beaus had lost, three-zip. He stood up to shake the man's hand.

"So, that's how you get to the end of the story—feed the hungry and all that. Works of mercy. That's what you believe?"

"What do you think I'm doing out here? Comforting the sorrowful." He handed Bryant a card before rising from his seat with a power squat. "Drinking beer and comforting the sorrowful." He turned and started walking away to exit the section.

Bryant looked down at the card. It read:

Father Howard Brown
Caretaker
St. Patrick Catholic Parish

20

Bryant parked his black F-150 on the street between the cathedral and cemetery, and the engine came to a rest with a shudder, rattling a giant steel tank in the bed. In purchasing the truck, he picked out one with an extended, eight-foot bed for the extra capacity, but it was rarely full. The clanking tank reminded him that he forgot to tie it down and now had nothing to string around it to anchor it to the truckbed.

He got out of the truck and stretched the canvas cover over the truck bed and began to snap it into place, thinking that it would at least prevent the tank from jumping out when he hit a pothole. He was just finishing with the cover when Vivian pulled up behind him.

"Hey—'morning," she said, as she stepped out of her car. "Thanks for letting me know you're stopping by. I was just headed to campus, so timing worked out great."

"You bet. It's nice to be here with other people sometimes," Bryant said. "It's so still. I like to hear another voice around."

They both walked through the gate flanked by a cast-iron fence—ribbons of black rails ran up to two small stone towers marking the entrance. An iron arch spanned the two towers—Bryant always lifted his eyes to read the phrase it contained: WHO IS LIKE UNTO

GOD.

At Estelline's grave, they stood quietly, recollected. Bryant heard a squirrel scolding them from the blue spruce behind him; car tires on the roads around them sounded like a soft breeze from where they stood.

"I never know what to say, but it feels good to be here," Bryant said.

"I think she'd like the quiet," Vivian said. "It's what she appreciated about baseball games—the quiet moments in between pitches when you could hear the crowd."

"Did you know she hated baseball?" Bryant said, turning to Vivian.

"What? No way," Vivian replied. "I never heard her complain about going to the park."

"Her older brother was on a traveling team, and she spent half her childhood wasting time at hot and sweaty ballparks while her parents watched his games. She swore to never waste another minute at a baseball game when she left for college."

He looked at Vivian and saw her staring at him with a furrow between her eyebrows.

"Then she met you in lab, and you suggested going because it was a change of pace from campus."

"I suggested that we sit near the visiting team's bullpen because there are always hot guys to look at," Vivian said. Bryant noticed an underhanded smile. She turned away and said quietly, "The catchers, I mean. God, I'd never date a pitcher."

"And then she realized that she felt at home there," Bryant continued. "No clock. No screens. A good friend."

He remembered loving that about Estelline—

that she was willing to set aside a firm conclusion or preference if it would feed a relationship. The memory of it tugged at the corner of his heart because he knew the generosity of spirit that he admired was buried before him under six feet of dirt. He bent down and yanked some of the grass that was starting to grow tall around the headstone where the mower blades couldn't get close enough.

"We miss you, Stella," Vivian said. "Every day, girl. Every damn day."

Bryant stood up and breathed deeply. He thought of what that fat man had said at the ballgame —about seeing her again. The thought carved a small, empty hole in his chest that asked to be filled. *Feed the hungry*, he recalled.

They turned to walk back to their vehicles. "Hey, you still helping with that study—that one with the brothers?" he asked Vivian.

"Yup—headed there this afternoon," she said.

"I think I need to do some community service or something—get outta my head, do some good. Think one of those brothers has something I could help with?"

***

Bryant confirmed with Vivian that the Andre Center was only a few blocks away from the old plant, so the next day, after moving half a dozen boxes of bottles, he decided to walk there. He approached the address she gave him, and was glad he was on foot—he easily would have missed it if he had been driving. The one-story building was five or six decades from its prime as a warehouse, and the whitewashed walls looked worn but clean. He could see the outlines of former windows and a loading door now filled in with cinder blocks. In the building's current incarnation, it was clearly a place for people, not industry. "Andre Center" was painted in careful, hand-made lettering above doors that opened onto a hard gravel parking lot.

Bryant paused before approaching the doors to study a mural painted in a bricked-over bay of windows. The painting showed an older-looking man—a saint, Bryant judged, based on the halo around his head—wearing a black robe and extending his hand in a gesture of welcome. Bryant could hear voices of children from inside the building—they sounded intent and energetic, like a team of young Wall Street traders.

He was about to reach for the door when it opened toward him. A tall, thin man gestured for him to enter.

"Hi—I'm looking for Brother Martin Taber? I told him I'd be by to talk about doing some service—my name is Bryant Black Fox."

Even as he was talking, he saw the man's angular face crack a knowing but hospitable smile—this was Martin, himself. His blue jeans were well-worn to the point of appearing faded, and Bryant noticed the outline of a silver cross flanked by anchors hanging over Martin's blue dress shirt.

From his quiet voice on the phone, Bryant imagined a small and round, shy man, and he was struck by how tall and sharp Martin appeared. He had a lean and well-tended mustache firmly atop his upper lip that did not extend past the corners of his mouth. Bryant had the impression that Martin could have been a logistics officer in the Army—orderly, disciplined, someone who facilitates important work.

"Welcome, Bryant," Martin said. "Good to meet you. Yes, Vivian told me you'd be along. We're always looking for help, so we'll have no trouble putting you to work. Come on in."

He showed Bryant around the center. The kitchen held three teenagers who were making sandwiches and packing lunches. Bryant smelled the green sweetness of snap peas—a side table held a box full of plastic baggies that had been stuffed with them. Martin explained that they keep a pantry stocked with donations from area parishioners, and they hand on whatever fresh fruits or vegetables might come in from local farmers or grocery stores. Volunteers pack large lunches so that the kids take food home, Martin explained. Bryant was surprised to hear that for every child who is here, there were three or four other family members at home who are either working or too young to be without adult care.

They passed through the back of the kitchen into a room arranged to display racks and stacks of clothing, with two sets of washers and dryers chugging in the corner. The far wall was covered by a series of shelves that held first aid supplies. Martin explained the range of maladies they respond to, from skin rashes due to pesticide exposure to pneumonia and broken bones.

They passed back through the kitchen and re-entered the large gathering space. Tables had been pushed to the side and ten huddles of children were sitting cross-legged in groups of four each around a teenager, who was explaining an activity that had to do with a tray of craft supplies in the center of their circle.

"Tutoring is what they're here for nominally," Martin said. "Retired seniors come in and help kids with their homework during the school year, and in the summers, we bring the young kids in for games and learning—like this—led by teens, usually older siblings. It keeps them all active when the parents are out working.

"When we can, we try to help the parents with their English. It gets them out of the fields and into something more stable—construction or landscaping. It really helps a family when one of the parents doesn't have to follow the harvests up and down the coast.

"But what we're really here to do is to simply be a part of these people's lives. Once we get to know the family a little, we have opportunities to see who's hungry, who needs medicine, who's in distress. Our volunteers know to share these kinds of stories with us—to notice what's going on with these families. We're building a community, really."

"Quite an operation, Brother Martin—I'm in," Bryant said. "I'm a brewer, so I'm comfortable in the kitchen preparing food. Packing lunches, working with the pantry, that kind of thing would be perfect."

Martin stopped and turned to Bryant, meeting his eyes. "Vivian said that you're Estelline's husband. I was very sorry to hear of her passing," he said. He was not probing—Bryant sensed a flat honesty. "You must be torn apart."

"Yeah. . ." Bryant wasn't sure what to say—the comment caught him off guard. When he looked up, he saw Martin's continued gaze, which seemed capable of the wound he had uncovered. "It ain't been easy, I can say that. Feels a lot like my whole life was buried in that grave," Bryant said. He folded his arms and took half a step back to lean against the wall. "I need some fresh air, a change of scenery."

Brother Martin nodded. "Understood. When you're stuck in a tomb, something has to change," he said, "or it starts to stink."

***

Martin introduced Bryant to the teenagers working in the kitchen, and then left to help wrap up the morning session. Bryant helped pack what food was left in lunch sacks, trying to smooth over an awkward, stilted conversation with the teens. Martin reappeared to roll up the aluminum grate covering the service counter that connected the kitchen to the hall, and they handed the bags out to a line of kids. The youngest kids appeared first—Bryant could only see their wrinkled foreheads and bright eyes over the counter as each reached up for a sack.

After the oldest ones had passed by, Martin entered the kitchen and asked Bryant to step into the hall with him. They watched the children tear into their food, and Martin pointed out a young boy sitting quietly among a cluster of chattering kids. Bryant guessed he was about ten or eleven years old—he had short black hair, evenly cut across his head, and thin eyes that seemed to convey either a scowl or mischief, Bryant wasn't sure which.

"That's Rafael Villahermosa—Rafa, we call him," Martin said. "I'd like you to work with him."

"Brother, I'm fine in the kitchen," Bryant felt a small panic rising inside. He imagined that feeding the hungry could be done at a safe distance—working one-on-one with a boy sounded way too involved. "I can keep those teens on task. I might be able to see about other donations, even. I just don't know much about teaching or tutoring."

"He's got a tough story," Martin continued, plowing right through Bryant's caution signs. Bryant's mind began grasping for another excuse. "His family is in trouble—real trouble. His father was killed this spring—he was organizing workers to improve conditions in the fields. They found his body in a ditch.

"Rafa is one of four, and his mom is trying to keep her head above water holding everything together. The kids are all hanging together, but Rafa's acting out. It's not so much that he's causing trouble—he's gone silent."

Bryant felt a jolt of recognition. "Completely quiet? He won't speak?"

"He's ten, right, so what's he going to do? His father stands up, and they murdered him. The kid's world is falling apart, and screaming at the chaos only makes it louder, so he's exercising power over that world with the only thing he can control—his own body.

"Honestly, he's doing fine with his studies—he finished the school year okay. He's a smart kid, but he's angry, and that'll sprout into trouble down the road. I've seen it happen before. He needs someone outside his family to see and understand him. You are an outsider, you're objective, and you're a man, so standing in that pain with him will mean something."

"Brother, I'm not a counselor—I can't fix that," Bryant said. He felt out of his depth; this was a task way beyond his capacity. *I don't have my own shit together,* he thought. *What am I supposed to do with this broken kid?* "I think you'd be better off handling this."

"I can't," Martin said. "I'm not objective—it's my job to care for him and his family, so it's nothing special for me to show some compassion. And there's a chance I could bring more trouble—working with this community puts me on the radar, you might say."

Bryant admitted a thrill at the feeling of alarm that came from hearing this. His *unjee* came to mind again—he remembered hearing from a neighbor how she fired a shotgun over her husband's shoulder the second time he came home with a belligerent attitude and gin on his breath. He learned from her that the first step in suffering no bullshit was to recognize its stench, and whatever was lurking around this family stunk.

"Look, I'm not asking you to fix him," Martin said. That sly smile was back—the one he opened the door with. "We'll give you some reading to do together, to keep busy and to give you something to talk about. It's summer, okay, so this is gravy. Come on over at lunch time every day and we'll keep you busy with meals. Two, three times a week hang around and you can meet with Rafa and chat about this. . ."

Martin set a book down on the linoleum-covered serving counter. Bryant concluded it was science fiction from the cover—an image showed hands gripping a steering stick in the cockpit of a spaceship screaming past incoming lasers. The title read *Permadeath or Power Up.*

"It's a story about video games," Martin said. "I'm told it has a good ending."

21

"We all here?" Gary asked, walking in to the small conference room. He paused at the door to glance at the faces of the coroner office staff, which included Britt, Bruce, Isabel, and their young new administrative assistant, Ashton. He flicked off the lights, took his seat around the table, and said, "All yours, Isabel."

Isabel had been in the conference room for half an hour already, reviewing the computer slides she prepared last night after Parker went down. The projector fan was already whispering, and the sound it made in the quiet moment everyone turned their attention to her reminded Isabel of when she was a girl riding in the backseat of the car, breathing on the window to draw faces. *Breathe*, she though. *You got this. Breathe.*

"Okay, so we got an inquiry on Monday about mid-year mortality rates. I did some digging, and found some unusual patterns. Gary asked me to do more research. When we talked yesterday, he told me to prepare something for today's staff meeting."

She tapped her computer keyboard and this slide appeared on the screen behind her:

Marion County Mortality Rates

Yearly Average	**Year-to-Date**
2,766 deaths	883
(~0.8% mortality rate)	(~1350 expected)

Investigated Deaths per Year

548 (8 year average)		181
256	accidental	131
107	violent	44
153	natural	6

Average Natural Deaths Per Month

184 — Trending to 0?

"So, as you know, we average between 2,500 and 3,000 deaths per year, which is right on track with the national mortality rate of eight per thousand for the population of our county. Here, halfway through the year, we're below 900, significantly under that average.

"Not an alarming number—fewer deaths is good, right? But then I looked at the deaths we investigate. We should be well over 200 at this point. The accidental and violent deaths we've investigated are slightly below average, but look at the figure for the cases that resolve as natural deaths—six.

"That led me to look into the numbers reported to us from our public health partners—the natural deaths that are not investigated. Over the past eight years, Marion County averaged 184 non-investigated natural deaths per month, but that number has been in decline since this spring and over the past two months, we've been trending toward zero."

"What's that mean?" asked Bruce. He was holding his chin in his hand with an elbow on the table, and Isabel detected skepticism in his scrunched-up nose. She didn't know if it was because she was new or because he was being a prick. "I mean, why would the death rate be changing?"

"That's the question," she replied. "Of course, numbers will fluctuate, but this is beyond the standard deviation." She intended the statistics term as a shot across Bruce's bow, and stood up to turn the light on. Gary seemed to be listening closely and thinking.

"I made a visit to St. Joseph Hospital yesterday, just to see if they're noticing any of these trends. I figured if fewer people are dying, they must be seeing this, too. They have a guy in charge of 'informatics'—he does technology and planning around efficiency.

"So this guy was just through the roof with these numbers—he said their strategic planning's really starting to pay off. Lots of patients going home from the ICU—they're approaching a 100 percent recovery rate. Their in-patient and diagnostic services are improving, but not that drastically—apparently people are still getting sick, but just not dying. He was preparing a submission for a national health care award."

Bruce sat back. "So, what, the regional hospital system has found a way to cure everyone who's sick? Sounds. . ."

Isabel jumped in—she didn't want Bruce to be driving these conclusions. "It sounds odd, I know, and I think there's something deeper going on here." She left it at that, though—she didn't want to introduce her conversation with that bishop. Gary asked her to start this investigation, and it was turning into something important, so she wanted to make sure she stayed in front of it in case it turned into an opportunity. Her goal for this meeting was to come across as completely competent to follow through with this line of inquiry.

Gary inhaled sharply, sat up, and leaned his sternum into the table. "I'm taking this to Indy at the end of the week, so I'm going to need more data. Given the potential here for what could be a major public health impact, this has to take top priority for the rest of this week. I'm asking Isabel to take the lead on this, so let's figure out where else we should be collecting data to round out our numbers. Bruce and Britt, you can report your findings to Isabel. Isabel, let's you and I work on putting the pieces together Thursday. We'll regroup Friday morning to try to make sense of it all before I head down."

Isabel was hoping Gary would stick with her, and felt her heart vault when he identified her as the lead. The meeting adjourned and everyone gathered their writing pads to stand. Glancing around the room, she noticed no reaction from Britt, but thought she caught a smirk on Bruce's face before he caught her eye and smiled. Prick, she concluded.

She let the others leave as she unplugged her laptop. On her way back to her desk, she stepped in to Gary's office.

"Hey, I wanted to ask you about that investigation down in Wilmot," she said. She was pleased to be placed in charge of researching the death rate issue, but didn't want to lose sight of what she thought was going on with the migrant workers. "We've had more evidence turn up."

Gary broke in without looking up from poking

through the papers and folders and binders layered on his desk. "Didn't we pass that case on already with our recommendation?"

"Yes, but no one's moving on anything. I thought we could maybe bring some attention to the problem with the media."

"A reporter around here is the last thing we need —we have no idea what's going on with these death rates, so we gotta keep our heads down until we get ahead of this."

"Okay, what about a follow-up call with the detectives to keep this top-of-mind?"

"Isabel, listen." Gary stopped his search and looked up at her finally. She felt part of her stomach flatten against her backbone. "You did your job. There's nothing new going on down there. We're not criminal investigators—we can only do so much. There's other important work we need to attend to now."

"Alright, I hear you," she said. As she walked back to her desk, she started to line up the people she was going to speak with today about those death rates.

22

Father Howard Brown pressed the black plastic nozzle lever on the five-gallon aluminum coffee maker and filled his Styrofoam cup half full. He stepped to the side to pick up two packets of fake sugar, two thimble-cups of creamer, and a red swizzle stick. There were three other pastors waiting behind him, conversing, so he carried his goods to the opposite side of the church basement where he could set them down on the fall-board of the old upright piano.

Turning his back to the assembly of gathering priests, he pulled a flask from his jacket and filled the rest of his cup with Irish whiskey. Then he ripped open the sugars and cracked open the creamers to make it appear as though they'd been used before walking back to the coffee station to toss them in the small trash can under the folding table. He turned the swizzle stick in the cup as he strolled to find a seat in the second row of steel folding chairs.

He found a seat and pulled out a pocket-sized notebook and pen and began writing. No one—ordained or otherwise—ever bothered him when he looked like he was composing a homily.

Bishop Newell separated from a small group of priests clustered near the front of the room, and moved to stand behind a portable lectern positioned in front of a black-curtained stage. The church hall quieted, and the remainder of the twenty-five priests in the room quickly moved to find a seat.

Howard was curious to see the bishop at one of these quarterly meetings—typically, they just featured a blowhard from one of the growing suburban parishes yammering on about the new dental coverage or some recycling program.

Howard knew the bishop was a small man, but he was always surprised at just how slight he appeared—it's as though the man took on stature in the subconscious because of his position, and then whenever he saw the bishop in person, his actual body subverted this memory. *No wonder he can hike like a deer*, he thought, putting away his notebook.

"Thank you for gathering here tonight," Bishop Newell announced. "Sorry to interrupt this deanery meeting, but I have a pressing matter that needs our attention.

"Before I begin, I have to insist on confidentiality," he continued. "It's essential that this conversation not leave this hall. This is a situation that is currently unfolding and I'm not prepared to answer for it publicly, but I have enough evidence that to delay responding any longer would be irresponsible."

Awfully vague, Howard thought. *Might be the first intriguing meeting in the history of this deanery.*

"I am reading signs that indicate that people in this diocese are in the midst of some kind of transformation—their bodies are changing somehow. As their needs and questions and relationships shift, it means we're going to have some work to do to catch up to them and then lead them."

A bald, angular priest sitting behind Howard

interjected: "Do we need to sign up for a fitness program? Because I'm all for that."

"Sit down, Frank," came a voice from the back.

Howard heard someone behind him mutter, "I'm not going on a diet."

Father Doug Lawrence had salt-and-pepper hair and a large, affluent congregation on the north side of town. He asked, "What exactly are you asking us to do?" Others in the assembly murmured their assent to the question, and Howard heard the low chatter die down as they waited for Newell's answer. He took a deep sip from his coffee and placed a leg over a knee, enjoying the show. The buzz was kicking in right on time.

"This doesn't leave the room." Newell shifted his weight. "I'm working with county health officials to better define what we're seeing, but as many of you have noticed, fewer people are dying. I think it's pointing to some kind of . . . renewal."

Doug spoke up again: "People living longer—isn't that a good thing?"

"Of course it is, but what's it going to ask of us?" Newell said. "We have a responsibility to read those signs and then lead—we're shepherds." His voice adopted a stronger tone and Howard assumed this meant he was not welcoming further inquiry. The room began to squirm, which amused Howard. He saw what was going on—the men behind him had established a comfortable rhythm of life for themselves. They wanted to take on more duties like he wanted to go back to rehab.

Newell asked for volunteers to form a group of consultors from among the pastors present so that they could study the facts more and start to form a plan. The room took on the heavy silence of a courtroom watching a jury return. A chair creaked.

The three words a pastor fears most, thought Howard: *ad hoc committee.* He looked over his shoulder to scan the room, but everyone was averting their eyes, studying their shoes or examining the water-stained ceiling tiles. Someone cleared their throat.

Howard saw Newell assess the reticence, recover, and decide to briskly conclude. "Okay, look," Newell said. "You'll be hearing from me in the next few weeks as we figure this out. I'll be calling on you to help me shift our ministry when we know more." Howard recalled, once again, that this bishop was not one to waste time or energy on laggards. "For now, though, just know that we need to prepare for something new taking shape within our congregations—within us, even. Ready yourselves. Ready your people."

He turned from the podium and strode quickly out the side door with his head down. The room reluctantly woke and began discussing in muttered tones.

Howard stood up, slowly pushing his chair back six inches with an obnoxious squawk. *Without a doubt, the most interesting—and shortest—deanery meeting I've ever been to,* he thought.

"What's this all about, Howie? Any ideas?" Howard turned to see Father Charles Mix looking at him with a mischievous smirk behind a grey beard. He was the exception to the rule in this room.

"Thoroughly confused, Chuck," Howard replied. "But something's up. For damn sure."

***

Martin Taber shifted the box to his hip and used his left hand to awkwardly knock on the screen door of the Villahermosa family's cinder-block home just outside of Wilmot. The box held a bag of rice, a tangle of green beans, and three zucchini the size of footballs. It was getting late, but the light lingered so long on these summer evenings he figured the kids wouldn't be off to bed yet.

He heard the patter of a child's feet rushing toward the door and saw Maria through the screen door. "It's *Hermano*!" she called back into the house with glee. "¡*Hola, Hermano Martin*!" She opened the door and he stepped in.

"*Hola,* Maria, it is good to see you. How was your day today?"

"It was good," she said. "After camp, Miggy pitched to us for home runs."

Aurora approached from the kitchen with a smile, but let Maria finish describing the backyard whiffle ball home run derby.

"Aurora, people keep sharing the fruits of their gardens with us," Martin said. "We can't eat all of the vegetables that show up on our doorstep. We're drowning in zucchini—can you help us?"

"*Por supuesto, hermano,*" she said. "*Gracias*."

He handed the box to her and asked, "How's everything going?"

He was studying her eyes, but did not see any glint of fear. She began talking about Rafa, and he took it as a good sign that this was the biggest concern she had at the moment. Rafa had not begun speaking yet, she said, but seemed to have a lighter disposition. She thanked him for the book and for the conversations he had arranged with the tutor.

"We're eating dinner now," she said, turning her body back inside the house toward the kitchen. "*¿Tienes hambre?*"

He was meeting Bishop Newell at Leola's in half an hour, and he knew it took twenty-five minutes to drive there from here in Wilmot. This would stretch him, but he was feeling stronger.

"*Por supuesto, hermana,*" he said. "*Gracias.*"

***

Newell left Leola's and began his walk back to the cathedral rectory. He strolled with his head down in concentration—his feet knew the way home. Meeting with Brother Martin at Leola's had made for a strange evening, full of both confusion and clarity, and he had a lot to think about. He felt grateful for the cool strains of breeze reaching through the heavy, late summer night air—it seemed to encourage his mind to stretch out.

At least he was driving at something now. He gathered his conclusions. A response to this new phenomenon was necessary, but he couldn't work through normal channels without raising alarms—that much was clear from the failed deanery meeting. Getting everyone on board would have to happen at some point, but he wanted to buy more time. What he needed was a scout force—a select group to step deeper into this reality, explore it, and start figuring out how to respond. He felt like there was a lot to learn—he just needed the right people to learn it discreetly and effectively.

The brothers were a good option, and he could see a way forward with them, but he didn't know what the catalyst could be. He sensed Martin was right—they needed some sort of practice to further tune their evolving bodies to their expanding spirits—but he had no idea what that could look like.

He was deep in contemplation and the next thing he knew, he was turning the key to unlock the back door of the rectory. It was the first he had been back home since leaving for Mass this morning. He walked in and dropped his round bulge of keys into the glass bowl on the nightstand at the base of the stairs—the clank echoed through the empty rectory. He turned on the small lamp next to the bowl and began examining the stack of mail left there for him by his housekeeper, an old Polish woman named Florence Ziebach who smelled like garlic and rosewater.

He stopped flipping through the bills. He heard a voice. He couldn't make out any words, but it wasn't quiet—it sounded like it was coming from behind a closed door somewhere. The hair on the back of his head stood up. The voice was coming from inside the house.

He cocked his head and began walking further down the first-floor hallway to see if he could discern any directionality. It seemed to be coming from the kitchen—or at least that end of the rectory. He recognized a male tone. The voice seemed at ease, but clear—as though someone was telling a story.

There were no lights on in the kitchen, but the voice was coming through more clearly now. He began to catch some of the language—something about a river in Tennessee. He moved beyond the kitchen into the pantry, near the back door. The voice was very clear now.

He reached out and slowly grasped the knob of the door leading downstairs, and in a hurry turned and swiped it open. Nothing, and no change in the tone. The sound continued—a stream of consciousness of sorts—but did not seem to be coming from the basement.

He turned around—behind him was a closet. "Hello?" he called. "Do you need help? Who's in there?"

He grasped the knob and flung the door open. Florence's cleaning cart filled the crowded, dark closet. Light from the kitchen illuminated a small, black, hand-held radio resting face-up on an overturned bucket on top of the cart. It was tuned to a baseball game.

". . . Cliff takes ball three outside. It's fun to hear him tell a story like that with his drawl. Says he'll never touch catfish again. It's a muggy night here in Andover—feels like Tennessee, or what you'd imagine Tennessee to feel like if you've never been there. Here's the three-one . . ."

Newell reached up and pulled the string that hung from a naked bulb so that he could find the off switch for the radio. The harsh light filled the cramped closet.

"Kangas swings and rips it down the right-field line! McGillick will score easily, and here comes Sanroy—they're waving him around third. . ."

He reached for the knob; his fingers froze around the dial, but not because he was listening to the play.

23

Rafa gingerly closed the back door of his home so that it made no noise in the pre-dawn darkness. His mom and siblings were still sleeping and would not be up for another hour and a half. He had set an alarm on his watch for 3:30 a.m., just like he used to do to help Papa pack his meals for work. He grabbed his hand-me-down bike from the back corner of the house and walked it to the gravel road, breathing in the cool, still air. He turned the front wheel toward Wilmot, hopped on, and began to pedal.

If he met any cars, which was rare, he could see their headlights well ahead, which gave him time to slip his bike and body into the ditch until it passed. It was a fifteen-minute ride into Wilmot, and he felt like a grown up being out and doing something important when everyone else was asleep. The birds would begin calling on his way home at 4:30, but all was still now except for crickets and some toads calling from the wet drainages. His eyes were adjusting now, and with the ambient light he could see well enough to avoid potholes and sections of washboard. The wheels on his bike made a dusty grinding noise on the gravel.

He reached the edge of town where the orange glow from the high-hanging streetlights began, and dumped his bike behind a large, tin-sided machine shed. The ride was routine now, and his body had adjusted to the distance—he left home with enough time to avoid rushing, and he was hardly out of breath.

He carefully tip-toed his way toward the town's intersection, winding around the edge of the few mechanical shops and equipment yards, careful to look around each corner before advancing. His feet were wet with dew from the tall grass, but he had slipped on an old pair of Miggy's sneakers, so he could let them dry on the back deck when he got home.

He reached a repair garage across the street from the convenience store near the stoplight. An unmarked school bus, painted sky blue, sat parked on the incoming road facing him; he could just hear its grumbling idle. From here, he could stand behind a stack of tires with a clear view of the line of men assembled in front of the store. He recognized many from the times he accompanied his father.

Earlier this summer, he found a used digital camera at the thrift store for $4.50, and returned the next day to purchase it with a ziplock bag full of change. He pulled it out now and turned it on, disabling the flash. He nestled it in a gap between the stacks of tires where it wouldn't move and cause blurry pictures.

***

Bryant thought Rafael looked tired, and he wasn't at all sure that anything was sinking in—that this "tutoring" was doing any good. It was their third meeting, but they had to space out the chapters they read because school had started and the kid had other studies to attend to, on top of helping at home.

"So, *Permadeath or Power Up* . . . any of this make

sense to you?" Bryant asked as they left the Andre Center. He usually met Rafa there after school and then they walked to Bryant's warehouse, which was slowly starting to fill in with equipment. The first time they visited, Rafa seemed interested in all the tanks and burners, so that was their routine meeting place—it was a short walk and it was better to be moving than staring at each other.

Rafa nodded his head immediately, and his eyes seemed to indicate that he had read it.

"Did you read through the first two parts?"

Again the nod.

"Did you read further? Did you finish it?"

Again the nod.

"Dude, don't tell me the ending—I'm only to the beginning of part three."

These sessions ended up being less discussion and more hanging out; Bryant filled the space with talk that usually rambled around himself. There was only so much you could pull from a kid who wasn't speaking.

"So, I know Faulk got the tracer planted, but was shot down and crashed into the Grindle mud pits. Were you surprised how Corson reacted? I mean, he's always been a little loopy, but he just went nuts."

Rafa picked up a stick and held it to his hip as though it were a fire hose or machine gun and whisper-screamed as though he were spraying down a hoard of attacking Mornuds.

"Exactly—I figured one of them wouldn't make it, that one would 'power up' and one would 'perma-death,' you know, but I thought it would be the other way around. Corson's gonna have to pull himself together or the Movement is doomed. There's just too many Klobotters."

They were approaching the old factory now and Bryant slung open one of the iron doors and they entered. The smell of salt and the sight of that furnace never failed to pinch his heart.

"I can identify with Corson, I guess. He's not accepting her death because it just seems unfair. Faulk was the smart one, and did everything right. It was a fluke that got her, just a lucky shot. What do you do in a situation like that? I mean, Corson's full of anger, so revenge feels good, and I liked reading about how he wiped out all of those Windinks, but now what? I'm not sure that was the smart move..."

Earlier that week, Bryant had begun repairing the ignition mechanism for the furnace, using a thick manual covered by a hard plastic three-ring binder that he had discovered in the back office. Gas line pipes and strands of electrical wires descended down the side of the furnace on the opposite side of the large iron door they entered.

"Give me a hand here," Bryant said. "I'm trying to get this furnace fired up so that I can play around with making some glass bottles." They moved to the back of the furnace and squatted near the nest of wires. Rafa picked up a heavy gas pipe that was bent at ninety degrees and studied how it might fit the broken hanging line.

"It's a mess, isn't it?" He handed Rafa a wrench and took the pipe from his hands and began fitting it to the open line. "Let's thread this in here . . . go ahead and tighten it down with that wrench. Yup—give 'er all you got."

When it was secure, Bryant said, "It seems to me that if Corson really cared about Faulk, he'd finish what she started: lock in to that tracking device and follow the Canktots back to their underground bunker in Mulvaria. That woulda been a better way to honor her death. Maybe he will in part three..."

Rafa shook his head.

"No? Does he find the XactinSaw?"

Again he shook his head.

"The heck. . . What kind of story is this? Don't make no sense."

Rafa grabbed an ignition switch and pretended to pull a pin on it as if it were a grenade, then lobbed it through a porthole in the furnace and covered his head.

"Ohhh, he goes after the Klobotter mothership, I see... Well, I guess that would do it."

He grabbed another section of pipe—this one with a valve in it—and placed it in the line and they tightened it down.

"I guess I would have done it differently. If I were Corson, I'd start working on Faulk's mission. That's what my wife taught me—she was good at that," Bryant said. "She'd set aside everything if she found someone who needed something."

They both sat there, holding their tools and thinking quietly.

"What do you think? What's the best way to honor someone who's been taken from you? What would make them proud?"

The question settled into the tangle of wires at their knees.

"She died this spring. We were having a baby, but things went wrong one night, and they both died in the hospital. I feel like doing something with this . . . knot in my gut. There's a lot of anger in there, but I don't think it's smart to let that unravel—it'll just make a bigger mess. I'm trying to do something that'd make her proud."

Rafa leaned over and picked up a flat, snub-nosed carpenter pencil and a dusty instruction booklet. The lead was worn down to the wood and he had to hold it up near his eyes and apply it at a severe angle to write. When he finished, he handed the edge of the booklet to Bryant and he read in the margins what the boy had scribbled: *Dads work isnt don yet.*

Rafa reached in his front pocket and pulled something out—it was small enough to be hidden in his half-sized fist. He reached his hand out, palm down, to Bryant.

"What's this?"

Bryant placed an open hand below Rafa's, and the boy dropped in it a small, black plastic square. It was a sim card that goes in one of those old digital cameras.

***

When Bryant got home, he picked up Estelline's backpack, which was leaning against the wall next to the closet in their bedroom, right where she left it. He unzipped the main pouch and looked inside. He was looking for her laptop, but first pulled out a brown paper sack. It was lunch she had packed for herself so she could get to the lab first thing that morning.

He looked inside and nearly gagged to see the ham and cheese sandwich rotting inside its Ziploc. Mold grew on it like a winter coat of fur and it had inflated the plastic baggie. *Good thing that was sealed,* he thought. The only other things in the sack were some desiccated baby carrots and a can of sparkling water. He stood up and walked the sack straight to the garbage bin outside and tossed it in.

Returning, he took out her laptop. Knowing that the battery had probably run down in time since she last used it, he plugged it in and hit the power button. The machine began to whir.

The screen flipped to a desktop with a vibrant photo for the background: the sun setting over the water on a Key West beach. It was taken from the vantage of their seats in short lawn chairs at the edge of the surf. He remembered her saying she believed it was the first time his pale thighs had seen the sun. Her legs were the sculpted, bronzed blades of a wind turbine; his were downed branches with the bark peeled away.

The sound of the surf came back to him—the endless rhythm, each wave repeating with several lingering phases: crash, spread, sift, then a brief moment of quiet stasis before another crash. They had closed their eyes to the crimson and cerulean of the departing sun and just listened to the day's metronome.

He came back to himself. How long had he been daydreaming? He shifted his weight and pulled the card from his pocket and placed it in the small drive on the side of the computer. A file folder appeared over the lime in her beer on the desktop. He clicked twice on it and a folder opened up with a grid of dark thumbnail images.

He opened the first image—it seemed to be taken at night. He could see the outlines of men filing onto a bus. He skipped down and picked another photo from a different row—seemed to be the same scene. He scrolled down and opened two more. Two men seemed to be present in most of the pictures—one was a thick man with thinning, curly hair. In most of the images he was walking up and down the line. The other was fatter and held a clipboard—it looked like he was writing down the names of the men in line.

He looked at the bottom of the window and saw that there were 574 pictures on this card. He scrolled down more and saw a series of thumbnails that were noticeably brighter. He clicked on the first one—it looked like the same location, only much more was visible in the sunlight. The bus was there again—light blue —and men were stepping off of it and walking toward the store.

He clicked through several more photos from this daytime scene and noticed the two men again—the thick one watching the men and the fat one writing something down. In the daylight, he could better see the posture of the men coming from the bus. They seemed to lower their heads when they came to either of those men. The fat one was handing the workers something before they entered the store—it was a small slip of paper.

He scrolled through the grid and could see a basic pattern of a dozen or so dark images followed by a dozen or so light ones. What was this kid up to?

24

Bryant held the front door of Columba Hall open for Vivian as she lugged the heavy, insulated box of lab samples out the exit. It was a brilliant, early fall day—the leaves in the canopy of oaks and sycamores lining the drive were just beginning to entertain the suggestion of changing colors. It was a day that would have looked like summer in a photograph, but felt like fall in person.

"Thanks for stepping in to help, Bryant," said Vivian. "When Madison called in sick this morning, I didn't know how I was going to do this. Would've been in a tight spot without you."

"It's the least I could do," he said. "And it keeps me connected to Stella's work. It's interesting to see these guys after everything she told me about them."

They walked around the side of the building to the loading dock area, where their vehicles were parked in a maintenance spot. As he helped Vivian place the equipment in her car, he heard men laughing. A dozen brothers were filing out from a back door in the hall and ambling into the center of an expansive, mowed field behind the building. The first two were carrying green canvas duffel bags full of sports equipment—Bryant heard the clacking cluster of wooden bat handles that were sticking out of one.

Two brothers just emerging from the back door

looked at each other and broke into a dead sprint to race to meet the pack of others. They were laughing as they ran, and Bryant chuckled at the incongruity. They looked seventy, but their bodies moved with fluid strength. They showed none of the temerity of elders who might have carefully picked their footing on the uneven grass to avoid a fall. When they reached the main group, one of them chucked the shoulder of the man carrying the bats, knocking him off balance. The other put his shoulder at the waist of the brother in the lead and hoisted him across his neck like a sack of dog food.

Bryant heard a car door shut on the other side of his pickup, and looked up to see a short, thin man with glasses striding toward the congregating brothers. Bryant thought his face looked like it was drawn by a mid-century cartoonist: his beard stubble appeared to be shaded with dark pencil in a sharp outline around his jaw. He looked like he was fixing a whistle to his mouth.

"That's the bishop, I think," Vivian said in a low voice. "I met him here once."

A sharp *twheet* ricocheted across the field. Bryant watched the men turn and begin to form a large circle. One stepped into the middle and they began doing jumping jacks.

"Wish Estelline were here to see this," Vivian said. "Our lab work is beginning to pay off—we're finally starting to understand some of what's going on here."

"What do you mean?" asked Bryant.

"Well, Dr. Bowdle gave this talk two weeks ago that drew some of this data together. He studies flatworms, and some of them have cells that survive interminably. They just keep dividing and reproducing. So, he's already proven that death on the cellular level is not an absolute certainty.

"Death in a body is simply the result of the cellular systems in our bodies reaching a tipping point where they switch from preservation and restoration to decay and dissolution. The thing is, nothing says those cells absolutely have to die after X amount of time. In theory, they could just keep restoring themselves, like the flatworm. Bowdle's hypothesis is that aging and death is an evolutionary mechanism to sharpen our focus on reproduction."

"Wait," Bryant said. "So we're still evolving? I thought we'd reached the top of the heap."

"Evolution isn't just going to peter out," Vivian said. "Just look at wisdom teeth. Dr. Bowdle was telling me yesterday that it's a good example of evolution at work in us today. Used to be that we ate lots of tough food—roots and leaves and nuts—that wore down our teeth. We needed big, powerful jaws and new, replacement teeth, so wisdom teeth would descend after childhood. Then, we learned to cook—we began eating cultivated, soft food, and our jaws started getting smaller. Our jaws today don't have room for wisdom teeth when they come in—they impact the rest and have to be removed. As a result, our bodies are learning from our behavior and the number of people born with no wisdom teeth is growing right now. So, we're very much still at the mercy of the forces of evolution."

"But age and death don't sound like evolution," Bryant said. "Why wouldn't it be advantageous to just live forever?"

"Think about it," Vivian said. "A village of early

humans impervious to cellular death, who don't age, would never have propagated the species. What would drive them, what would motivate them? As soon as they secured a reliable food source, they'd just sit back and relax.

"Also, keep in mind, violent death happens—a caveman resistant to natural death could still be killed and eaten by a saber-toothed tiger. So, eventually, the species wouldn't have survived. Better to have a short lifespan, relatively speaking, that motivates us to reproduce and pass on what we know before kicking the bucket."

"But now that there's no threat from saber-toothed tigers, these guys are 'evolving' past the aging process?" Bryant asked.

"Exactly," Vivian replied. "Connect the dots and it's actually not surprising that it's happening here first: these men have no concerns about where their food comes from, medicine has supported their survival for their whole lives, the threat of accidental death is remote, and they are not concerned with reproduction. Their bodies are learning they don't need the aging mechanism—they're letting go of cellular entropy. Our lab work is showing a biology of preservation and repair on the cellular level instead, which is leading to growth and rejuvenation.

"Anyways, I gotta get these samples to the lab," she said, climbing into her car. "See you later this week?"

"Yup—right. I'll be there," Bryant said.

25

Bryant was up at 3:30 a.m. and skipped the shower, tossing on his Wranglers and a greyed white undershirt and work boots. He grabbed a Mountain Dew from his mostly-empty fridge and hopped in his truck. He was glad he had a flannel shirt—the sun would warm things up when it rose in a few hours, but for now the night air was cold and damp.

It was a short drive to Wilmot. Yesterday, he traced the route out Hurley Road and scouted a place on the edge of town where he could park his truck inconspicuously in the corner of a farm supply store lot. After nearly missing the turnoff to County Road 40 in the dark, he rumbled the seven miles into town on gravel. There were no other cars, and he thought of how Rafa got himself to Wilmot—on a bike, maybe? The kid had moxie to get his butt out of bed in the middle of the night and ride in the dark, he thought. He wondered if he'd be there this morning.

He parked his truck and reached for the plastic grocery sack on the seat next to him. It held a sandwich, an apple, a bottle of water, and a dirty 'Beaus hat. He slapped the hat against his thigh and a small cloud of dust exploded over his leg and scattered in the light from the lone pole illuminating the lot, and pulled it low across his brow. The store from Rafa's pictures was only a few blocks away.

He felt nervous, and the hesitation gave him a chance to recall the conversation he had at the Andre Center with Brother Martin earlier in the week. Brother had explained that Rafa's dad, Raymundo, was organizing workers before he was killed. He crossed the supervisors out there—he called them *capateces*—and Bryant had immediately thought of the two figures overseeing the men coming and going from the blue bus.

"Slavery seems like an outdated term, and it's odd to think about using it today, here in Indiana in the twenty-first century, but that's exactly what this is," Brother Martin said. "No one cares enough to see it."

That's when Bryant decided he needed to get his own eyes on the situation. If Rafa was out here fooling around, Bryant wanted to know why. And, more importantly, who he was observing.

He left the truck and did his best to walk with a strong stride, engaging his core muscles to draw his lagging leg forward at the same pace as his other one. A few workers were already gathering at the corner in the dark. Street lights bracketed the store in a gap of darkness. He tried to exude confidence to show he had been there before, and walked to a specific spot he had picked out before crossing the street. He stood next to the side of the store farthest from where he expected the bus to be, judging from Rafa's images.

From here he could look out across the street at a mechanic shop and see a stack of tires on one side. He guessed that's where Rafa hid to take his pictures.

By 4:30, other workers had arrived and were muttering to each other in low tones. The line filled out from the far corner to where he was standing, and he turned his body and stood with the others. He wondered how much of a hurdle it would be for him not to know Spanish very well, and decided that he'd just keep quiet. Brother Martin had said that some of these workers were from rural Central America where they spoke their own indigenous languages, anyway, so he thought he could pass it off. With his hat pointed low, he tried his best to study other workers, on the alert for what to do next. He focused on calming his breathing.

A large, dual-wheeled pickup truck pulled up to the store and parked behind the workers, gravel snapping beneath its weight. A bus came in behind it and turned down the road that emptied into the intersection. Bryant recognized it as the same bus he had seen in Rafa's pictures—light blue—and it executed a three-point turn and pulled up to the corner, facing out. The workers hushed, collected their things, and fell into a more orderly line.

Two men got out of the pickup truck and walked up and down the line—they didn't say anything. The one holding a clipboard had fat around his torso that made his arms stick out to the side as he walked. Bryant noticed the heels of his cowboy boots were nearly worn through because he walked with a pronounced backward lean to keep his weight from pulling him forward.

The other carried nothing, and wore muddy penny loafers and a button-down linen shirt that seemed too thin for the weather. The strands of his curly hair were pasted to his head and didn't cover his scalp well. He seemed to be inspecting the line.

The line held maybe fifty workers—mostly men with a handful of stocky women—and Bryant started to move forward with them. The man in the linen shirt evaluated each one, giving tacit approval as they stepped in front of the fat man with the clipboard and gave their name. Then they stepped on the bus. Before long, four women had been culled from the line, as well as a tall, pre-adolescent boy. Curly pulled them out of the procession and dismissed them.

Bryant kept his head down and stepped forward, his heart banging like a speed bag whacked by a boxer. He knew Curly was looking him over, so he kept repeating in his head the name he had come up with—Matteo Benitez—and was about to say it out loud when felt a hard jerk on his shirt sleeve. He turned to see the man staring at him with a snarled, disapproving brow. Bryant could smell the stench of cigarette smoke emanating from his shirt. He pulled Bryant's arm harder, causing him to step out of line with a stumble because of his leg. The man huffed condescension through his nose and said, "Not today hop-a-long—we're picking melons."

Bryant turned, his only thought to walk away. Then the man tossed a phrase at his back: "Fuckin' cripple." Bryant stopped. *Not here,* he thought. He slowly stepped off the curb and walked across the abandoned street. It was the first time in his life he had ignored someone calling him that.

As he neared his truck, he heard quiet steps behind him, and turned to see Rafa running out of the darkness to him. In the circle of light cast by the one parking lamp, he could see that the boy still had pajama bottoms on, wet and dirty below the knees, which slapped against his ankles as he ran. Rafa plowed straight into him, clamped his arms around Bryant's waist, and plunged his bed-wrinkled hair into Bryant's chest. That fighter in Bryant's chest got up and began beating on his heart again.

***

Rafa walked around to the passenger side of Bryant's truck and reached up to open the door. He vaulted himself into the truck using the inside door handle, and turned to watch Bryant through the flat back window as he secured his bike in the corner of the bed with a short bungee cord. Dew had soaked through the thin cotton of his pajamas and felt cold against his shins. He sat forward in the seat to make his legs hang perpendicular so that they didn't rub against the wetness.

He's got that limp, but he's still strong, Rafa thought. It had been so long since he'd been near a man who did things just for him. Brother Martin was nice, but this was more. The way he felt reminded him of wrestling with his dad. Papa would wrap him up in a blanket, tucking in the edges, and carry him through the house to give him to Mamma like a present, and she'd act surprised and grateful and curious about whatever the gift could be.

His eyes did not leave Bryant as he climbed into the driver's seat. Bryant did not look back—he put the truck in gear and began driving out of town to avoid being seen by the bus as it was departing.

"Which way do you live?" he asked.

Rafa pointed east.

"Can you get there going this way?"

Rafa nodded his head and made the signal for an upcoming right-hand turn.

"Okay," Bryant said. Rafa could not tell how he

was feeling—he seemed tense.

"Listen—it's dangerous here," Bryant said. "You can't be out here anymore. I can help—I'll go out there so that we can figure this out, but you gotta stay home, okay? If they see you with a camera, you'll end up like your dad."

Rafa knew this already and had decided that if his dad wasn't scared, he wasn't going to be either. Well, he was scared, he admitted, but he wasn't going to let that stop him. *Eff those guys*, he thought.

***

The cemetery was being buried in leaves falling from the old sycamores that surrounded it, and workers were beginning to clear the colors in the far corner this morning. Bryant figured it would take them all day to clear the ground around all the headstones, and by the time they finished, the place they started would be covered again.

He was alone in the cemetery and when he reached Estelline's grave, he peeled an ochre leaf that the night's dew had pasted over the date of her death on the granite marker. Autumn felt strange this time around, he thought. It was usually a season for heavier beer and for spending the evening with a dramatic baseball game on television. *Unjee* would be filling her pantry out of habit; Estelline would start drinking coffee in the mornings darkened by the shortening light. But this time around, all he could see was the world giving up and letting go—death reasserting its governance.

"Getting colder, isn't it?" Vivian called to him as

she walked up in the noisy detritus of leaves. "Snow'll be here before long."

"Wonder what those brothers will do this winter," Bryant said. "Maybe they'll take up hockey."

Vivian smiled. "Wouldn't surprise me. It's fun to watch them. . . I can't stop thinking of her when I'm there. Still not over it."

Small-engine leaf blowers droned on in the distance, just above the sound of traffic. Standing here, he was always a little offended that everyone just kept going about their business around this plot of land that held all these dead people. Each person buried here was precious to someone and had work they once considered important, yet the world keeps turning and the seasons come and go, he thought—didn't seem to matter if we are above ground or below.

Bryant thought of his *unjee*—her education had not gone past eighth grade, but she was the wisest person he knew. She didn't know the first thing about evolution or calculus or chemistry, but she did know how to live. Somehow that groundedness came from the way she knew her place in the world and her relationship to everything. It reminded him of explaining his beer brewing with her. She struggled to follow the mechanics and biology of it, but understood that he was putting things in relationship with one another, and that those ingredients knew how to cooperate to turn into something that transcended the sum of their parts. She was the one who introduced to him the idea that his beer could do the same for Andover. It wasn't a "product" that he needed to pump out to grow a business—that was a *wasi'chu* way of thinking, she explained. She helped him see himself as a caretaker—of the ingredients he gathered as well as the people who gathered around his beer. He had the power to turn them into something greater than what could just be measured and explained. To do anything less would be to diminish what he'd been given, and himself.

They both looked up from the grave and took a deep breath.

"My *unjee*—my grandma, she's the one who raised me—she had a strong sense of the supernatural," Bryant said. "She didn't really have a name for it—she was just herself, but you could always tell that there was something more to it all for her."

He took a deep breath and continued, "She would say Estelline's here with us, only in a different way. It feels to me like I have her near, but maybe I'm just groping in the dark for something to hold on to."

"I'd like to think she's somewhere else, but that's just it—what the hell do we know?" Vivian said. She knelt down and traced the engraved lines of Estelline's name in the granite. "I know she'll always be with us in our memories, though—that's what I'm holding on to. She was extraordinary, and remembering that helps me live up to her example. She doesn't have to be bouncing around a cloud in some heaven for me to be a better person because of her life."

Bryant could see how that made sense, but he didn't dare tell Vivian how Estelline was starting to fade from his memory. He had trouble admitting it to himself. Her smell, her face, her voice calling his name —those things remained, so far. But he couldn't hold on to every single particularity about her, and was afraid that he was conjuring those details as they fled. How did the flecks of green line up in her irises? How did she cross her legs when she sat on the floor? And what about the things that annoyed him? He remembered how she filled both sides of the sink with dirty dishes when she was cooking, but what about her other stubbornnesses? They must have been the first things his mind jettisoned. Which meant that the person he was remembering was increasingly a construct of his own imagination.

Which meant he truly was losing her.

26

Bryant consulted an agricultural calendar for Indiana late-season harvests and knew they'd be moving to pick peppers around Wilmot in November. He resolved to try the picking crew again—he wouldn't have to handle heavy melons, and there would likely be fewer workers to choose from.

The night before he headed back to the store at Wilmot, at what should have been the height of the bell pepper harvest, he filled his bathtub with hot water and dumped in three boxes of bags of black tea. He stirred the water with a paddle he used to mash barley and water at the start of his brewing process. It steeped to an opaque, flat, black, steaming puddle, and was already starting to stain the sides of the tub.

He stripped his clothes, picked up the snorkel he found at the St. Vincent de Paul thrift store, and set a timer for fifteen minutes. He climbed into the tub, put the snorkel into his mouth and slipped under the warm water, closing his eyes. He could feel his body begin to float, so he braced his arms to the sides of the tub to keep himself submerged. The warmth was relaxing.

When he heard the timer go off, he stood up and let the water run off. When he looked in the mirror, his jerked his head in surprise because for an instant, he failed to recognize his body as his own. It was two shades darker, and evenly shaded through the tan lines on his arms.

This would stain his towels—he hadn't thought ahead to pull out an old one. He used the green towel hanging near the shower and gently dabbed the tea off his body. It smudged slightly, but he could see that there was a deep tint below that would not rub off.

He got himself ready for bed, wanting to get enough rest for a day of work tomorrow. His head began to feel light, though, and he could feel his pulse pushing against the inside of his wrists. The tea—he had just absorbed a month's worth of caffeine through his skin. This was a wrench in the plan—he might be looking at a day of work without any sleep.

***

Early in the morning in Wilmot, he waited for the line to begin to form before joining it. As he walked up, one man smiled and nodded at him with an uneven look. Bryant guessed he had suffered a stroke—half of his face didn't work. As he fell into line behind him the man reached around to greet him and he could see that he had been injured in some kind of accident—a deep scar formed a crevice across his forehead and down the side of his nose to his mouth. It looked like a fault-line—everything to the right of the scar was inanimate. The eye on that side was clouded over below a slumped brow and the corner of his mouth sagged like a flat tire.

The man was speaking to him in garbled Spanish, but Bryant just gave a half smile and said, "*Sí, sí.*" When the pickup truck pulled up with the bus behind it, the man turned to Bryant and puffed out his chest, motioning for him to do the same. *Stand up tall and look strong,* he seemed to be saying.

Only about twenty workers stood in line, including three women, and as they slowly moved forward and on to the bus, Bryant stood tall and looked straight ahead, feigning nonchalance with a twinge of impatience—as though he were used to this routine. The man with the curly hair was not inspecting the workers very closely—he stood near the fat one with the clipboard and just observed. No one was pulled from the line.

Bryant gave a name quickly—Matteo Benitez—effecting the best accent he could muster. No one looked at him—the heavy one just wrote down his name in a fresh column on the clipboard.

He climbed aboard the bus, and soon they were bouncing down the washboard gravel road west of town. Everyone had their own seat, and most of the workers slouched down and were resting. After twenty minutes, they turned onto a dirt road with grass in between the tire tracks.

The bus came to a stop, and when Bryant looked out the window on the left side of the bus, he could see the first few rows of green plants in a field and then darkness beyond. Two pickup trucks were parked just off the two-track in front of the bus on the right. Next to them loomed a windbreak of trees.

With the end of daylight savings time, they had gained some light back in the morning, but the sun was still an hour away from rising. The horizon was just starting to brighten at the edge.

No one spoke—the workers just grabbed whatever they had brought and stood up to file off the bus. It was cold outside—in the forties, Bryant guessed. He could see his breath linger in the air in front of his face. The diesel engine in the bus shuddered to a stop and the only thing he could hear was the breathing of the workers. They all seemed to be waiting for something, so he hung near the back to see what would happen.

Four men got out of the pickup trucks and walked into the field without acknowledging the workers. The bus driver—a large, solid man; Hispanic, thick about the torso with long arms—followed them and the workers bunched their lunches on the ground near the bus and fell in behind him. They walked out into the field on soft earth between two rows. The rows held four-foot swaths of thigh-high bell pepper plants, and more rows extended into the darkness on either side of the marching platoon.

Bryant was second-to-last to enter the field and could only see dark outlines and shapes ahead of him, but the stars were bright above. As they moved into the flat field the sky seemed to unfold over him like a vast, twinkling, silent umbrella. He was immersed in it like the tea-bath, only the suspending fluid was above, not below—three-dimensional and luminous.

The group walked for two or three minutes and then slowed and gathered together. Ahead, Bryant could see the outlines of machines—tractors, each connected to a trailer that held several large, wooden bins. The tall and narrow tires of the tractors and trailers precisely spanned the rows of pepper plants.

The two men from the pickups climbed into the cabs of the tractors and started their engines, which made chugging coughs. The other two men climbed onto the trailers and unpacked several stacks of plastic tubs from inside the wooden bins, handing them down to the workers, who then distributed the tubs around to each other. Bryant received a red one, round, with rope handles. The workers spread out behind the tractors and began picking; the tractors slowly pulled ahead to keep in front of the workers.

Bryant found a spot and bent over to the plants, but kept his eyes up, watching closely how the others worked. He keyed in on one woman, short, with a grey hooded sweatshirt and blue jeans. He noticed that on the bus, she wore the hood over her head, but now that she was working, it was laid across her back, revealing short, stringy black hair.

Both of her hands worked independently of one another, reaching out to snatch peppers and snap them off their stems. She pulled with a small twist and jerk and then, in the same motion, flipped her wrist so that the peppers fell into the bin between her legs. After two or three pulls from each hand, she stood, lifted the bin, and took several long strides to the side to bend down for more picking. It took less than five minutes for her to cover ten feet in the row, which filled her bin with peppers, then she hoisted it to her shoulder and walked it up to one of the trailers being pulled by a tractor. With a small hop, she hefted the bin up to one of the men who had handed out the containers at the start. He grabbed it and dumped it into the large wooden box on the trailer. The peppers tumbled into the empty bin with muffled thumps. He reached into a coffee tin and pulled out a small blue plastic token, tossed it into her bin, and then handed the bin back to her. She reached in for the token and put it in her pocket, and stepped back to where she left off.

Bryant discerned the system—each side of each

row had two or three workers, and the first one picked quickly and left some for those who followed. The last one made sure everything was off the plant. He needed to be in the front—he knew he'd have trouble keeping up with only one decent hand, and didn't want to be obviously lagging behind, so he could make that first pass and leave some for the workers behind him.

He stepped ahead of two workers in one row near the edge of the group and began picking. The plants dropped dew on his arms as he pulled, so he pulled up the sleeves on his flannel shirt. His arms felt bone-cold, like he was reaching into the tub of ice water he used to cool tubs of hot wort back when he was brewing in his garage. The peppers smelled like wet dirt.

After several pulls, he took large steps forward. The sun wasn't above the horizon yet, but there was enough grey light to see the peppers. When he looked up, he could see the expanse of the field—they were a small flotilla on a green sea. The diesel engines of the tractors had settled into a comfortable rumbling purr. He put his head down and continued working.

It took him close to ten minutes to fill his bin the first time, and by his third token, the ache in his back was reaching down the hamstring on his right leg. He tried squatting down to pick, but then his shoulders began to ache from reaching out and up for the peppers. He was beginning to doubt if he could last the day.

27

On the bus ride back to Wilmot, Bryant was too tired to check the time. He laid across a seat on the bus with his legs hanging into the aisle. The springs in the seat had long ago surrendered their form and he could feel the outline of the seat's frame in his back. He closed his eyes. Why was he doing this again?

Rafa. Raymundo. What was Raymundo fighting? What was Rafa documenting?

His arms itched below his elbows. Must have been pesticide residue on those plants. He was starting to get a rash, and he couldn't rest with that itch nagging him.

The commotion of workers standing up woke him. He didn't realize the bus had stopped. He stood and walked outside with them. The pickup truck that arrived with the bus that morning was parked back in the same place, and the two men from Rafa's photos were tracking the workers as they came off the bus. As they passed the heavy man with the clipboard, each worker set a stack of tokens on the clipboard. The curly-haired man counted them and dropped them into a coffee can with a tumbling twang. He whispered to the fat one, who wrote a few small figures on the spreadsheet on his clipboard and then scribbled on a slip of paper and handed the receipt to the worker.

Bryant was starving. He had taken a break mid-morning and downed his lunch. He took another break just after noon, but only to rest while everyone else continued to work. At that point, all his food and water were gone. He paced his work even more slowly for the afternoon and stumbled to the bus when the day was done. Now his stomach was an angry cavern, and he just wanted something to put in it to calm it down—anything. He walked to the store.

He saw a counter to the left that had refrigerated bins of prepared meat with a steaming grill behind it. A dry-erase board on the wall behind it listed a range of options in Spanish, but there were no prices. A teenage boy stood ready for his order.

He looked around and saw other workers gathering cans of beans and bottles of Gatorade. They were already checking out. He held up two fingers and said, "*Tacos, pollo.*" The kid started heating two pairs of corn tortillas on the skillet; it screamed when he placed a pile of meat next to them. The smell bounced around Bryant's stomach like an echo.

He grabbed the biggest Gatorade he could find and took the tacos from the teen, who motioned to the cluttered checkout counter next to the door. He walked over and set the food down and pulled out the receipt for his day of work. He handed it to the severe-looking woman behind the counter.

She opened a discolored ledger book with a black cover, the pages dog-eared and swollen from being handled and spilled upon. She flipped to the front and scanned for his name under the B section. Not finding it, she glanced at him and then wrote, "Benitez, Matteo" on a new line and placed the numbers 250 and 8 next to it. She looked at the tacos and Gatorade and wrote 10, then summed it all to 268. Then she picked up his receipt and subtracted 62.

She flipped the book around and started speaking in Spanish to him, pointing to the numbers. He waved her off and said quietly, "*No español.*"

"*¿Inglés*?" she asked.

He showed her his good hand and pinched his fingers together. *A little.*

"Okay," she said. She continued, speaking slowly and pointing to the numbers. "Registration fee 250. Transportation is 8—for the bus. Your food is 10. You earned 62 today. Are you in the barracks?"

He shook his head no.

"Okay, so you still owe 206."

"Okay, okay," he said. She flipped the book back around and looked to the worker behind him. He gathered his food and walked outside, trying to wrap his mind around the fact that he had only earned $62 for the whole day in the field. A fast worker could earn twice that, maybe.

He squatted next to the exterior wall of the store, cracked open the Gatorade, and poured it down his throat—he could feel it splashing in the emptiness below his lungs. The tacos disappeared in the way newspaper is consumed by a well-stoked fire. He rested and watched the workers make their way out of the store. A few stood in line next to a payphone around the corner. Dusk was already starting to fall. If he was going to try again tomorrow, he was going to need some sleep. It seemed like weeks since he last felt rested.

He remembered that she asked about the barracks—they must charge for rent, too. He wondered where the workers stayed. He stood and looked around

—there were still two men standing near the payphone, twiddling plastic cards in their hands, waiting. He looked around the corner and could see a trail of eight people who were in the field with him, walking out of town. He decided to follow them.

***

After walking for about ten minutes, he reached a compound with a chain-link fence around it. A strand of barbed wire was looped around the top. The fenced area could have held two football fields, he guessed. There were four rows of square, cinder-block structures with corrugated tin roofs and one small window in each wall. Each row of huts held four bright blue portable toilets stationed at intervals. A small cloud of dust rose from the area in the waning light. He could hear children playing.

The fence enclosing the small village gathered to an open gate that faced the gravel road. The people in front of him walked into the compound. He continued walking past the gate, looking in and observing as much as he could as he passed. The first house inside the gate had no door and there were three ATVs parked near it. He recognized the bus driver standing just inside the door, talking to someone further inside. Dirty tricycles and kids' toys were littered around several of the huts. He could see rope strung between the barracks holding drying clothes. He kept walking.

He passed the far side of the compound and nothing but empty cornfields stretched before him, an expanse of dry, brown stubble broken in the black soil. He had to find a way to loop back toward Wilmot so he could get to his truck and get home. He was exhausted, and needed more food. And a hot shower. *Lord God in heaven, a beer would taste good just now—a cold pour of Last Stand in a frozen mug.* His mouth was watering.

It was nearing dark now, and he saw the glow of headlights approaching from ahead. They glared brightly for a moment as the car passed him, and he kept his head down to shield his eyes with the brim of his hat.

He heard the vehicle come to a grinding, sudden stop behind him. He looked back and saw the white taillights come on—the car was backing up. It was a black sedan with dark tinted windows. He turned back around and walked quickly. Should he start running? What could anyone want with him out here?

A door opened, followed by a shout from a male voice—it sounded tense. "*Ai, amigo! A dónde vas*!" He did not turn around and kept walking. "*Cabron*!"

Footsteps. He turned to see a young man jogging toward him. A larger, older man was getting out of the car, which had been turned off. The headlights were out and all Bryant could hear was the urgent crunch of gravel as they approached him. The stars were coming out—the same ones that enveloped him with mystery this morning. They seemed impassive now—two dimensional and remote. Darkness was closing in.

The young man passed him and stood in the middle of the road and put his hand up. Bryant stopped. He could hear the other man walking up behind him slowly.

"Hey man, I'm just going home after a long day," Bryant said. "I don't want trouble."

The young man jerked his head back and smiled

when he heard the English. "Whoah, did you hear that, Spinks? *Muchacho* has the *inglés*. The fuck you doing out here, man?"

Bryant knew he couldn't out run these guys, and if he were lucky he could hold his own with the one in front of him in a fight, but not both. He'd have to talk his way out of this. The adrenaline was narrowing his vision, and the words weren't coming. He couldn't think.

"I worked all day, okay? I'm going home."

"You work in the field, your home is back there. Why you leaving? Where you going?"

Bryant could see the tattoo of a snake winding down the other arm of the young man. He stepped toward Bryant. "You can't leave, *amigo*. Surprised you fuckers don't learn."

Bryant started to put his hands up, expecting a confrontation. He turned to check on the big guy behind him just in time to see his long arm flying toward him. A violent jolt rocked the horizon like a see-saw and then his cheek was pressed against gravel.

Disoriented, he had his hands up; his eyes were clenched closed. There was a rush of noise flooding his head. He had to move. He tried rolling over and getting up. There was an impact on his rib cage and he could hear his lungs empty through his mouth. He laid on his side and sucked for air. Pain everywhere.

They were picking him up, one on each side. He calmed his body, let go of the tension, and tried to fix one problem at a time. He had to breathe. He expanded his chest and tried to suck air in through his nose. Half an inch at a time, his lungs regained their footing. They seemed to be taking him to the car. They'd have to adjust their hold as they opened a door—that would be his chance, he thought.

"Hardly worth making an example of you, since the season's about over. Most everyone's been shipped south already. So, what we going to do with you? What good are you?"

The large one who'd been called Spinks stayed silent.

"Siego will know."

Bryant could feel Spinks adjusting his grip as they neared the sedan. *Now*.

He kicked his legs and tugged his arms in and his torso fell to the gravel as he fell free from Snake. The side of his face dragged on the rocks as Spinks stumbled backward, still holding onto his arm. Bryant twisted and with his free arm reached for the big man's sausage thumb to pull it loose from his wrist. A blow to the back of Bryant's head smacked his neck down. The world started filling in with white and he lost control of his muscles. He fell backward and his head hit the ground, harder this time. Everything was black. He could hear the men moving and speaking, but the words floated past his consciousness like traffic by a bus stop.

"Fuck that hurt! Get him in there."

A latch released and a door squeaked. He was being lifted again, then tossed, horizontally, into a hole. His limbs were being handled, he felt his body rocking. Maybe they were binding his hands and legs? A door slammed again. He was wrapped in a cocoon—the air felt close. The floor beneath him rumbled and his body rolled backward.

***

He was only in the trunk for a few moments when the car came to a stop, and he had to brace from rolling over again, sending pain through his ribs. When the car engine stopped, he heard voices outside the car. He tried to move, but his legs and arms were wrapped tightly together and against his body. He couldn't open his mouth—duct tape.

The latch cracked and the trunk door squeaked. He could smell fresh air—cool and mixed with exhaust and road dust. A flashlight flooded his eyes and he pulled his head back and away. Someone grabbed his hair and pulled him into the light.

He recognized the voice of the man with curly hair who had studied him in line that morning. "I remember him in line this morning, but he didn't say anything. He was walking past the barracks?"

He heard the voice of the young man who had stopped him in the road—the one with the snake tattoo. "He was limping down the road past the gate, out of town. We stopped him and were going to teach him like the others, but he started speaking English. Good, like, too. And, we only got a week left in the season, so I didn't know if it would be worth it to fuck him up."

"If he got English, he's connected—either we can't touch him, or we gotta end him. And we already touched him, didn't we. So looks like you two got a long night ahead of you.

They're going to kill me, Bryant thought. Dread pooled in his chest and his head felt fuzzy as it sunk in. *No one can help me. I gotta get myself out of this.*

"I'll call my guy up in Michigan City—the one we used this summer. He'll be ready for you."

The one named Spinks reached in and dislodged a tire iron from the wall of the trunk behind Bryant. He grabbed Bryant by the hair and jerked his head up, lifting half of his body upright. Bryant tried to yell, "Stop!" but his breath bottled up against the tape over his mouth and cheeks. He shut his eyes as Spinks swung the iron toward the side of his head.

28

Bryant emerged from black nothingness into a penetrating cold wind steadily blowing in his face. The left side of his head felt wet. His vision remained black not because he couldn't see—it was dark outside. His equilibrium caught up to the fact that he was in a moving vehicle with winter air blowing on him. He startled awake and cussed, remembering the danger he was in.

He marshaled his faculties and did a check of his body. He was slumped in the back corner of some vehicle—was he in the bed of a pickup truck?—his hands still bound behind his back, his legs mashed together. He tried to open his eyes, but the cold air buffeting his face made his eyelids squint and tremble.

His torso felt broken—any movement at all sent a crack of pain across his chest. The slightest twinge of a neck muscle unleashed brawling badgers through his brow. The crackly, wet sensation on his left cheek was blood, probably freezing now—he remembered cringing for the blow from Spinks.

Spinks—where was he? He wedged his eyes open and closed to clear the tears accumulating in the corners of his lids. He could make out two figures—Spinks and Snake—standing inside a glass door ahead, blowing into cupped hands to warm them. They were in a cabin with one other figure, who was driving. It was a boat! He was in the back of a large fishing boat.

He remembered the honeymoon in Key West, walking along the docks and reading the names of all the charter boats—this looked about that size. A waist-high gunwale enclosed the back platform where he was stuffed into a corner. The white outlines of the boat caught the disappearing ambient light from shore—everything else was night. The boat was rocking against a steady beat of waves—they were speeding out across the open water. He guessed they were on Lake Michigan.

They're going to dump me in this lake, Bryant thought with terror. He had no chance resisting—he couldn't feel his hands lashed behind his back, much less move them. Even if he could get free, he couldn't take on three men. He knew his time was limited—they would stop the boat at any moment and kill him and throw him in the water.

I might have a chance in the water, he thought. *Maybe the water will loosen the tape around my hands. Can I even stand?* With every second, he knew he was getting farther from shore if he had to swim. *Am I strong enough?*

I have to jump. It's my only chance.

Bryant twisted his knees under his body, keeping an eye on the outlines of the men in the cabin silhouetted against the navigational and steering lights. He levered his body deeper into the corner and lifted his hips—his back rose along the gunwale. The pain felt like he was breaking in half. The blood drained from his head and he worried he might pass out.

He hopped to drag his feet closer. They caught on something. He looked down—his legs were bound together and a plastic rope was threaded through the thick layers of tape and looped around a cinder block.

He heard shouts and looked up. The men were all turned toward him from the cabin. They were opening the door and rushing toward him. The boat suddenly stopped and they both staggered backward, toward the cabin door, from the loss of momentum. With his weight braced against the gunwale, though, Bryant stood stable.

It has to be now! he thought—*go!*

He heaved his body with a thrust and tossed his head backward. His waist rose over the gunwale, dragging the block, which banged against the wall of the boat. Spinks was reaching out for him. He pulled against his legs again, feeling the rope tug the cinder-block up and over the edge of the boat. He fell backward and took the deepest breath his ribs would allow.

The water struck him with a thud—more than anything it felt dense. Then the cold settled in, soaking through his jeans and flannel shirt—it was a gripping, ruthless cold and it nearly forced the air from his lungs.

The cinder block jerked hard on his legs and he began sinking at an astonishing rate—he felt like he was falling out of a building, underwater.

He jostled his wrists together, working them up and down frantically. He felt the water reaching beneath the binding tape and begin to loosen it. His smaller hand scraped loose.

He was still sinking—the water pressure pressed on his ears.

His heart battered the door to his lungs.

He reached down for his feet and could feel the rope, but couldn't find the knot.

A retch convulsed his chest, and he struggled to

keep it in. His body heaved for air and he was overcome with a fit of coughing. Thick, icy water poured into his throat and down to his lungs and his body stopped responding to his diminishing orders.

This is it, he thought. *This is how I die. I can't believe this is it.*

He heard the motor of the boat throttling up and speeding away. Far above him, he saw a white trail of surf from the boat's wake streaming away like a distant comet.

His last thought was a flash of recognition, a memory. *Yes—this is death: they go on without me.*

He was swallowed by the dark and cold, and was gone.

PART THREE

The End of Ending

29

"Hello? You still here?"

Slouched in the chair inside the confessional booth, Father Howard Brown snapped his head up, suddenly awake. He heard someone bending to kneel behind the screen next to his head. It was dimly lit and quiet as a closet, and he had been waiting for penitents. Did he pass out or just fall asleep? What time was it?

"Yes, of course," he mustered in the most patient and ready voice he could find. He looked at his watch —it was after three o'clock. He'd been here since noon. He sat up straight, the crick in his neck and cramp in his back busting through the door of his consciousness like a SWAT team. He breathed in deeply through his nose and filled his lungs—he needed to get with it. "May the Lord be with you to help you make a good confession. In the name of the Father, and of the Son, and of the Holy Spirit."

"I've never done this before." It was a female voice, and he guessed her to be in her twenties. He could hear the rustling of her puffy winter coat as she settled in; peaches with a hint of rosemary from her shampoo reached out to him through the opaque screen. "I'm not sure what to say next."

"Usually, this is for the confession and forgiveness of sins, but we can talk about whatever you want. Why don't you tell me what brings you here today?"

"Okay . . . well, I'm dying, Father," she said. "I'm sick and dying. They told me yesterday that I have MS." He heard a loud sniffle. "I don't know what I'm gonna do," she broke down.

A lunker, he thought. A few times each year, he found himself in a position to have a come-to-Jesus talk with a complete stranger—the kind of exchange where something real is at stake, where someone's come to a crossroads in their story. Last spring, there was a runaway teenager he caught breaking into the rectory garage, and then he happened upon that cripple at the ballgame this summer. It was like fishing—you go out every day and throw in a line and every once in a while something really big bends your pole: a lunker.

"Well, multiple sclerosis is hardly a death sentence—it affects quality of life more than anything," Howard said. In his time as a priest, he had known two people with this disease, and was impressed with their resiliency. "It's certainly something you can live with."

"Sure, Father, but who's going to love me like this? I'm twenty-eight and I'm going to spend my life alone in a wheelchair. I can't stand that thought—it's such a waste!"

He could hear her weeping quietly, and made quiet room for her grief to bloom. After several moments and loud sniffles he could hear her gather herself back together.

"You haven't said yet why you're here," Howard said. "If you think it's all over—that there's nothing for you to live for—then what're you doing here?"

"Jesus, Father, I thought you'd try to help me," she said with a snap. "I'm *dying*, okay? I had this picture of my life—I was supposed to establish a career and then get married, have a family—and now it's all gone. I'll die alone!"

"Okay, listen—we all of us die alone. I'm trying to help you see that being here means something." He was used to the escalation: prick the despair and he usually found anger. That was a good sign. "The fact that you haven't just wandered off to swallow a bottle of pills counts for something. You're looking for hope, and if you didn't think you could find it, you wouldn't be here."

"But, Father, that's just it—I don't have any hope. There's no good way for this to end; there's no way to make sense of it all; there's no way through."

"Hope—like faith and love—has nothing to do with where your head's at. There isn't a way to make sense of it. It's not a calculated risk. And contrary to the BS you see on your Instabooks and Tweetsnaps, it's even less a feeling. In the end, it's about where you put your butt. And you brought yours here, so what's that mean?"

Silence.

"It means that hope lives in you much deeper than you can say or understand. That's what it means. It'd be a lot easier to say to hell with it, but here you are. Follow that line and you'll find something on the other end. You're not alone. There will be a way."

He heard her take a loud sniffle and clear her throat. "You know what? Fuck you," she said. Her voice was sub-zero cold, and then he heard her coat rustle suddenly as she stood to leave. "You were supposed to show me the way."

"Look, I didn't force you here—you got here by yourself. So what are you looking for?" Howard asked.

"I'm trying to help you see: The capacity for hope is nothing less than hope itself."

The door to the confessional slammed shut. This is often how it ended, but he wasn't there for fun. His job was to set hooks, and most fish objected to that proposition.

30

The beach—Sully loved the beach.

Yes! Here it is—the big water yard, the sand!

There were so many scents near the water, and he loved the freedom to run wherever he wanted. Or walk. He could walk or run on his own, as long as he stayed close. The beach was literally the best place in the whole world.

Do not mark the seat. Do not mark the seat. Mark outside—outside! Open the door!

New smells always seeped up from the sand, calling him to uncover them. Sometimes he discovered a fish or a bird that didn't move and was coming apart. He liked to pull them out of the ground for Master.

The logs and branches on the beach did not look or smell like branches in the yard. They were a lot heavier and they smelled like the clean, wet dirt at the bottom of a new hole. It was a perfect place to find out if Others had been here. The wood stayed marked for a long time. It was also a perfect place to let Others know he had been there, which was an important duty.

As they began to walk, Sully perceived Master to be happier here. She was sad at home but she was not sad here. This was their first trip back to the beach since the days started getting longer, and once they started moving it didn't feel so cold. Sully ran back to check on Master, and she smiled at him and said, "Good boy,

Sully! Go run!"

Sully wheeled and looked ahead. The lake had tossed chunks of broken ice here and there, but they never smelled like anything. He spotted a log on the beach a good throw away—water was lapping around it with the same steady and deliberate licks he used to clean peanut butter from the empty jars Master gave him once in a while. Maybe it had been marked, he thought—he ran to find out.

As he got closer, he stopped in surprise. It wasn't a log at all—it was another Master! He looked like he was asleep, but Sully had never seen another Master sleeping outside like this—partway in the water with his face in the sand. He cocked his head, confused, and listened for any sound. Nothing. He tried to smell if the Master had an Other that might be nearby, or some food, but the Master only smelled like a new hole.

Sully barked at the sleeping Master, but he didn't move at all. His skin was blue. Something was wrong. "Something is wrong here!" Sully called to his Master —"I found another Master but something is wrong!"

Master ran up and said, "Hey! You okay? Yo! Are you okay?"

Then she said, "Oh, shit!" but Sully was not push-squatting. He did not even feel like push-squatting. Sully looked at Master. She seemed to be worried and thinking.

She stepped closer and bent down to look more closely at the side where the Master's face was partly showing up from the sand. A small wave reached up and stroked the man's cheek, briefly flowing into and out of his mouth.

"Aw, shit. Get back, Sully. This is bad, bad, bad."

Master pulled out her shiny stick and touched it.

"Hi, my name is Kimberly Ball. I'm calling to report a dead body. I'm on the north end of Dunes State Park. I was out for a walk and found it washed up from the lake. I'm maybe a quarter mile south from the lot at the end of Lake Front Drive.

"Yes, sir, I'm sure. He's not breathing and he looks . . . blue. There's ice in his hair and face. He might have been dead for a while, I don't know.

"Male, maybe in his thirties. Dark hair. Wearing jeans and a flannel workshirt. No shoes.

"Okay, thanks. Should I . . . move him out of the water?

"Okay, I won't touch him. I'll just stay here 'til someone arrives.

"No, I'm fine. It's just a shock, you know. Wasn't expecting this. I think I'll be okay, thanks."

Sully observed Master to see what she was feeling. She wasn't happy, but she wasn't sad. That feeling Sully had when Master left home most mornings—he wanted to go, but he had to stay and make sure nothing went wrong—that's what Master looked like: full of longing and duty, waiting for things to be right again.

Sully stood by Master so she wouldn't be alone.

***

Sheri Daniels rolled the stainless-steel table under the examination light and unzipped the black plastic body bag. A musty damp smell released into the medical examination room in the basement of the Porter County Municipal Building and she felt relieved not to recognize any scent of decay.

"Okay, let's take a look here. This guy was pulled from the lake this morning—a lady and her dog found him. We'll document a prelim to see if there are any distinguishing marks, then I'll have you set up the instruments while I do a quick search through the missing persons database."

Bennett was the third forensic technician Sheri had to train in the past six months. The previous two gave good reasons for leaving the morgue, but she suspected it really came down to working with cadavers every day. It took a toll on most people—it opened questions they didn't want to spend most of their time thinking about. This work wasn't for everyone.

Bennett was off to a good start, though. He was still learning, but seemed earnest. She didn't have to repeat herself to him and he seemed physically capable—he moved quickly around the morgue and she appreciated his responsiveness. It was a big help to have someone with a large frame to help move the bodies.

She liked her tools and instruments arranged just so, and went about her work methodically. It was their job to speak for the deceased, to say what they couldn't say, so she wanted to make sure they didn't miss anything. Bennett seemed to get that.

The body from the lake had arrived mid-morning, and the coroner indicated it took top priority because the press was showing some interest.

"Should I write on the same form we used last time?" Bennett asked.

"No, I can already see injuries on the head," Sheri said, peering over the body. "This'll be a criminal examination, so we'll need the pink one. I'll just say what I'm seeing and you write it in the notes as bullet points. I'll fill in the top later.

"Okay, so we're looking at a male, in his thirties. Hispanic or American Indian heritage, dark skin tone. Though it appears mottled in places. Short-cropped black hair. Evidence of blunt force trauma in the temporal and parietal bones of cranium, left side."

Sheri scanned the rest of the naked body. "Deformity in his right hand. And his right leg below the knee—see the difference in muscle tone in the calves? A few abrasions around lower legs above the ankles.

"Time of death is tough to say—typically, we'd be looking for the pooling of blood and stages of rigor mortis, but this body's been in cold, cold water—only a degree or two above freezing. Suspended like that, the blood doesn't aggregate anywhere in particular. If the body was at the bottom of the lake, there'd be very little oxygen for microbial decay. Obviously, the body is just now coming up to room temp. We'll need to do an autopsy to determine if he drowned or was dead before immersion.

"Anyway, that's enough for me to do a search. We'll need a full set-up for an autopsy—should be able to finish the external exam before lunch, then this'll be the afternoon, probably."

Sheri walked to her desk against the far wall and waited for her computer to light up. She clicked on the tab in her browser that connected her to the state's missing persons database and logged in.

It took only a few moments for her to find a clear match: Bryant Black Fox, thirty-three, from Andover in Marion County. The file said he was American Indian with a partial disability and missing since November 7. *That's a long time,* Sheri thought. *Hard to believe he's been stuck under the ice since then, with the condition he's in.*

She decided to call the Marion County coroner now as long as she was here. There was going to be a lot of exchanges back and forth as the investigation developed, and she liked to know whom she was working with. She looked at a dog-eared and smudged half sheet of paper taped to the wall above her computer monitor, scanning for the number of the coroner's office in Andover, then picked up the phone and dialed.

After half a dozen rings, the call went to voicemail. She listened to the message and said, "Hi, Isabel—this is Sheri Daniels, medical examiner in Porter County. We have a body under investigation that matches a missing person from your neck of the woods. We'll handle the investigation, obviously, but I figured you'd want to see if you can find his family. We can work out a transfer of the body soon as we're done. Just wanted to let you know so you could start making arrangements on your end.

"Appears to be a Bryant Black Fox—that's Bry-ant with a T, Black-Fox, spelled just like it sounds—missing since November 7. He was found this morning washed up from the lake in Indiana Dunes State Park. Call me with any questions—I'm at 202-495-2700—otherwise, I'll let you know when we're ready to release the body."

Just as she hung up, she heard a clang in the room behind her—like someone dropped a cymbal.

"Ah! Sheri! Sheri—come take a look at this!" Bennett sounded alarmed.

She stood and turned, thrusting the rolling desk chair behind her with a clatter, and strode quickly toward the examination table. Bennett had stepped backward and knocked over a metal cart he was setting with tools; it lay behind him like an anchor, the swiveled wheels still rocking from the topple with a quiet *sh-sh-sh*. His hands were trembling within the purple latex gloves that covered them—he held them out like he was preparing to catch something.

"Bennett, what is it?"

"What the hell is going on?" He pointed to the face of the body on the table.

Sheri saw white foam emerging from the nose and mouth—it had filled the breathing cavities and was starting to dribble down the right cheek. After eight years examining corpses, she had learned to skip over any feelings of repulsion and jump right into the task of comprehending and diagnosing what she was seeing. For the span of three heartbeats, she had nothing—then it came to her. She straightened her back and stepped toward the body to look closer.

"Ah. Freaky, huh? Totally normal, though—it's a fine foam expelled by the lungs in drowning victims. Just air and mucus that mixed together when he breathed in water. It actually makes our job easier—proves that he drowned. He wasn't dead before he hit the water."

"That's pretty friggin' weird, man," Bennett said. He sounded suspicious. "Why's it coming out now?"

"It's . . . the body's warming up . . . but . . ." Sheri paused and cocked her head. "But, it's odd. Froth like that is a sign in freshly drowned victims—bodies that took on water hours ago, or at most a day. This guy's been gone, what, five months? He was reported missing in November. . ."

She took a deep breath. There was a story behind this—they'd just have to figure it out. "So, yeah, I guess.

Kinda . . . friggin' weird."

***

Isabel noticed the red indicator light on her desk phone as soon as she returned from checking in with Parker over lunch. She sat down and punched in her PIN and put the message on speaker as she hung her coat on the hook behind her door. She didn't recognize the name or voice—Sheri Daniels—but wrote down her number on a blue pad of sticky notes.

She tapped her computer to life as Sheri continued to speak. Then she thought she heard Sheri say the name, "Black Fox" and immediately dialed the button that skipped backward ten seconds in the message. Yes, she definitely said "Bryant Black Fox."

Isabel immediately opened the bottom drawer of her desk, which was deep enough to hold file folders. She kept most of her investigative files on her desk if they were open; closed ones she stored in the locked beige cabinet against the wall. The few that fell into neither category—she kept those in the bottom drawer. It was one of the most important and fundamental lessons she had learned in her two years on the job: keep everything. Nothing ever ends unresolved, she learned, so it pays off to lay down a paper trail. It maybe took months, it maybe took years, but the stories always came back around. The lives described by these files found ways to make sense in the end.

She picked up the file marked "Black Fox" and set it on her desk. She replayed the message one more time to ensure she heard it correctly, and confirmed the phone number, then dialed it.

The phone picked up after four rings with a

voice that sounded harried. "Yeah Med Exam Sheri here."

"Hi Sheri, this is Isabel DuPree from Marion County returning your call from this morning."

Silence. For a moment, Isabel wondered if they had been disconnected. "You called about a missing person found at Indiana Dunes—a man named Bryant Black Fox?"

"Yes—right! Yikes! Yeah, a lot's happened since then. Okay, so Bryant Black Fox—not dead, turns out. Took him to the hospital a few hours ago."

"What?"

"Yeah, I know—so messed up! After I called you, we finished the external exam. Turned him over to look at the back and all this water poured out his lungs. We heard a choking kind of a cough and he twitched. Thought it was muscle contractions—I've seen bodies do that kind of thing before. And then he coughed harder—like a real hacking cough—so for sure I'm thinking brainstem activity. Then color starts coming back. We kept him on his stomach and whacked his backside and he kept coughing. Never regained consciousness, but began breathing.

"Of course, we don't have any lifesaving equipment here, so all we could do is keep him warm. Called the ER and they sent an ambulance—first time they'd ever done a pick up at the morgue instead of dropping off."

Isabel squinted her eyes and scrunched her brow, wondering what kind of Mickey Mouse operation they had up there in Porter County. "You're sure this is the same guy? He'd been missing since November, right?"

"Definitely the same guy. Bryant Black Fox. Had a

disability on his right side, arm and leg. And the photo was a positive ID. No one knows what to make of it. EMTs suggested the cold water shocked him into stasis. If that was the case, they said, the best way to revive him would be slowly bringing up his core temp, which is what we did without knowing it, I guess. Poor guy's probably brain-dead, though—that long without oxygen."

Isabel didn't know what to say.

"Listen, Isabel, I know what you're thinking. I've been doing this eight years and I've seen some things here, but this—this takes the cake. After they took him away, my tech looked at me and just said, 'I quit' and walked out . . . So, it's been a day."

"It's been a year, Sheri, let me tell you," Isabel said. "So what's the status of his missing person report?"

"That's been passed back to the state police—they're already in touch with the person who filed. They'll close it all up."

"Well, it's good news, though, I guess." Isabel said. "What hospital did you say he was at?"

31

Vivian was consciously pushing the speed limit as far as she could on her approach to Michigan City when she suddenly remembered she should call Grant to tell him she'd be late coming home tonight, if she came home at all. He had no way to know what happened.

At the first stoplight she came to on her approach to town she pulled out her phone and touched Grant's name.

"Hey, babe—what's up," he answered.

"Grant, listen—they found Bryant," she blurted. "They found him near Lake Michigan and he's in the hospital in Michigan City. I got the call an hour ago and I jumped in the car. I'm almost there."

"Wha—? Hospital? How's he doing?"

"They just said that he's in the hospital and stable —I didn't get to talk to him—gotta go!" She hung up as the light turned green and gave two insistent honks to the driver in front of her.

***

The retiree at the hospital information desk directed Vivian to the third-floor trauma center to find Bryant, which didn't sound good. When she stepped out of the elevator she turned to the beige double doors on the right that had "Trauma and Life Support Center" painted across them in maroon letters. She could feel her pulse thumping in her neck as she charged through the doors.

A nursing station with a curved counter stood inside like a bulwark guarding the wing. The hallways were flooded with light that also shone up from the waxy tiled floors. A huddle of four people in scrubs were talking and smiling behind the desk—relaxed, as though they were on break. One round man in a light blue uniform looked up and greeted her with raised, expectant eyebrows.

"I'm here to see Bryant Black Fox."

"Are you Vivian?"

"Yes." She took a deep breath to quiet the blood throbbing in her ears.

"They said you'd be coming up from Andover. Come with me and we'll have the doctor fill you in."

He stepped around the front desk and started walking to her left, toward the corner of the wing, and motioned for her to follow him with the nonchalance of a host showing her to a seat in a restaurant, which pissed her off, because didn't he understand the urgency here? Past the wheelchairs and light blue curtains, Vivian could see a carpeted waiting room ahead. He deposited her in the quiet, empty room—even the television hanging from the ceiling in the corner was dark. The whole wing was strangely still.

"Doctor Garrity will be by to speak with you in just a sec."

"Can I just see Bryant?"

"Oh, sorry, no—the doctor wants to meet with you first. She won't be long—another quiet day here."

She didn't feel like sitting, so she took off her jacket and set it on a chair. A quick look at the magazines showed them all to be out of date by six months. The remote control for the television sat on a corner table, but having that thing blabbing at her was the last thing she needed. She had to talk to someone—in moments like this she really missed Estelline, even still.

She pulled out her phone and dialed Grant again.

"Yeah—how is he?" he answered.

"He's in the trauma unit, so I'm waiting for the doctor to come hold my hand."

"The trauma unit? The hell?"

"People are being weird here, Grant—something's odd. The doctor's making a point of talking to me before I see him. Hold up—she's here." She turned the phone off and lowered it into her pocket.

A short, thin woman strode past the glass walls of the waiting room and slipped through the door frame into the waiting room. She had short-cropped hair flecked with grey, but the flushed red in her cheeks softened the severe angles of her face. Vivian guessed her to be a marathoner; her white lab coat hung off her like a set of curtains.

"Ms. Ward? I'm Dr. Garrity." She reached out her hand—she had a strong, vigorous grip. "Thank you for coming so quickly."

"I'm just relieved to hear Bryant's been found," Vivian confided. "No one's heard from him since November. I was shocked to get the call today."

"Yes, good news, isn't it?" The doctor's smile faded quickly. "I wanted to meet with you to shape your expectations. Is it okay if we sit down?"

Vivian felt skeptical about the request—was

there bad news?—but lowered herself to the edge of the chair.

"Bryant is in intensive care, but he is stable. He was found on the shore of Lake Michigan early this morning—he appeared to have drowned. When they. . ."

"Drowned?!" Vivian had been so excited after the call this morning that she hadn't even considered what it meant that Bryant was found at the lake. The idea of him drowning—of suffering in any way—felt like a firecracker going off in her hand.

Dr. Garrity reached out to Vivian and grasped her shoulder with a firm, warm hand. "But, listen—when they brought him in for examination, he revived, okay? The water cleared his lungs and he . . . just started breathing again. It's pretty extraordinary.

"But he's not out of the woods. For a person in his situation, we'd expect severe damage to the brain when it's been deprived of oxygen for anything more than a few minutes. There also seems to have been a wound to his head"—*bang!* another firecracker —"which is probably a factor here.

"There's a lot we don't know—how long he was in the water, for example, or any of the conditions he faced. We're still running tests, but you should know he won't be conscious when you go in to see him—he's unresponsive."

Vivian put her hand to her mouth as a geyser of anxiety erupted within her. "He's in a coma?"

"I'm afraid so," she said. "His body systems are stable and improving, but there's just no way to know what to expect from here regarding the brain. He could be like this for hours or months—we can't say. And if he does regain consciousness, we don't know what functions might be impaired."

"Oh, my God," Vivian said. She had a thousand questions, but more than ever just wanted to see Bryant.

"Now, I will say that we've advanced this unit of the hospital and have been seeing dramatic results in our patients over the past six months, so he's in good hands. Once we get a better read on where things stand with him—particularly his brain—we'll be able to apply more precise treatment.

"There's just a lot we don't know yet, and I wanted you to know what to expect before you go in there."

"Thank you, doctor," Vivian replied. "I'd really just like to see him now, if that's okay."

***

After Dr. Garrity left, the host-nurse returned and led Vivian farther down the hallway around the corner from the front desk. He stopped only four doors down —Bryant was only a few yards away this whole time! —and extended his hand into the entrance on the left, tapping the doorframe twice with his open palm.

"Just ring if you need anything," he said, and walked back to the desk. The smug bastard.

Vivian stopped in the doorway at the sight of Bryant nestled in the hospital bed. He was neatly tucked in with his arms resting on the covers, IVs and sensors sprouting from them like tender shoots from light brown soil. His head was resting on two pillows with his face pointed up, as though he had fallen asleep listening to music. Clean, white gauze covered his hair like a cap, but his face looked peaceful. A thin tube piped oxygen under his nose.

The scene blurred for Vivian as the reality sunk in: he was back, alive; and yet he was unconscious, wounded. A worried gratitude swamped over her and she couldn't breathe. She staggered in and collapsed on the chair at the side of the bed, leaned forward and placed her head on the chlorine-scented starchy blanket and cried.

***

That evening, Vivian's stomach rumbled and she began to think about dinner. How long could she stay here? What if this turned into months? And what if it turned out his body was alive but his brain was dead?

A knock on the door startled her and she stood instinctively. A bear of a man ambled in wearing a brown state trooper uniform and holding a wide-brimmed, stiff campaign hat with both hands. His hair was so short he could have been bald, and the sides of his head bore an imprint from the hat ring.

"How's he doin'?" he asked, looking at Bryant. A smile made dimples erupt across his face.

"Hard to say, I guess, but he's here," Vivian said, standing up.

"Dewey Campbell—I'm an investigator with the state police. I cover this northwestern corner of Indiana. Can I ask for a moment of your time, ma'am?"

"Sure," Vivian said. She sat down and pointed to an extra chair in the far corner. The investigator grabbed it by the arm and dragged it to the foot of Bryant's bed. His leather belt squeaked as he walked, and Vivian looked apprehensively at the gun and all the other equipment strapped to it.

"I've been looking at this case today—I happened to be here in Michigan City when the call came in this morning, so I was on the scene right away. Don't know that I can explain what happened—when I saw him, he was in bad shape. I certainly thought he was . . . you know. . .

"Anyways, I pulled his file and engaged all of our units in this area. We found his truck—it was parked at a casino here in town, the Plucky Pelican."

Vivian felt her face flush with anger. "What? Why wasn't that found earlier? I filed a report in November when he went missing."

"Ma'am, when he disappeared, Bryant had full mental capacity and no threatening medical issues, and because he's an adult, all we do is file the report. Even if he were still missing, we wouldn't be out looking for him. He's a free man."

What a load of horse shit, Vivian thought. He was in trouble and they could have found him if they had just looked.

"Besides, even if we had investigated, he was reported missing in Marion County, so we wouldn't have looked this far north. Detectives there would have focused on local leads. I know it's frustrating, ma'am—you must have a lot of questions."

The first "ma'am" was already one too many. At this third one, Vivian turned her gaze to Bryant to hide her narrowing eyes.

"Did you ever wonder if he had a gambling problem?" officer Campbell asked.

Ever since he came in, Vivian felt like he'd been tiptoeing around the flowerbed of decency, and with this comment just kicked right through it with those thick black boots. She couldn't contain her outrage. She stood up and turned to him—she didn't care what was strapped to that belt—and took a deep breath to unload on him.

"Just what are you suggesting? You don't know anything about him!" She stood with her legs wide, as though she were guarding Bryant's body, and crossed her arms. It was silent for a full minute as Dewey studied the angles of his hat as he turned it in his hands. The steady beep of the monitors attached to Bryant kept time. She made sure her glare did not relent.

"I can see you don't suffer fools, so let me just tell you how this is stacking up and we'll cut through the crap," Dewey said. He stood up slowly and met her glare with an even look. It dawned on her that he was being generous in accommodating her resentment—he didn't have to, and it didn't affect him. He had probably seen much, much worse.

"We may never know the whole story, but here are the facts as we have them now. His new wife died, pregnant, last year. He took out a loan to buy a warehouse and invest in heavy equipment for his brewery, but he's been behind in payments on that loan since August. Three months later he disappeared, and his truck was found at a casino."

Dewey stopped talking, and looked at Vivian.

"So, what?" Vivian asked. Part of her shriveled inside but she stuck with the glare now out of principle. "That doesn't tell us anything."

The trooper stood up. "Ms. Ward, Bryant seems

like a nice guy. Maybe he's just down on his luck. There's a million ways he could have ended up on that beach, but we don't have unlimited resources to connect every dot. We have other priorities. I'm letting you know that for now, we're closing this case as a missing person who's been located. If Bryant wakes up and remembers something and wants to pursue a criminal investigation, give me a call."

"Not if—when." Vivian growled. Dewey extended a business card to her but she didn't budge. He set it down on his chair and left.

32

In the beginning of Bryant's dream, he woke to a drum beating outside somewhere. A girl, maybe twelve, maybe Rafa's age, was waking him with a gentle, persistent nudge on his shoulder in time with the rhythm. She stood next to the bed in a plain white cotton shirt that hung long on her thin body. It was fringed at the arms and bottom; eagle and owl feathers hung from the neck. Her long hair was tressed back by two thin braids looped above her ears.

"*Keek-ta-yo*," she said, beaming. "Time to rise and shine." She looked like she'd been waiting all morning to wake him with that line, like it was a secret she'd been harboring and finally allowed to set free.

He knew her, somehow. *Keek-ta-yo*—that was the Lakota phrase his *unjee* said when she woke him up for school every day. He could tell the girl was charged, but she was being patient with him, as though she knew what it was like to be confused in this situation.

Something about the way her eyes sparkled told him it was Tally—the daughter he'd never known, the child who died with Estelline. The warmth of familiar love and affection radiated from his gut, even through the dim awareness they'd never known each other. Seeing her felt new, like meeting a distant cousin for the first time, but also easy and dear.

He sat up and dangled his feet over the bed and

filled his lungs. He felt well-rested, alert and perceptive. He was in a bedroom in his gram's trailer, and the window next to the bed was open. He could hear people arriving and being greeted outside.

In the summer, his gram often cooked outside over an open firepit, or on a propane griddle set up on a picnic table. A shade shelter extended from the trailer's patio—wood poles holding up a blue tarp. When they were expecting family or guests, she often made a large pot of *wojapi*—a thick soup made with chokecherries and raspberries—to be served over frybread. When they could find fresh milk and eggs, though, she'd make pancakes from scratch.

Now, under the tarp, Bryant could hear arriving guests sharing conversation as they prepared breakfast. The day was underway and moving toward some kind of event or gathering, but it wasn't too late to join the fray.

The girl put her hand in his—it was small and warm. "Wait a minute," he said, realizing his nose was coming alive. He cocked his head back slightly and inhaled slowly and deeply.

The smell of coffee darted about the room like a woodpecker, probing and full of energy. The toasty warmth of pancakes came ambling after, patient and round with vanilla. The two scents danced in his mind for a moment and he closed his eyes to explore the feeling below what he sensed: the start of a day full of abundant food and laughter.

There is a beer in here somewhere, Bryant thought. An ambition took form inside of him: there must be a way to capture that feeling in a bottle so that people could pour it over their tongues and, just for a second, light up inside.

He looked at her hand in his and rose.

***

"There he is." It sounded like a male voice—friendly, but unfamiliar. Bryant opened his eyes and struggled to focus them. A nurse or doctor with round cheeks leaned over his bed and peered into his face. "Bryant, can you hear me?"

Bryant tucked his chin down to nod yes.

The man turned over his shoulder and yelled, "Yo—someone stop that woman! Vivian!" He looked back at Bryant. "Hold tight there, bud. She's been here sitting with you for days. Be right back."

He left and Bryant closed his eyes. It felt good to breathe, to expand his chest and feel the eddies of air tumbling into his lungs. Clean, simple, stupid, plain old air. So sweet.

His head began to clear. He opened his eyes again and had trouble focusing enough to read the hands on the clock on the wall across from his bed. He seemed to be in a hospital, but was too tired to be worried about it.

A rustling, hurried sound and then a shock of black hair in his face—"Bryant! You're here!" It was Vivian. He tried to lift his hand to return her embrace, but it seemed tangled in something. She rose and stood back, holding the hand he couldn't lift. He couldn't make out her eyes, but her presence was unmistakable. Very little about his situation made much sense to him, but he was glad Vivian was on the job—he trusted her to handle whatever was going on.

"How you feeling, big guy?" Must be a nurse—sounded too casual for a doctor, Bryant decided. He was on the other side of the bed fiddling with something.

"U-kay," Bryant forced out.

He grabbed Bryant's toe firmly and tugged. "Can you feel that?"

"M-hm."

"How 'bout your fingers? Can you move them?"

Bryant looked down at his right hand and wiggled his fingers.

"That's really good, Bryant. I'm going to let the doctor know you're awake."

"Do you know where you are?" Vivian asked.

He closed his eyes and turned his head to the side—no.

"You're in the hospital in Michigan City. You've been injured in the head, and you were found on the shore of Lake Michigan."

He heard the words, but they sounded like a news report from a distant land.

"You don't understand, do you?" she said with melting compassion in her voice. "That's okay. Don't worry. We'll figure it out. The most important thing is that you're back—you're here."

***

Bryant woke up to the phone ringing next to him. He pushed the button to slowly raise the head of his bed and leaned over to stretch out his arm for the long, beige receiver with its flashing red light.

"Hello, Vivian."

"Good morning, Bryant! How you feeling?"

"Tired. But better."

"That's good. I'm at class today and catching up on some things, but just wanted to check on you. Doctor Garrity was by last night while you were sleeping. She says you're making really great progress for only being three days along."

"Did she say." Bryant took a breath. "When I can go. Home."

It was work to string together enough words to make a sentence. He had to look for them in the swampy recesses of his mind, then hold them all together as they came to his tongue. He couldn't carry more than a few at a time, and sometimes he dropped one on the way.

"Dude, your language has come a long ways, even from yesterday. Nice work—keep it up."

She was not the cheerleader type, but was a good one to have in your corner.

"All depends, she said," Vivian continued. "They're treating you with protocol for a traumatic brain injury—she knows you had water in your lungs, but there don't seem to be any effects from that and your body seems fine. It's just a matter of getting your noggin up to speed."

"Okay. Keep plugging away."

"That's right, man. Keep grinding. Don't watch any TV. Talk to the nurses when they help you to the bathroom. Stay limber.

"Hey, Grant's coming up this afternoon with some clothes for you. Anything else you want him to grab?"

"Recipe book. Black. Living room desk." He woke with a hankering for coffee and wanted to review cold-brewing.

"Black recipe book from the living room desk—got it. Anything else?"

"No. Thank you."

"You got it. Hang in there, okay? I'll be back up to see you tomorrow."

***

The next afternoon, after a nap, Bryant decided to test his strength and coordination by walking a loop around the wing. He pulled out the lariat of tubing from under his nose, sat up, and swung his legs from under the covers to the floor. The shiny epoxy surface shot shocks of cold through his bare feet. *Slippers*, he thought, and made a note to ask Vivian to bring him a pair next time she came up.

He slowly eased his weight forward and lifted his hips from the mattress, his hand gripping the cool chrome rail on his bed. The blood drained from his head and as his heart adjusted, he could feel his pulse pressing in his temples, a throbbing rhythm of pain. He evaluated his strength and balance—not bad. It felt good to stretch out his spine and stand tall. His legs had a hint of a pins-and-needles feeling, and he felt his face flush as his body adjusted to a new circulatory pattern. The pain in his head subsided to an ache.

When he felt steady, he moved his right foot forward. His joints felt sore, like the morning after spending a day hefting brewing tanks and kettles, but he detected strength there. He willed his left foot to match his right, and let go of the railing. As he brought his arm around, though, his hand snagged—an oxygen sensor with a red light was clamped over his index finger. He tugged his hand closer to his body and it snapped off. A low, urgent beeping alarm sounded. The cords streaming from his bed ran up the sleeve of his gown and tugged on the skin over his chest. A slight tug popped several free, but a louder, buzzing alarm sounded now.

His feet were cold, but felt steady on the floor. He took another slow step toward the door, then another. He felt like an explorer on a glacier, testing the security of each step before entrusting his weight to it.

"Hey, bud, you're up and moving." It was Dallas, the pudgy nurse, and he sounded startled, probably from the alarms.

"Feeling stronger. Thought I'd try moving around," Bryant said. "That okay?"

"Sure thing—just be careful. Don't push it. Moving's good, though—go for it." Dallas stepped behind Bryant and helped him into a robe. "Let's maybe close the back door, though."

It took Bryant twenty minutes to complete the expedition around the wing. As he was returning to his room, a tall, Hispanic woman appeared—she was studying the door numbers. She reached his door before he did and entered, then reappeared, looking around.

"Looking for me?" Bryant asked.

"Bryant?"

He nodded.

"Yes, hi—Isabel DuPree. I'm from the Marion County coroner's office."

"You shouldn't say that. Around here."

She smiled and waited for him to plod his way into the room. He made his way to his bed and fell in, drained. Just the ability to relax the tension it took to stand up straight and carry his weight around put goosebumps on his arm. His head began to throb again —the pain was catching up and he could feel his heartbeat pressing against the bandage around his crown.

Isabel stepped to the side to make room for Dallas who helped him settle back into bed, making sure to re-attach the finger sensor and oxygen tube. She closed the door behind Dallas when he left.

"Bryant, I'm here because of Brother Martin and Rafa Villahermosa," Isabel said. At Rafa's name, Bryant's stomach sank—that kid had been through so much already. What had the past five months been like for him?

"I want you to know I'm committed to getting to the bottom of whatever happened to you," she said. "When you went missing, Rafa told Brother Martin, who checked with Vivian. That's when she filed the report, but she didn't know what you were doing with Rafa. Martin and Rafa brought me photos of workers in Wilmot, and pointed you out in the line."

Isabel handed Bryant a manila file folder with pixelated color photographs inside. The images were foggy and dark, and the figures were blurry, but he immediately recognized them as part of the series of photos Rafa had showed him of the parking lot and *tienda* in Wilmot. He could make out the curly haired one and the fat guy with the clipboard.

"Rafa swears this is you," Isabel said, pointing to a man with a flannel shirt. Bryant nodded his head.

"Well, I was obviously sympathetic to what they were saying—I'm doing what I can to help them build a case for Raymundo, too—but all I had was a blurry picture that could have been taken anywhere of anyone and a kid who won't talk. And, I had no body. As a coroner, that gave me zero to work with.

"I went to Carlos Siego—he's the one here," she moved her finger to the curly haired one. "And asked him for the roster of workers who'd been through there recently, but your name didn't come up."

Bryant remembered the name he had fabricated —Matteo Benitez.

"And he seemed a little put off by my asking. I'm guessing that's when they moved your truck. . . I had my suspicions, but not a shred of evidence, so I kept the file and waited. And here you are.

"So, Bryant, my question is this: What happened to you?"

If Brother Martin trusted Isabel, Bryant decided he could, too. Clearly, she knew the backstory with Rafa, and she understood something of what Siego, as she called him, was doing in Wilmot.

"I worked in the field all day," Bryant said. He sat up to summon the concentration to coordinate his thinking and breathing. "But they paid me in store credits. I was already at a deficit.

"I followed workers back to a compound. When I left, two guys jumped me. Spinks was one."

Isabel took out a notebook and jotted down the name.

"The other was skinny. Snake tattoo on his right arm. They were in a black sedan. They hit me with a tire iron.

"Then I remember being in a boat at night. My feet tied to cinderblock. I knew I had to get out, so I jumped. And I woke up here."

"Bryant, that was five months ago."

"I know."

"Does it make sense? What do you think?"

"Doc says if I was in water, it coulda been cold enough to put my body in hibernation. I can tell she has no idea, though."

"Well, I have no idea, either, but strange things have been happening all over, so I'm not ruling anything out. I know the state police were here. Did they close their investigation?"

"Yes—they think I have a gambling problem. I wasn't awake when they came."

"Right. I'd like to connect this to the case I have open on Rafa's dad, Raymundo. He was killed a year ago. And I think we can put it all together in extortion and slavery charges, on top of attempted murder, obviously. But we have to do it right. They won't take us seriously if all we have is a mute kid and a guy with a head injury and debt. We need evidence.

"I picked up the clothes you were found in from the morgue here—the jeans have glue residue around the ankles from tape. And maybe Rafa's pictures can give us more. That's a start.

"So, for now, get better. Let's meet in another week or two when you get home and feel stronger, and I'll take down all you can remember. We'll make a plan from there."

33

It was a rare evening that found Newell in his rectory before eight. Committee meetings, pastoral visits, fundraising dinners—his schedule conspired against quiet nights at home.

Knowing he had an empty evening before him, he turned off the lights in the kitchen and dining room and entered the living room, which used to serve as a salon or sitting room back when this place held half a dozen priests. Now there was just the two of them, and Father Harney was always up late as he completed his studies, so Newell unbuttoned his collar and collapsed in a large, overstuffed leather chair—finally able to relax.

He sat for a moment thinking that the situation seemed to call for a glass of single malt Scotch in his hand, and maybe a cigar. He looked around the room and imagined it full of priests chuckling at jokes on a Sunday night after the Masses and a big dinner, but he never understood why people felt the need to chemically alter their personalities in order to socialize or unwind. He often studied other priests in those situations, wondering what they were seeking and finding in tobacco or alcohol. Whatever fires were burning inside them never seemed extinguished, he noticed, no matter how much they poured down their throats. Usually, it was just the opposite, actually—it just gave the flames more fuel.

He stood up and turned to a record player console, dark-stained walnut, that stood against the wall behind the leather couch. It had been part of the living room when he arrived—it probably was original to the early 1960s. Its round legs were sheathed in corroding tin at the bottom, and one of the knobs on the cabinets was missing, but a working turntable was nestled under the divided surface. On the few nights he had alone each month, he liked to listen to music to unwind. He lifted the middle third section of the table top.

Some previous bishop or rector had been a jazz fan and left behind a sizeable collection of vinyl albums from mid-century artists. Newell was partial to piano jazz because of its simplicity—fewer moving parts—and though Thelonius Monk immediately caught his eye for the name alone, he kept coming back to Bill Evans. There was a precision, an arithmetic to his pieces that put Newell at ease. He could rest in the tones and movements—he could let himself go. The feeling inside was something like what he experienced in prayer, but it was like someone else was doing it for him and all he had to do was hang on to it and be pulled along. The joy felt like waterskiing.

He turned on the player and set the needle at the center of "Everybody Digs Bill Evans" and sat down. Fuzzy tics and bops soon gave way to a rasping cymbal chasing dancing chords.

He returned to the chair and sat back. His mind wandered to baseball and the game coming up. A hitting lineup had taken shape in his imagination as he observed practice over the past few weeks. The question was where to place everyone in the field. He needed more speed in center—Brother Fulgence was maybe ready for that.

Lordy, he's come a long way, he thought. He remembered Fulgence as a young man. Newell played in a Catholic Youth Organization basketball league in primary school, and Brother Fulgence coached a rival basketball team—he remembered the brother because he never yelled from the bench. He just sat there with his legs crossed, watching. Then, in time-outs in the huddle he'd stand over a clipboard like an architect over plans and calmly describe court positions and movements. His players had a devastating, frenetic full-court zone press that prevented most teams from even getting past half-court.

"Young and Foolish" began to play, and Newell thought of how he'd seen Fulgence grow old. By the time Newell was named bishop and arrived in Andover, Fulgence had been running a food pantry from the back of the social hall attached to the cathedral for two decades. His body had become frail, and though he'd never lost that spark of competition, he walked with a shuffling limp and wore thick glasses.

Newell smiled and rubbed his eyes. Now here he was, coaching the old man—young man?—in a strange reversal. At practice yesterday, Fulgence chasing down fly balls reminded him of a golden retriever tracking ducks—a mature golden retriever, to be sure, but his body posture, strength, flexibility, and coordination were of a different order. *Needs a little more pop in his swing, though,* he thought. *I'll get him on the medicine ball.*

Newell recalled he owed a report to Monsignor Groton—the "devil's advocate" who visited from Chile. He'd received a hardcopy preliminary statement from the coroner's office and it detailed the dramatic decline in natural deaths. He could pass that along. And the transfiguration in the community at Columba Hall was undeniable now.

Then there was his own little experiment. If the ontological change of baptism had anything to do with what he was observing, as he suspected, then he should be experiencing some change, himself. At forty-nine, he probably wouldn't notice a dramatic physical rejuvenation, but he decided to put his body to a test. The percussive opening to "Night and Day" snapped to life in the warbling speakers.

Two weeks ago, he decided to fast from food and take in only water. Fasting was nothing new to him, but he'd never gone longer than a day. He began on a Monday, and it felt much like any other penitential fasting he'd done—hunger reminded him what he was doing, but he suppressed it with a prayer and sip of water. The hunger pains continued through Tuesday, but he noticed they hadn't grown any more demanding. In fact, they simply appeared at his regular meal times, and then went away—as though his body was learning a new routine.

By Wednesday, he felt somewhat diminished in energy from the lack of food, but it was the kind of tired he felt after a day of hard physical labor. An afternoon of desk work and he was back on his feet. His mind was sharp and he worked with alacrity.

When he stepped on the scale on Thursday, he was shocked to see that he had only lost three pounds —probably in his ability to retain water. Aside from having to rise more often to urinate, he slept soundly. He was certain the administrative staff, who worked so closely with him through the day, would notice circles under his eyes or gauntness, but not a word, even on Friday. If anything, his cheerfulness invigorated them.

He broke his fast on Saturday by baking bread —sweet, wheaty, dense dinner rolls his mother had taught him to make. The smell woke up his stomach and his gut squirmed with anticipation all afternoon as the dough rose. He set out two bars of butter to come to room temperature. When he pulled the buns out of the oven, he split them open with his hands and slid blocks of the melting butter on each half. The steaming bread was nearly too hot to hold and it turned to pure pleasure in his mouth—the salty butter running over the chewy bites of tangy malt in his cheeks. He baked two dozen rolls that night, and after eating three buns, he took the rest to the intersection two blocks away. He sat down with the panhandlers there and chatted as they ate.

The incongruous "Oleo" pulled him from his reverie; his mouth was watering. He sat up in the chair and reviewed the main outline of the letter to Groton: Isabel's numbers, evidence from the brothers, and his own experience—five days fasting without any diminishment. The conclusion took form in his mind: *If the changes were simply a product of evolution, we'd still be constrained by other natural forces. This has to be from somewhere else, a movement of the spirit—something purposeful that is building a new capacity within us.*

He twisted the knob to the console and the turntable slowed to a stop and fell silent. It was a conclusion that didn't feel conclusive because it only raised another question: Why? A capacity for *what*? He recognized this as a fruitless search, so climbed the stairs to his room to go to bed.

One foot in front of the other, he thought. *Tomorrow's a brand new day.*

***

Rafa gripped the knot in the white plastic grocery sack that sat next to him on the concrete steps of the front porch to his home. Fresh tamales wrapped in tin foil and paper towels radiated humid warmth through the thin bag. His butt was getting sore, but he couldn't stop his heels from tapping the stairs as he waited.

He could hear birds singing behind the noise of his brothers and sister playing homerun derby in the backyard, but the cacophony didn't distract him from studying every car that passed.

After a few moments, a light blue minivan pulled into the driveway with a slight whine and Rafa saw Brother Martin wave to him from the driver seat. Nursing the toasty tamale bag, he climbed in next to him.

"Nice day, isn't it?" Brother Martin said. "Got your mom's tamales?"

Rafa nodded.

"Alright, let's go. It'll be good to see him again, won't it?"

Rafa's smile could have parted clouds.

A ten-minute drive took them to a neighborhood Rafa had never seen before. It was full of small, square houses, all the same size. He watched Brother Martin stretch his neck over the steering wheel to peer at the house numbers and then they pulled into a steep driveway next to a tan house.

Rafa was out of the car and already slamming

the door before Martin finished asking, "You ready?" He waited on the front step with his finger on the doorbell until Brother Martin reached him.

"You forgot these," Brother Martin said, handing Rafa the bag of tamales.

Rafa heard the chime ring inside, and immediately the door opened. A pretty woman with dark black hair smiled and greeted Brother Martin. "And you must be Rafa!" she said. "My name is Vivian. Very nice to meet you."

Rafa shook her small, strong hand but quickly stepped past her into a living room just inside the front door.

"Rafa! Haw!" Bryant was standing slowly from a couch—Rafa took two leaps and embraced him around the waist and a patient grimace tinged Bryant's smile. Rafa was surprised to feel his eyes water; a knot formed in his throat. He was certain Bryant had been swallowed by the same thing that took his dad, and he never thought he'd see him again.

The gloom of that certainty had settled over him in successive layers of despair over the winter. He overheard his mom telling Brother Martin that he was even quieter than normal, if that was possible. He felt imprisoned in his body—sentenced to move it around between school and home, to feed and wash it until something changed. Then, when Brother Martin told him Bryant had returned, the news clanged in his mind like the bell at the end of the school day. This hug sloughed off something old from Rafa, like he was molting. He felt new again.

"Ho-lay smokes, bud! It's been a while! Good to see this one. What'd you grow, a foot?" Then Bryant held Rafa by the shoulders and lowered himself to eye level with him. "Hey, listen—I'm sorry I was gone. I didn't mean to leave, and I know you were worried."

Rafa blinked firmly to squeeze the rest of the water out of his eyes, and wiped his tears with the heels of his hands. After a long sniff, he nodded lightly to Bryant: *It's okay. I'm okay.*

Rafa watched Martin give Bryant a long and slow handshake, then Bryant slowly lowered himself back to the couch and Rafa settled next to him. He listened to the grown-ups talk—all the information and questions went through Vivian, who seemed to be in charge—and looked around the room. A stack of bills in white envelopes with small plastic windows was overflowing from a small basket on the counter.

"If the state police aren't doing anything, will you press charges?" Brother Martin asked.

"I was just explaining everything to Vivian on the way home. . ." Bryant said. Vivian interrupted with exasperation: "I still can't believe you pulled that, Bryant—going out into the fields was bat-shit crazy!" Rafa saw her lower her intense gaze from Bryant to him. "Sorry, Rafa. That's an adult word."

Rafa wondered what made bat poop crazy. Or crazier than other kinds of poop.

". . . and I was just saying," Bryant continued, "the county coroner, Isabel—ah, Doopy? Drupie or something?—wanted to put a case together."

"Dupree," Brother Martin said, "Isabel Dupree—you can trust her. She's good people."

"Isabel heard me out and thought we could connect it to a previous file," Bryant said, and tilted his head toward Rafa. Rafa knew they were being polite, so he looked down as though he were uninterested. "She even went down to Wilmot to look for my name in the ledger at the *tienda*. She didn't find it because I made one up that morning—Matteo Benitez—but that thing'll show exactly how they're extorting workers with all the extra fees they can't work off."

Rafa locked the name Matteo Benitez in his mind. He knew exactly what ledger Bryant was talking about. When Rafa was waiting for the worker bus to return one afternoon, he grew impatient and brazenly walked right into the store to look around. The woman behind the counter watched him with a fake smile that revealed her missing teeth. He picked out a can of green chiles to make it look like he was running an errand and took it to the counter. She had asked if he was from the camp, and started to pull out a book full of lined paper with names and numbers and notes, but he paid with money he had taken from his piggybank.

"She thinks if we can carefully put enough pieces together—hard evidence—then federal investigators will have to take it seriously," he said. "I'm supposed to rest up and get stronger—she said she'd be in touch in another week or two."

Rafa's mind was spinning. He had a lot of photos to go through—he could do that at the library after school. He could definitely pick out the ones with Bryant—they were in the last download—but he had to save the time signature on them. Probably wouldn't hurt to pick out some of the other workers—Lucas or Gerardo, maybe—and show them coming and going, too.

"Well, we should let you do that, then, Bryant," Brother Martin said, standing up. "Rafa has brought some tamales from Aurora—some real food for you." Rafa handed him the wet, warm sack.

"I know you have a lot to get in order, but I have an idea for you. The bishop's been spending time with us brothers and he's made us into a baseball team, of all things. He wants to put together a community event—a game—for the workers and their families as they arrive for the planting season. This'll be next weekend—we'll have a meal after, and I was thinking some beer would be nice."

"Yeah, let's do that," Bryant said. "I need to get over to the warehouse and see what's up there, but I've got a lager that's been racked since November. If it's in good shape, it'll need to be moved, so that could be a perfect fit. It'll be good to get things rolling again."

Rafa followed Brother Martin to the door. "Would it be okay for Rafa to drop in and see how you're doing from time to time?" Brother Martin asked. Rafa looked at Bryant to see what he said. Maybe he didn't want to get involved again.

"Yah, you bet," Bryant said, looking at him with a grin. "I could use the help."

Rafa waved goodbye. He could probably get the photos organized and lined up this week, he thought as they returned to the car. A dark smirk dimpled his cheeks as he imagined an army of police cars with flashing lights and wailing sirens screeching to a stop outside that *tienda* in Wilmot.

All he needed was that ledger book.

34

As soon as Bryant was strong enough to get through the day without a nap, he decided to walk from his house to his brewing operation in the old glass factory. He felt the need to occupy his hands with something familiar. As long as he was idle, the conversations and theories about what happened to him—and, more confusing, what it meant—kept circling in his mind. He was tired of thinking about it, and decided to use his returning strength to get at least one area of his life back up to speed. He knew how to control his brewing, if nothing else.

As he approached the building, he saw a bright orange posting stretched across one of the iron bay doors. He read its block letters from across the street: "NOTICE of FORECLOSURE."

Even this, he thought.

He had first bent his life around brewing, then around Estelline, then Rafa. It felt like the more he invested in something, the more tenuous it became. What did Vivian call it—entropy? It was like the universe was designed to strip things away from him. Every door in his life had a neon "NOTICE of FORECLOSURE" sign posted across it.

Bryant grimly gripped the cold iron lever and thrust it back—the metal yelped and the posted notice ripped in half. *Just keep moving forward*, he thought.

The doors swung open with their familiar dry wheeze. A layer of dust had settled over everything and the new air coming in created turbulence that thrust dust particles through the slanting sunlight. Without any recent activity, the scent of the building reverted to its inert, dry earthy bricks and beams instead of the living brewing atmosphere of steaming cereal and yeast. Mice had opened some of the grain bags, leaving several small avalanches of barley along the row of stacked sacks. Those little buggers were going to cost him, but he knew they were just looking for a way through the winter, same as everyone.

Bryant entered and examined the first of four eight-foot stainless steel tanks standing at attention to the right of the furnace. He remembered filling it with forty-five barrels of lager back in late October. His intention had been to condition it through the coldest winter months, but he would have bottled and kegged it more than a month ago.

Assuming it had over-ripened, he reached for a tall glass next to his toolbox, blew in it to clear the dust, and wiped it out with his shirt before pulling a pint from a small valve on the side of the tank.

He plunged his nose into the glass, bracing for a sulfurous, skunky smell. He inhaled and was greeted instead by clean spice, like frozen bay leaves. A chipmunk-sized shard of delight scampered through him. Perhaps this lager had held together in the time he'd been away.

Tipping the glass, he took a sip and let the fluid run back and forth over his tongue. It felt crisp in his mouth and washed around with a broad, lively zing. There wasn't any bitterness—it tasted like snow and oatmeal—and as it sank through the throat it departed with the hint of citrus.

He held the glass up in surprised gratitude—the taste whispered in his ear that maybe not everything falls apart, maybe not everything is destined for decay. The beer was clear and sunny—not bright as midday, but with the gleaming golden haze of dawn.

Tastes like a brand new day, he thought.

***

The next day, Bryant was sweeping the floor when he heard the clatter of a bike hitting the crumbling cement outside the bay doors. He looked up to see Rafa peeking around the open bay doors.

"Rafa—good to see you!" he exclaimed. "How you been, bud?"

Rafa shrugged and gave a smile, but Bryant could tell it was forced. He looked more deeply at him. Rafa's thoughts were disturbed—he could somehow feel it.

"Hey—you okay? It's been rough, hasn't it?"

He walked over and touched the boy on the shoulder. Then it became clear: Rafa had been full of despair when he disappeared, but it had turned to anger after his return—he wanted revenge. No, he was *plotting* revenge.

Rafa stepped away from him and grabbed a flat-headed shovel to help Bryant scoop the dust piles up off the floor. Bryant followed.

"Well, things are looking up. Look what I found when I finally got back here."

He walked over to the tank of lager and pointed to the small glass window portal above the large emptying valve. Rafa leaned close to look into it.

"That's beer, dude. I filled this tank before I left and normally I'd let it age for a few months. It's been here for almost six, and guess what? It's still good. I think I can use it for the baseball game coming up, and then I can get this operation rolling again. It just needs a kick—something to give it spirit. Here's what I'm thinking."

He had moved his workbench between the tank and his furnace, and he pointed to a jar on its surface. It held a long, black, skinny bean with a hooked end like a miniature shepherd's crook.

"It's a vanilla bean—here, smell it."

He unscrewed the top of the jar and held in front of Rafa, who sniffed and raised his eyebrows. Even at arm's length, the milky warmth reached into Bryant's nostrils.

"Smells good, don't it?" Bryant said. "I got this hankering for beer that tastes like breakfast, so I've been playing with coffee and vanilla beans. I think it's as simple as soaking them—I want just enough flavor to remind people of morning. I'm calling it 'Daybreaker.'

"Got two bundles of smoked beans and twenty-five pounds of Cuban Queen coffee on order from Key West, and when it gets here tomorrow, it's all going in this tank before I keg it for the ballgame this weekend. We'll see how people like it. You'll be at the game, right?"

Rafa tucked the corner of his mouth into his cheek in a terse half-grin and nodded before walking off to explore the back corners of the factory. He was putting on a good face, Bryant could tell, and it worried him to think of what the kid might try.

Stepping back, Bryant recognized something new coming alive within himself—like a deeper form of compassion. He not only knew what was on Rafa's heart, he *felt* it with him. Maybe he had lost that capacity when he buried Estelline. Maybe it was just another part of him that was recovering, and he was noticing its re-emergence. But it felt like he'd been gone a long time and was returning to the human family.

Looking at the lager tank, it struck him that this feeling of coming alive wasn't too different from working with beer. With the right touch, raw ingredients could come alive under certain conditions—and show resilience. For the first time since the darkness that descended on him with Estelline's death, he could see a way through. If this lager could hold together when it should be a stinking stew, then maybe he could, too. And maybe he could hold other things together as well: this brewery, Rafa and his family—maybe more. And if the effort poured him out empty, then it will have been a good try. At least he'll be moving forward instead of sitting on his hands.

He remembered that fat priest at the ballgame and his works of mercy. Feed the hungry, he told him. Giving a drink to the thirsty must be about the same thing, Bryant thought.

He heard a loud clank—Rafa had found a jumble of industrial steel debris against the back wall and was pulling it apart. Bryant remembered setting aside some enigmatic old equipment when he moved in—it was too heavy to easily toss out and he thought he might be able to scrap it for a few bucks some time.

Rafa untangled one contraption and pulled it out. It had a heavy frame with brackets for attachment to the floor. A skinny, iron lever reached up like a modern art interpretation of a tree sapling rising from a pot. Four or five such mechanisms rested together in a nest.

Bryant walked over, intrigued, as though he was seeing it for the first time. When he was moving in, it was just in-the-way junk, but now he was curious what it was supposed to do. He braced his foot against the bottom and pulled the lever, which opened the rounded frame on the bottom like a sideways clam. The inside was smooth and perfectly round.

"Know what you found?"

Rafa shook his head.

"This is a mold for a jug. It's a casing for glassblowers to make large bottles. "

He lugged the unwieldy appliance to the round furnace and, sure enough, discovered small hitches below each glory hole where the casing attached perfectly.

"Picture it," he said. "The kiln is full of orange flame: hot—like 2,500 degrees hot. Big men with leather aprons are pushing and pulling long, steel tubes in and out with melted glass on the end. They blow through the tube and a bubble forms inside the glass and it looks like glue. Then they spin it around, and blow some more, and the bubble gets bigger, thinner, wider. Then, when it's close to the right size, they step on this"—he stomped on the casing and it swung open. "They put it inside and it clamps shut. Then they spin, spin, spin, and blow, blow, blow. When they take it out, it's shaped like a jug."

Before his disappearance, he remembered fixing the regulator on the furnace with the thought that he might one day play around with blowing bottles, but the economics of that idea weren't great. His supplier could get him bottles for pennies, and he'd have to invest weeks in perfecting the blowing technique. But what if he could learn to use these casings to blow half-gallon growler jugs?

He glanced back at the door and could see the frayed edges of the neon orange foreclosure notice. "Hand-crafted growlers" had a distinctive sound to it. He could imagine clear glass jugs with the Black Fox Brewing logo embossed on them grabbing people's attention. He could imagine them selling.

He looked at Rafa. "Should we fire this puppy up?"

He walked around the backside of the furnace and opened the valve for the natural gas line, and the small cavern began to hiss. He quickly stepped to the regulator box and pressed the ignition button. The ricochet of two snaps sliced through the hissing before the gas combusted and thundered to life. Bryant heard Rafa inhale sharply in surprise. An orange glow emanated from the glory holes and Bryant could instantly feel the roasting heat pour out. The digital thermometer display on the regulator box began counting up.

"So this is what we're gonna do," Bryant said as he turned to Rafa. "I know you're mad those guys took your dad. You're mad they tried to take me. But if we get stuck playing their game, we'll lose. We're better than they are, so we'll do what we do best. We'll be us—we'll stick it to them by being the best we can be, by doing our best work.

"You got it? We can do this, bud, but you gotta stay with me. I know you're hatching something in your head, but you can't go back to that *tienda* without me, okay?"

***

Bryant woke early the next morning and drove to the spot in Indiana Dunes where he was found. He paid no attention to the surroundings—he didn't want to think about what his body must have looked like on the shore there. He carried a red spade over his shoulder with one hand, and his other hand held the handles of two five-gallon buckets.

The air was cool but heavy with moisture. He could hear songbirds along the shoreline, but once the sun came up, they'd be drowned out by scavenging gulls. Far up the beach, he could see one figure walking away from him, southward, a black dog trotting nearby.

After trudging out onto the beach for ten or fifteen paces, he stopped and cleared a spot and began to dig. He filled the two buckets with sand, then lugged them back to the truck and grabbed two more. Forty-five minutes later, he was pulling away from the beach—the ten plastic buckets that had rattled around empty on his drive up were now solid as stumps.

The bed of his truck rode ten inches lower from their weight, but he figured there was enough left in his suspension to hold a few more bags of material from the industrial supply warehouse in Michigan City. He had spent the night researching glass production and knew he needed sodium carbonate, lime, dolomite, and a few other ingredients to stabilize the silica when it melted.

Reaching up to turn on his blinker, he felt a tightness in the bicep of his right arm. He squeezed his withered hand into a fist and raised it to his shoulder and flexed—it was a swollen knot of muscle. Come to think of it, he had no trouble carrying those buckets of sand. Each must have weighed close to fifty pounds. They were heavy, sure, but when he exerted himself, the strength was there to handle them, even with his limp.

He checked a box in his mind: fully recovered.

35

Rafa stopped running—he thought he heard his name being called. The current of children playing cops and robbers flowed around him.

"Rafa! La pelota!"

It was Miggy—he was calling from right field and pointing. Rafa shrank back when he noticed that the rest of the players on the field were facing him. His eyes followed the line of his brother's hand to a baseball that was just rolling to a stop in the shade between him and the sunny field. The baseball field had no fences except for the backstop behind the catcher—just white lines that couldn't stop foul balls.

He ran to the ball, picked it up, and closed his eyes to heave it as hard as he could to Miggy. When he looked, he saw the ball traveling on the right line, but felt a twinge of shame when it fell short and bounced and rolled to him.

Miggy just scooped it up and shouted, "Thanks, Rafa!" He seemed unconcerned and the attention from the players on the field followed the ball, leaving Rafa out of the spotlight, mercifully.

Dislodged from the herd of kids momentarily, Rafa sat at the pillared base of an oak tree to watch the baseball game for a moment. The branches from all the trees in the park reached together to surround the baseball field with shade. He could hear his brother and sister shrieking with friends from one of the four playgrounds that anchored the corners of the park. It was his favorite place in town because there was so much space to run, and the four playgrounds made perfect base forts to run between.

He smelled the *asador de carne* and his stomach rumbled. He looked up and saw clouds of smoke wafting through the trees turning to small, solid thunderheads when they hit shafts of sunlight sifting through the oaks and evergreens.

His eyes followed the billows toward the area behind the backstop that was lined with picnic tables. His uncle, Berto, was one of the men shuffling orange-pasted meat on one of the large grills back there—he could hear it sizzling. His mom sat there at a table, smiling with two other women—maybe Felipe's mom and Javi's *abuela*. When he had risen to watch cartoons this morning, Mom was already up making tortillas.

Beyond the grills billowing with smoke, Rafa saw Bryant pumping a lever on a grey metal barrel that sat inside a big bucket of ice. Must be the beer he was working on—he decided to go greet him.

The sizzling got louder as he walked around the backstop, drowning out the chatter from the field where the players were talking and jesting. Bryant saw him and waved him over as he began to pour beer into a plastic cup.

When Rafa reached him, it was half full, and Bryant lifted it to him. "Give it a sniff," he said. "Whaddya smell?"

Rafa placed the cup below his nose. It smelled a lot like beer with that familiar spicy yeast scent, but then he detected the vanilla bean that Bryant showed him in the factory. He raised his eyes and smiled.

"Can you smell the vanilla?"

Rafa nodded.

"And the coffee?"

Rafa put his nose into the cup again, and sure enough—he picked up the scent of his mom's coffee cup.

"Pretty cool, huh? *Wash-tay*—that means it's good." Bryant raised the glass and sipped it.

Rafa saw his sister, Maria, wandering by looking lost and he flagged her down.

"What's the score?" she asked. Rafa shrugged.

"I don't think they're keeping score—they're just playing three outs to a side and switching," Bryant said. "It's just for fun."

"How will they know when the game is over? I'm hungry," Maria said.

"Guess they'll just play till they're tired," Bryant said. "But there's food over there—see your mom? She'll get you fixed up."

Rafa followed Maria over to Mom, and noticed that the black-haired woman who was Bryant's friend was up to bat. He heard Bryant heckling her.

"Give 'em hell, Viv! Hey batter, batter!"

She swung at the first pitch and dribbled it to the shortstop, and Rafa saw her run awkwardly to first base in flip flops. She was out by a mile, but she was laughing.

His mom had plates ready for them when they walked up. She was squeezing a lime over their open tortillas. Strips of thin-sliced, crispy meat was blanketed in crumbles of white cheese, slabs of buttery avocado, and flourishes of cilantro. She pointed them to the next picnic table, which held round coolers full of aqua fresca. Rafa pulled the nozzle on one with slices of watermelon in it and poured a glass for himself and another for Maria and sat down at the end of the table to eat and watch.

Vivian was the third out and now the brothers were in the field. They looked old, but they moved well. Someone yelled for Berto to hit—he took off his apron and grabbed a bat and jogged to the plate. Rafa didn't know Berto could play ball—he'd never seen him do anything athletic, and he had trouble imagining how his thick, callused hands could hold on to the thin bat handle. The bat looked like a pencil coming out of his fist, but he handled it with fluidity and grace—it reminded Rafa of his mom turning tortillas. It was Berto's waist, Rafa noticed—he could twist his beltline around in time with the bat and it made him look sleek and powerful.

On the second pitch, Berto cracked a screamer right over the pitcher's head. Rafa followed the ball with a sharp twist of his head and the corner of his eye caught a figure—it was Brother Martin!—sprinting back from his position at second and lunging for the ball. He knocked it down with his glove—he didn't make the catch, but it kept Berto at first.

Rafa liked to listen to the players banter—there was a lot of chatter on the benches and in the field. He finished his plate and went back for more.

***

The patch of sunlight was slowly crawling past Vivian, so she scooted to the end of the picnic table—butt on the top, feet on the bench—to watch more of the game. Baseball had always been, for her, part entertainment, part sunbathing. Grant asked if she wanted another cider, but before she answered, he got up to refill his cup and grab another bottle from the six-pack of cider Bryant had brought just for her.

Bryant was up and drilled the second pitch—*th-crack!* The ball streaked past the third baseman and shortstop on a rope before they could even move and he easily reached first.

There's nothing like that sound, she thought. That resonant, solid concussion was the result of everything clicking into place the way it should at precisely the right moment, and the satisfaction—labor meeting craft—felt rich, even if it was for a fleeting moment.

Despite her taunting, Bryant was taking a cautious lead off of first. She recognized the next batter from her lab at Columba Hall and tried to see if she could recall his name. Brother Edmund, maybe? His spine had a pronounced curve at the shoulders, causing him to look up whenever he walked somewhere. She noticed that the curve was still present, but less so—his shoulders swiveled freely in the on-deck circle.

Ed drilled a pitch to left-center, and because there was no fence around the field, it bounced into the shade under the trees out there. Two outfielders raced to pick it up, and she looked to see where Bryant was. He was running—running! she'd never seen him do that before!—past second looking for a sign from the brother behind third.

The brother waved his arm in a big windmill motion and Bryant put his head down and kept chugging. His limp made him look like he had a flat tire, but he was moving fast.

The shortstop cut off the throw from deep in the outfield and turned to see Bryant nearly home. Brother Ed was already around second, and the brother coaching third was starting to wave his arms up and down, bending at the waist like he was urgently worshiping the baseball god of the triple. The shortstop cocked and fired to the third baseman straddling the bag. Ed thrust his feet forward into a slide. The throw came in right at the chest of the third-baseman, who collected it and flung his glove down to hit Ed's thigh—his foot had already reached base.

Vivian clapped and then raised her fingers to her mouth to whistle loudly. Grant met Bryant as walked past the dugout, handed him his cup and returned for another. Bryant slumped down on the bench of the table next to her, huffing.

"You got wheels, man," she said. "You're really moving well."

"Yeah, I think I'm back to 100 percent."

"You look better than that—is that possible?"

"Dunno," he said, still breathing deeply. "Maybe. Feels good."

He took a deep drink of beer, then paused for more breathing. Grant returned and sat next to him.

"What do you think of Daybreaker here?" he asked Grant.

"It stands out with the coffee right away," he said. "But it's not harsh—it's . . . rounded."

"Vanilla," Bryant inserted.

"Yeah, it's good," Grant said. "I like it. I don't think I've tasted anything like it."

"I wanted to see what everyone thought about it here," Bryant said. "Got a stack of bills at home that I'm hoping this'll pay."

He took another sip and began to breathe deeply through his nose. "In fact, I'm thinking of firing up that furnace and making growlers to sell this by the half-gallon."

Vivian wondered how safe that old thing could be—it could have been decades since it was last used.

"Has that thing been inspected?"

"Not yet, but I'm taking it slow—step by step. Just got the gas line and ignition working."

"How hot do you have to get it to melt glass?"

"Pretty damn hot," he said. "About the same temperature that steel melts at—north of two thousand degrees."

Grant got up and asked Vivian if she wanted more to eat. She figured she'd fill up on cider for the rest of the afternoon and declined. As he departed for the grill, she heard shouting from the field. It was a shock to hear Brother Martin's voice raised—he was walking out of a cloud of dust around second base and heading for home. He was pointing his finger at the umpire.

She looked back at home to see the catcher stand up and walk away. The umpire took off his mask—he was the only umpire on the field, and she recognized the bishop right away. She thought it funny to see him dressed in umpire blues with that hat with the small brim. It was oddly out of context, like seeing your letter carrier at the grocery store.

"Was he stealing second?" Bryant asked.

"Musta been thrown out," she said.

The two met just in front of the pitcher's mound. The catcher and pitcher ambled over to the first baseman, where they huddled together to watch. Now it became clear that Martin was suppressing a smile as he shouted at Newell.

"This is horseshit!" he yelled, walking right up to Newell's face. "There's no way you can see that tag from home plate. I was safe! Everyone on this field knows it!"

"Oh shuddup, you don't know nothin'!" shouted Newell. He was doing much better at keeping a straight face. The pitcher and first baseman were cracking up.

"I know I was safe by a country mile—you've been dogging me all day, and I'm not taking it anymore!"

"Well, you're entitled to your opinion," Newell calmly replied. He raised a finger, but there was so little space between them that Martin bent backward to allow room for it. "But you're wrong. Now calm down and stop showing me up or you're taking a shower."

"Don't you threaten me! Don't you threaten me with that finger, you short-sighted midget! I'm gonna break your cane and shoot your dog!" Newell turned and shot his arm up in the air as though he was throwing a paper airplane. "Get outta here," he said, and started walking back to home plate.

Brother Martin leaned into his ear and kept barking at him, but started using Spanish.

"What's he saying?" Vivian asked. She and Bryant both leaned forward, enthralled with the spectacle. "Is that Spanish?"

"Yeah," Bryant said. "He's saying . . . 'Diarrhea has more consistency than your calls today.'" They both began laughing.

Newell remained stoic and when he reached home, he pulled on his mask and stood behind the plate. Brother Martin was chuckling now, unable to contain himself or keep the façade any longer, and kicked dirt on the plate before walking off the field. "I was getting hungry, anyways," he said, returning to a friendly tone. "Want me to put a plate together for you?"

Newell nodded once and smiled at him.

The crowd cheered and laughed.

"I didn't know you understood Spanish," Vivian said to Bryant.

"Yeah, I'm picking it up—not from Rafa, obviously, but from being around the Andre center with that hot-head," he replied, nodding to Brother Martin.

"You're starting to remind me of him," Vivian said.

"Who? Brother Martin?" Bryant asked. "What do you mean?"

"You're just . . . different. Since you've come back. People talked about how he got sick, and when he came back he was . . . somehow more alive."

"I dunno," Bryant said. "I'm a little worried where that line of thought will take me."

"What?"

Bryant took another drink from his beer—he seemed to be thinking, or weighing his words. "I was gone for, what, four, five months? And I'm back? What if I was dead? What if I died?

"Freaky. . ."

"Yeah, but. . ."

"But what?"

"How long is too long to be dead before you can come back?"

Vivian shot him a look, but he didn't return it.

Estelline.

***

Carlos Siego had heard of the game, of course—it was why the compound was empty, even of kids; it was why the store had a line at checkout yesterday, but was silent today; it was why even his crew chiefs were not responding to his text messages.

He turned down the *norteño* music in his white Cadillac and slowed as he approached the park. He could see the *asador de carne* smoke billowing across the street in the light breeze. He turned his car and slowly rolled along the wooded park, past the playground with running kids, past the cluster of grills and picnic tables. As he rounded a corner to circle the block, he studied the people in the field and along the dugout on the first base line.

There was Salvator, with a plate in his hands. He was stuffing his face, but should be gathering at least six workers to plant strawberries Monday. He better be ready when that bus arrives.

There was Manuel in the outfield. He was a mechanic at the shop across the street from the store. He owed $400 because of the *quinceañera* he wanted for his daughter last year. That's fine, though. He's on the books and would keep paying on that for a long, long time.

There was Juana on the mound. She drove a tractor in the pepper fields at the end of last season, and had shown quick thinking when it got stuck. She wasn't pretty enough to fuck, but maybe one of her daughters would be in a few years. Carlos made a note to keep her on the tractor when they went south for the cauliflower and cabbage.

There was Angel, pouring a cup of beer. Who was that he's talking to?

Siego pulled to the curb and put the caddy in park. He turned the radio off and rolled down the window to get a better look. Yes, the guy looked just like that gimpy *hombre* Spinks tangled with last winter.

Fucking Spinks. He'd told him exactly what to do. It's sloppy shit like this that's gonna bring attention —the last thing they needed. *That motherfucker thought this was catch-and-release?*

He powered the window up and turned the car off. He needed to find out where this crippled sonofabitch lived.

***

Bryant had a truck full of empty kegs, and it was getting dark. It would take him another hour to clean everything up back at the factory, but he couldn't pass by the cemetery without stopping.

He quietly shut the door to his truck, and stepped around the front bumper to let a dark, smoky-windowed white car slowly roll by. He let it clear the corner before walking to the entrance gate under that iron arch. He reached through the bars and lifted the stake that kept the heavy gate from swinging freely. An opening cracked just wide enough for him to slip through, and he pressed the gate back together again.

36

Rafa Villahermosa had a plan, and he kept it buried in a lead-lined box deep in his brain. He went through the daily family routine as if everything was normal, as if he didn't have a fusion reactor humming between his ears.

After school, he went with his siblings to the Andre Center where they had a snack and began plowing through homework in order to be able to continue their *Settlers of Catan* game. Then, when his mom arrived after getting off work at the recycling plant, they all climbed in the pickup truck to head home. He folded his legs into his chest to sit in the half bench behind the front seats.

As they all piled out of the truck and into the house, he went to his room, dumped his backpack on his bed, scribbled a note, and ran back downstairs.

Aurora was still unpacking her things from the day and sorting through some mail. Rafa tossed a note on top of her pile: "Dante's house. Back for dinner." The door banged *whumpf* before he could hear her reply. If she was protesting, she wasn't quick enough to stop him—he was on his bike and pedaling out the driveway.

It took a little longer than normal to get into Wilmot in the daytime because he had to share the road with more vehicles, which meant riding on the soft shoulder, not on the harder crown in the center of the road like he could in the early mornings. When he pulled into town, he propped his bike against the wall of the mechanic shop across the street from the *tienda.*

He walked around the shop and crossed the street, and suppressed a startle when the bell hanging on the door to the store clanged.

The *tienda* was quiet except for *norteño* music playing on a black AM radio behind the counter; it was empty except for the woman with a scowl and black hair looking at him from next to the radio. He looked away and walked into an aisle jam-packed with boxed and canned goods.

He grabbed two cans of chiles and then found the section of the shelves holding bottles of Jarrito soda. He stopped to review the steps in his mind. He knew things would happen quickly from here.

He reached out and knocked over two bottles of red pop. They broke on the tiled floor with a crash and a lingering hiss as the carbonated liquid spread like a pink stain. He waited.

"*Oye*, what the hell'd you do?!" The woman appeared at the end of the aisle—the scowl was now a distinct frown that revealed a gap where a canine tooth should have been.

He looked down and raised his feet in the sopping mess, making sure that pop coated his sneakers, and apologetically stepped away with his chile cans. His steps made a wet noise that turned to a sticky snicket as the soda he was tracking across the floor increasingly clung to his soles.

She returned behind the register with a huff and he placed the chile cans on the counter.

"You have to pay for that, you know," she said.

He gave her a sorry look. She rang up the cans.

"Ten dollars."

He was confused—the cans should have cost less than five dollars together.

"There's a clean-up fee," she said flatly.

He pulled out the five-dollar bill from one pocket and some spare change from the other and placed it on the counter, slowly counting it.

"That ain't enough," she said, sliding the money toward her across the counter with one swipe. She stuffed the bill and change into her pocket.

He put his head down and turned away, leaving the cans behind. The bell on the door clanged as he slipped out. He trudged toward his bike and when he reached the corner and was out of sight from the windows, he crouched between a blinking lotto sign and a money wire poster and peered back into the store.

The woman was shaking her head and leaving the counter. He watched her stomp toward the rear of the store. He walked back to the door, looking through the gaps in the window signs to track her progress. When she opened a closet in the back, he broke for it.

He carefully slivered the door open six inches and reached around to hold the cow bell hanging from the inner door bar, then slipped his body through. He could hear water running into a bucket in the back of the store.

After gently nursing the door and bell back into place, he quickly and lightly stepped toward the register. Crouching down behind the counter, his eyes scanned cubbies full of receipt boxes, old magazines, and cigarette cartons before they landed on the black-bound ledger he was seeking. It was tucked under the cash register in a gap left by the adjustable feet of the machine. With a finger he levered one corner free from beneath the register.

He paused to listen for the woman. He heard the squeak of a water faucet being closed in the back room, and then the rumble and rhythmic snap of small metal wheels crossing tile seams. Peeking over the edge of the counter, he saw her holding erect a wooden handle and pushing a yellow mop bucket on casters out of the maintenance closet. She disappeared across the back of the store as she navigated to the aisle with the spilled soda.

He immediately regretted not planning enough to think about making a mess in an aisle not pointed at the door. He wouldn't be able to leave until she had cleaned up the mess and took the mop back to the closet. Her mop made a greasy whisper as it slid around the tile, punctuated by a high-pitched growl whenever it caught and dragged a jagged piece of broken glass.

He decided to pull out the ledger from its hiding place so that he could make a quick exit when she was done. He squared himself in a crouch in front of the register and delicately pulled the corner he had exposed. The book rubbed against the bottom of the register as it slid out.

A loud, shrill clang suddenly sounded and the register drawer jumped at him. Rafa froze with his eyes wide. The ledger fell to the floor.

He listened in a panic to tell if the woman had heard the ring. How could she have missed it?

Dead silence—the only sound was the humming of the refrigerated coolers. No sounds of mopping, no nothing. He held his breath.

Then, he heard quick squeaky steps. She was leaving the aisle to investigate. He had to move. *Now*.

He picked up the ledger from the floor and ran for the door. The woman was just approaching the end of the aisle when he sped by.

"Hey!" she shouted as he reached the door. "*¡Alto!*"

He slung the door open as she lunged; the bell clamored with a violent jerk. He had a shoulder through when he felt her nails rip at his shirt. He tugged free and was through the door. He ran—without looking, he ran as fast as he could.

In the street, he didn't hear her behind him.

He veered behind the stack of tires across the road. Huffing, he hid the ledger inside a tire tread and looked back at the store. She was standing outside the store dialing a mobile phone, then holding it to her ear as she looked at where he was hiding.

He felt like he had nudged a small pebble loose at the top of a long hill and was watching it tumble into an avalanche below him. The situation was moving beyond him now—he was a twig in a crashing wave and would be crushed if he didn't get out of there.

He sprinted to his bike behind the building, hopped on, and cranked the pedals as hard as he could down the alley that paralleled the road, keeping out of sight behind the shops and stores for as long as possible. The alley dumped into the gravel road he came in on and he skidded to a stop and looked as far down the road as he could see. It was empty, but it would be hard to stay concealed for the whole ride home if someone was looking for him. He had to go, though—those guys knew everyone in town. No place was safe but home.

His legs were already throbbing. He gulped air and tore off down the road.

After 200 yards, he could see dust from an approaching car and he veered into the ditch and hunkered down until it passed. Seeing cars coming from behind would be more difficult. He wheeled the bike back up to the road and continued.

Twice more, he stopped to avoid oncoming cars. Then he heard a vehicle approaching from behind. By the time he braked to jump in the ditch, it was already passing—there was just not enough time to hide. There was no way to avoid being seen, and he was losing too much time stopping to hide. He knew he needed to get off the road, and the fastest way to do that was just to get home. The muscles on top of his legs were swelling and aching, and his mouth was dry as dirt, but he decided to just go for it.

The intersection with the county road that led to his home was in sight when he heard the rumble and snap of approaching tires on gravel. He looked back. A black sedan with tinted windows was already slowing next to him. A man leaned out of the window—there was a black snake on his arm. He was holding a metal bar and threw it at Rafa's bike.

The tire iron hit Rafa's front wheel and suddenly the bike jerked out from beneath him. The ground slammed up into his face, raking his chin and digging into his palms. He couldn't breathe and dust swirled into his eyes. The car ground to a stop ahead of him.

He heard the doors open on the sedan. Someone picked up his bike and savagely threw it into the ditch; Rafa saw the handlebars convulse backward as the frame bucked at an impossible angle. He was being picked up.

His chest heaved, his lungs desperate for air. What little he could coax into this throat was thick with dust and came coughing back out. His eyes burned as rage began to roar in his ears. These *cabrónes* did the same thing to Papa—he knew it was them, and he hated them for it.

He stretched his lungs as wide as they could go and let out a scream that had been pent up for more than a year, but the only sound that came out of his mouth was a hoarse, rasping static. Where was his voice? He cried out again as panic started to sieze him —nothing but a raw, heavy whisper.

He thrashed, but their grip tightened on his arms and shoulders as they dragged him implacably toward the rumbling car.

37

On Saturday morning, Bryant pulled his suit out of the closet with the sudden recognition that he hadn't worn it since the funeral. As he pulled on the pants, dried mud along the hem cracked and flaked to the floor. He remembered helping shovel dirt over the grave and having to wash the moist soil and clay from his dress shoes when he got home, but he had apparently neglected the suit.

As he pulled up to the cemetery, he put on a pair of sunglasses and waited for the funeral. Within an hour a hearse slowed and turned in to the driveway, pausing for a young funeral director in a shiny blue suit to hop out of the passenger side to open the gate. A line of cars followed—each vehicle grimly bearing a small, purple flag magnetized to the roof above the driver.

Bryant got out and slowly mingled with the crowd as they assembled around the open grave. A carpet of bright green plastic turf covered the mound of loose dirt. A chrome pipe frame stood around the hole in the ground, and the pallbearers and two funeral directors shuffled around it with the casket. They gently laid the coffin on canvas straps draped over the shiny poles.

After the rite, people started to disperse, but Bryant lingered to watch the burial process. Despite helping to fill in Estelline's grave, he was too distraught to remember specifics, so he was taking mental notes as the casket was lowered into the ground. The blue-suited funeral director turned a clicking winch embedded in the chrome frame and the coffin slowly descended by inches. When it reached the bottom, the director pulled out the straps. The last few remaining mourners stepped close for a final goodbye and Bryant joined them.

The casket rested inside a cement box, and Bryant remembered a line item from the funeral home expenses noting the cost of a grave liner. It had something to do with the graves not collapsing over time as the casket disintegrated. He stepped back and walked to the high entrance gate, but remained there to watch the rest of the burial process.

When everyone was gone, he heard the rumbling start of a tractor engine. Two workers emerged from a maintenance shed the size of a small barn on the far end of the cemetery. They walked next to a backhoe driven by a third worker and slowly approached the open grave.

When they reached the site, the two workers in overalls peeled back the plastic turf to reveal a mound of dirt black as wet coffee grounds. A flat cement slab rested on top of the mound like a book placed on a pillow. They slung a heavy chain through two iron loops embedded in the top of the slab and connected it to the backhoe arm. Each grabbed a corner of the slab to stabilize it as the tractor's engine revved and lifted it into place above the grave.

When it was in place, the two workers shoveled dirt into the grave and stepped down into it to tamp and stomp dirt around the liner. He could only see their chests and guessed the top of the liner to be about four feet down, which made sense—it placed the bottom of the grave hole at the proverbial six feet under. Then the backhoe swung its arm through the pile of dirt like an elephant swiping hay and black soil tumbled into the grave.

Bryant didn't see any way he could remove Estelline's casket without the backhoe. He could probably dig out the dirt with a spade and a few hours of hard labor, but he couldn't lift that slab by himself, let alone raise the casket out of the liner. All of that would require the hydraulics of the backhoe's boom. So he'd have to break in to the maintenance shed.

He was committed to starting that evening. Tomorrow was Sunday, so there would be no funerals—he'd called a funeral home to be sure. He could open the grave, remove the casket at twilight this evening, and then just line the hole with that plastic turf. To any visitors wandering the cemetery tomorrow, it would look like a grave prepared for a Monday morning service. He could return on Sunday evening to fill the hole back in—if he needed to. . . But everything would be back in place before workers returned Monday morning.

No one would be any wiser. Except for him.

***

Bryant was too nervous to eat the rest of the day. He watched four or five different video clips on his computer that described the operation of several different models of backhoes. After that, time seemed to drip by. He forced himself to wait until five o'clock, but couldn't find anything else to occupy his hands or mind—he just couldn't focus. For the last hour, he sat at his kitchen table, staring at the clock on the oven. When it finally ticked over from 4:59 to 5:00, he got up and went to his truck.

He pulled over in front of the cemetery gate and decided not to concern himself with being secretive on the theory that people notice a suspicious-looking figure more than someone just going about their business. But he did move efficiently, thinking that less time in the open meant less exposure. Plus, daylight was limited.

He pulled through the gate, closed it behind him, and parked the truck in front of Estelline's grave with the tailgate just over the top of her headstone. He had packed a canvas tarp in the back and he took it out and spread it on the ground so that the dirt from the grave wouldn't ruin the grass.

The maintenance barn had a broad rolling steel door that opened into its bay, like a garage door, but another entrance was cut into the side of the building—a normal exterior door with a small window the size of a sheet of paper cut into it at about shoulder-height. Bryant picked up a grapefruit-sized stone that was used to prop the door open and rammed it into the window. With a loud bang, it cracked. A second attempt shattered it, and with the third, glass fell inside the door. He carefully reached through and felt for a handle, but his hand felt the cold steel of a push bar. He clamped it down and the door opened.

He found a panel of switches inside the door for lights, and one flat button—he pushed it and the garage door started to grumble and rise. The light that flooded the dark space illuminated the backhoe parked in the center of the shed along with a sparse assortment of tools hung along both walls. In the corner stood a coat rack that held several pairs of dark navy work overalls. Bryant slipped into a pair and checked the backhoe—the keys were in the ignition.

He took a second to take in the levers and switches before him, recalling the videos he'd seen that day. The alignment wasn't entirely confusing, so he started the engine, which came to life and began rumbling beneath him with tremendous life. He put the tractor in gear and in the same instant, the cabin convulsed violently and a loud screeching filled the shed—an eagle screaming in his ear—and he stomped on the brakes. Below him, the concrete floor had a broad white scrape below the front loader. In parked position, the machine had its appendages lowered to the ground for safety. He looked behind him and narrower, corresponding white scrapes glared at him from below the narrow digging bucket and stabilizer legs.

He searched for the levers to raise the loader, legs, and bucket four or five feet, then proceeded slowly out of the barn. Bryant gently bounced in the seat as the shifting weight of the tractor made its way over the uneven path into the cemetery. He steered wide around the grouping of graves to meet up with the paved road that circled the interior of the cemetery and found a lane toward Estelline's grave.

Pulling into place, he put the tractor into park and remembered to lower the stabilizing legs. Then he began to dig.

***

Bryant turned the key off and the tractor engine coughed and fell silent. He opened the cabin door and stood above the hole he'd just opened in the black earth. There was no activity in or around the cemetery —no one poking around—and the sounds of the city were fading into the twilight.

Well, it ain't pretty, he thought, looking next to the open hole. The burial rite that morning had been conducted around a hole with sharp, square sides. This looked like a mammoth-sized badger had pawed a hole in the ground.

He inspected the far corner of the hole where the bucket had banged into something hard. Climbing out of the tractor and stepping into the crater, he could see busted concrete—he'd smashed the corner of the liner, fracturing and crumbling the cement in an area the size of a basketball. He stomped around the opening—the other sides of the liner seemed intact. He returned to his truck for the spade.

After scraping dirt away from the rest of the top slab, he wiped dirt free from the embedded iron loops. The chain the workers had used that morning was piled in a box in the tractor cabin and he strung it through the loops. It took some back and forth between the hole and the driver's seat to maneuver the bucket arm and chain, but it wasn't long before he could gently raise the boom and lift the slab. He swung the arm to the side of the grave and placed it atop the disorganized mound of dirt.

The casket sat inside the liner, clean and shiny. It was just as he remembered it: modest and simple— brushed steel with a dark bronze finish. The bouquet of flowers from the top had wilted to dried, black disintegrating twigs.

Did he dare knock? Or speak out loud? Was it crazy to think that she might be able to hear him?

He was suddenly taken aback at what he was doing. Up to this point, he'd been so laser-focused on the decision to act; once he fixed his will on doing it, all he considered were the steps to take. Now he was confronted with the reality of what he had done. Surely this was against the law. Did he really want to see what was inside?

Yes, he did.

He knew what was happening to him, and he'd never stop wondering about her if he didn't do this. That's why he was here. His heart was wildly tossing blood through his neck and head, but he was committed—he was all-in.

He decided to stay silent around the casket unless he could detect some sign from within. He'd already prepared things at the factory to open it there—he had to get somewhere private. So he carefully stepped onto the cement walls of the liner and began looping the chain around the pallbearer handles on both sides of the casket.

Once it was secure, he climbed into the tractor and lifted the casket, wobbling, out of the grave and reached the arm forward so that it hovered over his truck bed. He hopped out and arranged two 2x6 boards on parallel tracks in the bed so that the casket would rest on them for the drive—he had spread grease on the boards before leaving the factory so the coffin would slide over them more easily when it came time to push it out of the truckbed. Then he gently lowered the boom till the chain went slack. The truck bed gently sank over the wheels from the weight.

From there it was a matter of clean-up—shape up the dirt mound as best he could and return the backhoe to the barn. He found rolls of the green plastic turf stacked along one wall there and dragged one out to the hole. Once everything was covered up and looked moderately tidy and intentional, he fastened the tarp cover over the top of his truck bed and pulled away.

***

So far, so good, he thought as he arrived at the factory. He unlocked the two iron doors facing the furnace and backed the pickup in. He stepped out of the truck to lower the tailgate and open the window frame around the glory hole. It took some back and forth to make sure that the edge of the truckbed came right up to the opening. Then he shut and locked the wide iron doors leading out to the street.

Finally—he was safe with her. He took a deep breath. *Okay, Stella,* he whispered.

He found he didn't need the winch system he'd set up inside the furnace—the casket weighed about 300 pounds. He found that he could brace himself against the wall of the truckbed and find enough purchase to drive it forward. The greased boards eased the friction, and it fit through the glory hole with about six inches to spare.

With enough pulling and tugging he negotiated the casket into place on top of a smelting cradle along the interior wall, making sure that the side that opened faced the center of the furnace. He knew there was a latching mechanism in the coffin frame—a small handle that folded out and swiveled around to work a locking clamp under the cover. It took some looking, but he found it and worked it until he heard a click. The lid nudged loose and raised a quarter inch, free.

38

As evening fell, the voices echoing around the Andre Center had transformed from the high-pitched chatter of children to the softer and lower tones of adults talking in hesitant fragments. Brother Martin was leading a group lesson on comparatives and superlatives in English when he felt his cell phone buzz in his pocket two separate times.

After everyone had broken into small groups around tables for further conversation with volunteer tutors, it buzzed a third time. He pulled it out and recognized the number: Aurora Villahermosa.

"Hola, Aurora—cómo estás?"

A flood of words gushed into his ear. She was clearly distressed and spoke in frantic sobs. He couldn't grasp anything specific to understand. Something about Rafa, but he'd just been here after school today. Martin told her to slow down, to breathe, and start from the beginning.

***

Carlos Siego was annoyed he had to spend his day following this cripple who should have been rotting on the bottom of Lake Michigan. It was clear that he wasn't a desperate corn farmer from Guatemala named Matteo Benitez. So who was he? How long would it take for him to point a detective toward their operation in Wilmot? And what was it going to take to make him go away for good?

Carlos had cleared the whole day on Saturday, even packed a lunch. He intended to clean this matter up by the end of the weekend. Early morning found him parked a block away from the small house the guy slept in every night. And when he pulled out in his long, white pickup, Carlos was ready.

He followed the guy to the cemetery, and observed him observing the burial. He followed him back home and was ready when he returned to the cemetery that evening.

Peering at him from the darkened windows of his car parked on the street, Carlos could see through the wrought-iron fence. Clearly the guy was opening a grave. An anonymous call to the police would have put him behind bars, but he didn't need more law enforcement attention on this asshole.

So what the fuck was he doing?

After tidying everything up, the guy drove to the east side of town. It was not difficult to follow him unnoticed—there was not a lot of traffic this late on a Saturday so he could hang back several blocks. When they approached the dilapidated industrial section, Carlos parked his car next to an abandoned warehouse and got out to walk.

As he turned the corner on Webster road, Bryant's white truck came into view through the bay doors of a factory. Carlos stopped short across the street and took a step back behind the brick corner of an old storefront and leaned against the wall. He pulled out a cigarette and lit it. After a deep draw, he looked around casually as he exhaled—the surrounding blocks were silent.

Sure as shit, the guy had taken a casket out of the cemetery. He was pushing it into a brick hut of some sort inside the factory. Then he swung closed the iron bay doors with a careful, hushed clang. Carlos took a deep draw from his cigarette and studied the building across the street.

The tall smokestack seemed positioned right over that central hut—must have been a furnace of some sort. He could just make out the fading squared letters on the base of the chimney in the dying light: TYNDALL GLASS. He wondered what connection this guy had to such a strange building. Confusing as the incident at the cemetery was, why did he bring the casket here? Was he trying to cremate someone's remains?

He lit another cigarette and waited. He was curious, but not in a rush. He'd learned that patience rewards the observant. So many people were shortsighted and impulsive, grasping the first solution that presented itself. That was Spinks' problem—Victor's, too: no vision. He knew neither would be able to run that camp in Georgia.

The cool air of the evening was starting to sift down off the roof of the old buildings that loomed over him. A frog somewhere started calling.

After about twenty minutes, the levers on the iron bay doors turned and creaked. Carlos hid his third cigarette behind his leg so the burning red tip wouldn't emit a glow in that direction. The white truck slowly emerged and stopped. The guy got out to close the doors behind him, then pulled away.

Carlos was torn between following the target and

following his curiosity. He was confident he'd catch up with the guy again when he needed to—he'd end up at his house eventually. He wanted to know what the fuck he was doing with a casket.

He finished his cigarette to give ample time for the area to clear. It was completely dark by now. Then he crossed the street.

The iron doors were solid and would have been impossible to breach if they'd been locked. That was something to take note of. He gently pulled down on the lever he'd seen the guy move and the mechanism gave with a rusty yelp. He pulled the door open enough to slip in and closed it behind him.

Inside, there was only a little ambient light from the city filtering through the opaque glass panels above the bay doors. He flicked on his lighter and in its halo, he could make out a workbench and toolbox on the wall next to him. Examining it, he found a flashlight.

The round beam of light swung through the darkness like a lighthouse beacon and glinted off large tanks and barrels in the cavernous area to his right. It was the small brick hut he was interested in, though. He approached the round structure and lifted the beam—sure enough, that chimney sat right on top of it. It was a kiln.

He studied the series of portholes around the perimeter, each framed with an iron latch structure around a small window. And within each door was a smaller opening that could be manipulated open or closed. He reached the flashlight through one of those holes and peeked over his arm—the inside of the furnace was smooth brick. A series of small benches with troughs sat below each opening around the kiln. As he swung the light around to the right it began to bounce off something shiny. *Shit*, he remembered with a startle —the casket.

So did this thing work? He walked farther around the outside of the furnace and noticed gas lines emerging from the wall and entering some kind of control system around the back. Bright yellow rubber sheathing covered several levers attached to glimmering new valves. He tried one and heard a creeping *sssssss*. He closed the valve—gas was flowing.

He studied the pipe configuration further and discovered a metal-covered electrical box attached to the kiln at about chest height. He opened the latch and saw a glowing green digital display above a series of buttons.

Inside the box door was taped a dirty, dog-eared piece of paper. The top read, "FIRING INSTRUCTIONS." He scanned the text below it: "Heat furnace to preset levels by pressing start, then program number, then ignite. To fire furnace manually, follow the sequence of instructions below in order!!! Furnace must be ramped to at least 2,500 on the readout before introducing raw material. . ."

A trumpet blared a tinny solo and he jumped before he recognized it as his ring tone. He touched his phone and raised it to his ear. "What is it."

"Kid's not talking," Spinks said. "We're getting nowhere."

Carlos sighed. No vision.

He could feel rage unfurling in his chest. Here he is, cleaning up their tracks with this cadaver-stealing motherfucker, and they can't handle a punk-ass kid?

Then he looked at the dull green light emanating

from the control panel. He took a deep breath. "Okay, listen. I'm on the east side of Andover in the old industrial sector. Only one factory will have its lights on—the one with a big smokestack. Bring him here."

39

From his truck, the only sign of life Bryant could see in the brick rectory next to St. Patrick Church was a single light coming from an interior hallway. The front of the rectory was shrouded by a spacious porch and the light's warm glow reached through the shadowed stoop like a distant torch deep in a cave.

After turning off the engine, Bryant paused with his hand still on the ignition. It was really quiet out there—what did a priest do on a Saturday night? Would he be interrupting something? Would he be waking him up?

Bryant's mind frantically rummaged through images from the last hour when he opened Stella's casket. Like a drifting ship dragging an anchor, his memory snagged on the image of her skeletal remains.

The putrid smell that assaulted his nose when he lifted the lid still lingered in the back of his throat. Her skin had looked like a dirty bedsheet covering a wood pile; her hair was a grey tangled nest fallen out of a tree mid-winter. Mold and black decay circled the eyes and mouth; her nose was a shriveled prune.

He had pulled back in shock from the face—teeth were showing from the retreating, taut skin and the result was a tense, cruel grin. Turning back in disappointed grief, he caught a glimmer—the gold from her wedding band gleamed from her withered hand like a strand of tinsel snagged on the limb of a discarded, desiccated Christmas tree.

He'd covered his mouth and nose as a sob escaped his throat, chased by a wave of nausea. He'd turned to the side and vomited. The coffin lid slammed down and a thunderclap echoed through the furnace.

Right up to that moment, Bryant couldn't have admitted what he'd been hoping for, but whatever it was had disappeared fast as darkness filling a room after turning off a light switch. Despair curdled in his chest.

Reflecting on the experience as he sat in his truck in front of the rectory, he understood that the body inside that casket wasn't Estelline. He knew that. Still, he couldn't unmoor her identity from those remains. The body inside that casket was inanimate—it was just a thing now, its substance no different from everything else in this world scattered by time. Yet, those were *her* teeth. That was *her* hair. Those were *her* bones. He had loved *that* body.

Last summer, that night at the ballgame, when the fat guy sat next to him and they talked about Estelline, he'd handed Bryant a business card. Bryant held it now and looked at it: Father Howard Brown. Surely priests knew how to deal with crazy people, he assured himself. Because that's what he was now—a crazy person who had dug up his dead wife. On Monday, he'd be in jail and a local news team would be broadcasting his sad-sack story from the cemetery as workers filled in Estelline's grave.

He got out of the truck, closed the door quietly, and approached the cavernous porch. The night smelled like rain. Slowly, he climbed the concrete steps, following that dim light from beyond the front door, unable to see anything else in the inky dark. He lifted his hand to knock.

"Who you lookin' for?" A voice sounded from somewhere to his right in the cave-like porch. Bryant turned and peered. A black mound in the shadow shifted. Bryant thought he recognized the voice from the ballgame—it was firm, but languid and fleshy. "Father Brown?"

Part of the mound gestured toward what looked like an old couch disintegrating under a darkened window. "Have a seat."

"What're you doing out here?"

"I was telling myself it was prayer," he said, "but looks like I was waiting for you."

Bryant sat down and heard the clink of an ice cube in a glass. His eyes were adjusting, catching the ambient light from the spotlights on the church façade next door, and he could see Howard tilt his head back and finish his drink. "Quiet out here, isn't it?" he said after swallowing. An ice cube pocketed in his cheek turned each "t" into a "d."

"You said I'd see her again."

"You're the beer guy from the 'Beaus," Howard said, in no rush. "I remember you."

"I told you the worst part was that I'd never see her again and you said, 'You don't know that.' You said love was stronger than death."

Silence.

"Yeah, well, death is pretty fuckin' strong, ain't it." Howard said at last. Bryant heard him take in a deep breath and exhale—whiskey fumes wafted over him. "Didja think I was talking about a fairy tale? Because mothers don't bleed out in hospital beds in fairy tales."

The words tied the despair in Bryant's chest to a block of cement and sank it deeper into his belly. Why had he ever listened to this guy?

The sounds from a quieting city wafted into the porch. Someone down the street rolled a trash bin to the curb and the plastic wheels on cement sent out a grumbling rumble that bumped around the with thunder from an approaching front. Thumping bass spilled from a car a few blocks away.

"You gotta be pretty goddamned lucky to get a happy ending in this life," Howard said. "It's like I told you at the field: pages get ripped out of everyone's story."

Then Howard inhaled sharply and looked at Bryant: "Given. that. fact." — he spit those three words out and let them each sit for a full beat — "what're we supposed to do? Put'cher ass in the right spot to find some hope, and when it passes, grab hold and don't let go. There will be a way through to the ending."

"What *hope*?" The word came out of Bryant's mouth like a swig of sour milk.

"Well what other choice do we have." It was more a statement than a question, and Bryant detected heat in Howard's voice as it rose. Was this guy ever not sauced? "Give up? Fall into ourselves and despair? We have no right to be that selfish."

"Selfish?"

"Oh, as if there's no one else around you who's suffering," Howard said, wiping his chin. He puffed softly through his lips. "Shit."

The notion hit Bryant like a right cross and spun him sideways. He thought of Vivian. She'd been walking next to him through all of this—through Estelline's death, through his own, what, accident? Something beneath his sternum cracked to think of what she'd been through in the past year. Had he even once tried to buoy *her*?

And what about Rafa? The kid still wasn't speaking. Bryant had simply come to accept that as a fact about him, but the recognition dawned on him that this was a continued, on-going protest because he was so deeply wounded. Beneath the kid's ingenuity and spunk, he was still bleeding.

"Yeah everything falls apart," Howard continued. "It scatters, okay, I see that. I get it." He seemed to have come aware of the volume he was speaking at, or the impact his words had, and softened. "But we're made different. We're made to hold things together, even if it's just for a little while.

"So you can't control it falling apart, but you can hold on to the people you're with. There will be a way through."

"There's nothing left to hold on to," Bryant said. The crack in his voice sounded more like a plea than grief.

"She's not the only one needs holding," Howard said. "You know that.

"Besides, she's there in your memory. You remember her love—how she pulled you out of yourself, made you want to be better. That's not gone—she can still carry you forward to others. Set your sails to that memory, man. You're not leaving her behind if she's pushing you ahead."

"Even my memory of her is dying. It's turning to ash," Bryant acknowledged. Images from the casket were now permanently carved in the folds of his brain.

"Then lower your fuckin' sails and row. There—will—be—a—way."

***

Howard offered Bryant a glass of Jameson, and he accepted. They sat in silence on the dark porch for a good twenty minutes. The rain Bryant smelled when he stepped to the stoop began to shower softly, the sizzling murmur drowning out any other noise from the night. Moist, cool currents of air pressed through the porch and into their faces, scented like fresh fog. Droplets gathered at the edge of the gutter lining the porch, shimmering with the reflection of the spotlights from the church; they shattered into glimmering shards when they fell and splattered on the railing. When he breathed through his mouth, Bryant felt mist wash over his tongue and rinse the spice left there from the whiskey.

The rain, the quiet, the company, the whiskey—it was all a relief. It occurred to Bryant that for once he wasn't alone. He wasn't the subject of questions or the object of pity—he was just sitting on a dry porch observing the wet, falling world around him. His mind let loose and contemplated more deeply the contours of Vivian's and Rafa's experience in the past year.

The rain spent itself and a chorus of drips receded into the ever-present hum of the city. After finishing his glass, Bryant was starting to feel tired. He was ready to rest. He moved to get up and make his departure when his phone buzzed in his pocket. When he pulled it out, the display glared in the cavernously dark porch.

Brother Martin Taber was calling.

"Excuse me, Father, I should go," he said. "Thanks for the whiskey."

"Any time—stop by any time," Howard replied without moving. "Hang in there."

Bryant answered the phone as he walked down the stairs and back toward his truck. "Hey, brother."

"Bryant, have you seen Rafa?"

"No. Why?"

"He's gone missing. His mom just called me and she's worried—he left the house earlier this evening and isn't where he's supposed to be. His bike is gone."

Bryant's heart doubled its output—he felt his face flush and his fingers tingle with energy.

"Shit. I mean. . ." He started to apologize for the obscenity, but Martin cut him off: "I'm worried he's decided to do something drastic. Do you have any ideas?"

"I don't, but I can check my house to see if he's there for some reason."

"Give me a call either way, will you?"

***

Bryant pulled into his driveway, but the house was dark. He searched it anyway, calling Rafa's name loudly. He even double checked the yard and garage—nothing. He picked up his phone to call Brother Martin but suddenly paused. Rafa wouldn't be at the factory, would he? He'd just been there and hadn't seen him. . .

The factory was only a four-minute drive away, though, and it wasn't inconceivable that Rafa would have run there to hide in a corner if he was in trouble. If this was as serious as he worried it could be, it was worth being thorough. He wanted to be able to give Martin a definitive reply.

***

Bishop Newell's phone rang. The number was Martin Taber's.

"Martin, it's late—everything okay?"

Martin's voice was urgent, but controlled. "There's a family from Wilmot who's in trouble. Remember Raymundo Villahermosa? His son is missing."

"So you think it's time," Newell felt a charge of adrenaline brighten his brain with clarity.

"I think we're ready. Even if he turns up, might be good to run the house through the exercise."

"Okay, then," Newell said. "Keep looking and let me know where we should be. I'll get 'em ready and meet you there."

40

Bryant steered his truck anxiously though familiar streets and when he was still several blocks from the warehouse he could see a dim light coming through the opaque windows above the bay doors. Did he leave a light on above his work station? Or maybe Rafa had snuck in and was working on something?

As he neared the turn on Webster road—the drive leading to the bay doors was only a dozen yards in from that corner—another set of headlights spilled on to the road ahead. A sedan-sized car had pulled up to the intersection two blocks up and stopped. Bryant couldn't see much about the car besides its size in the dark, but it seemed to be waiting.

It struck Bryant as an odd coincidence that anyone else would be out in this part of town this late on a wet Saturday night. Any number of weekend nights found him out here working late and when he left for home, he'd rarely ever see another soul within a half a mile.

Something wasn't right. He slowed, and went beyond the turn to the warehouse. As soon as he crossed Webster, the car made its turn toward him. The two vehicles passed and Bryant peered into the sedan, but its windows were shaded and dark.

Bryant made a left on the road the car had turned from, but as soon as he was half a block in, he turned off his headlights and pulled into a deeply-rutted alley and parked. He got out and, after making sure the street was empty, quickly walked across the road to circle around the back side of his warehouse. The light inside brightened—someone had turned on the rest of the overhead lights in the front half of the space around the furnace. What the hell was going on?

As he picked his way through the wet weeds on the back side of the factory, he heard the iron bay doors on the front side of the building squeal open and close.

He startled with dread: maybe public health officials had learned of the casket and they were here to recover Estelline's body. That didn't seem exactly right either, though—it was a Saturday night, late. He figured they'd catch up to him sometime in the next week, but he couldn't imagine government bureaucrats responding with a SWAT team's urgency.

He reached the far edge of the factory and rounded the corner, passing the window he had taken Estelline through when he first showed her the building. He'd long since replaced the rotting plywood on the window, though putting in a real window there would have to wait until he got some breathing room in his budget.

He pulled out his keys, careful to make sure they didn't jangle, and eased one into the deadbolt in the back door. He retracted the bolt with a small knock, then switched keys to unlock the knob. It clicked free and he slowly pushed the door—as it opened, it sounded like 400 pages of a thick book tumbling past a reader's thumb.

Even though he rarely used this door, the space and dimensions of that back office were carved into his memory. He couldn't see through the pitch black inside, but he avoided kicking the round, orange cooler he'd left by the filing cabinet and stepped wide around the corner of the desk. The door from the office to the factory floor was closed but unlocked, and he reached for it, then hesitated.

He could hear voices now—at least two males. Their words echoed through the rafters of the warehouse. He guessed they were speaking Spanish. The tone was urgent but deliberative, like they were trying to figure out a puzzle against a timer.

He decided he could open the door into the main area of the warehouse and easily slide behind the pallets on the right that held layered sacks of malted barley. In the dark, and on this far end of the warehouse, they'd have to have the hearing of a guard dog to perceive anything. He hoped.

He began to twist the knob when he heard a sharp clack and then a jumping roar, as though a bear was bawling on the other side of the door. Orange light pulsated through the frosted glass window above his desk. The furnace! Shit—they'd lit the furnace!

Bryant immediately thought of Stella's body in the casket. He immediately pushed the door open and slid into the dark shadow by the pallets. A fiery glow winked off the steel tanks between him and the furnace. The voices sounded panicked now, and he could understand some phrases.

"Stop! Shit, turn it off!" one called. "It's fuckin' hot!"

Bryant edged around a steel tank to get a view of the scene. Against the glare of the fire, he saw two adult silhouettes—young and trim—backing away from the igneous portholes. There was a third voice coming from someone he couldn't see.

The rumbling furnace fell silent and the orange slowly died. No one talked—they seemed awestruck by the power they'd unleashed. All told, it must have fired for only ten seconds—fifteen at the most—which shouldn't have compromised the casket.

As his eyes adjusted to the re-emerging shop lights above the furnace, he discerned details in the figures before him. In a flash, it dawned on him—the voice, the body shape. Spinks. And next to him was that guy with the snake tattoo. They'd found him, somehow.

His stomach twisted like a stepped-on earthworm.

Then the third voice again, with an almost casual calm: "So, now you can see—you'll either tell us where it is, or you'll burn."

There was a panicked shuffling sound of struggle. "Shit, he's fiesty," Snake said. Then he stepped to the side and Bryant could see past him—it was the curly-haired supervisor who kept turning him down at the *tienda*, Siego. And he was holding Rafa!

Spinks and Snake had their backs to him and kept shifting positions, but for a moment he could see through them to Rafa's face—it was wrenched in terror.

"The little fucker hasn't said a goddamn word," Spinks said with disgust.

"See? He knows," Snake said. "But he won't give it up."

He had no idea how or why these men were in his warehouse, but they were more interested in Rafa than him or the casket at the moment. Rafa must have done something rash and drawn attention to himself—they caught him, and now they were ready to burn him.

They didn't know he wouldn't talk—hell, he might not even be *able* to for as long as he'd been silent.

Bryant knew he had to call for help. Speaking into the phone was impossible, though—they'd hear him. Could you text 9-1-1?

He pulled out his phone and entered 9, 1, and 1 into a message, then wrote:

Break/enter at 1842 Webster Road
Danger!!!
Send help ASAP!!!

When he hit send, the phone processed then immediately buzzed and emitted the sound of a bottle of beer opening—*psht!*—his notification for incoming messages. He clamped a hand over the device and looked up to see if anyone had heard him, but it didn't look that way. The incoming message read:

911 Error Invalid Number.
Please re-send using a valid 10-digit mobile number or valid short code.

He decided to text Martin—maybe he could coordinate law enforcement to respond:

Rafa at my factory
1842 Webster
911 DANGER
HELP!!!

The message appeared to go through; there was no bounce-back. Would Martin see it?

"Alright, enough of this," Siego said. "Put him in."

Bryant looked up from his phone. He could see Rafa trying to scream, but the only thing coming from his throat was forced air in choking sobs. He was thrashing with all he had, but Siego's grip easily controlled him.

Bryant looked at his phone. *Pick up! Reply!*

He had to do something or else he'd watch Rafa die right here, right now. But what could he do? He'd tried fighting two of those guys once before when his own life was on the line. That obviously didn't work—and now there were three of them.

Anywhere his mind scrambled, he could only see the situation creating two victims instead of just one.

Maybe he could buy some time—maybe state troopers were flying here with sirens on right now. Maybe Martin was calling the police. Maybe help was on the way.

Maybe.

Maybe not.

He didn't even have a weapon.

He looked around, as though he might have left a shotgun laying around. He peered back at the men—they were opening a porthole.

And there was Rafa, struggling alone.

Bryant stepped around the steel tank into the light.

"He gave it to me," Bryant said. Whatever it was, he didn't know, but he could tell that they were after something he'd taken. "Let him go."

"The fuck he come from?!" Snake shouted. He scrambled to pull out a gun from his waist line and raised it with a tense grip. He approached on Bryant's left with sudden jerks as he looked around, not knowing if others were lurking. Spinks locked in on Bryant with deadly intent—he didn't have a gun, but began stalking toward Bryant's right side at a patient, coiled pace. The supervisor, still holding Rafa, began backing away.

Seeing all their attention turn to him made Bryant's guts spill to the floor. His face drained. What had he gotten in to?

"I have. . ." he repeated, haltingly. What did he have? It didn't matter. "I have it," he said with determined force.

"I don't like this, Siego," Snake said. "Who *da fuck* is this?"

"Shit, we already killed this one—remember?" Spinks said dully. "We put him on the bottom of the lake."

"You don't have the ledger," said Siego, holding Rafa. "You haven't even seen this kid in the last two days. No, you've been busy with something else, haven't you?"

Bryant felt his plan falling apart like a sand castle in the tide. Spinks and Snake continued to approach on either side—they were now within twenty yards, at 10:00 and 2:00. Spinks bent over and picked up a long metal stirring rod.

"Okay, look," Bryant said, glancing at both men, but speaking to Siego. "Just let the kid go. It's me you want, anyway—I'm the one talking to the police. I'm the one who can identify you. What—they're gonna listen to a kid? Who's scared shitless?

"But they've been listening to me." He evened his tone to try to bluff his way to some power in the exchange. "And I won't bring charges if you let him go."

"Fuck you," Siego said sharply. "You won't bring charges because you'll be *dead*. Shoot him!"

Bryant broke right toward Spinks as hard as he could. The sound of a shot exploded in the cavernous space, causing Bryant's thighs to convulse involuntarily. He felt a splash of fluid. Blood? No—it was splashing on him more like water. It was beer—Snake's shot hit the tank next to him and a stream of beer was pouring out.

Spinks began to swing the rod around at him, and he ducked—it slammed into the second steel tank next to the furnace with a clang. Bryant cut to his right between the two tanks and circled back toward the office and the corner with the barley sacks, his heart a skittering rabbit bounding around his rib cage.

Beneath the sound of beer pattering on the cement floor, he could hear Snake and Spinks following with the same cautious steps. He reached the corner and couldn't escape any farther. *I'm going to die here,* he thought.

He desperately felt the grain sack—could he throw it at them? What could he use that would be dangerous?!

In a flash, he remembered the training for his safety permit for his brewing license. He pulled out his Leatherman tool and frantically levered out the largest blade and began gashing the sacks. Barley poured out with a growing hiss, the smell of toasty grain billowing out with the growing cloud of chaff and dust. He moved around to the front of the pallet and slashed those sacks, too, then moved on to the front of the second pallet next to the office door.

Snake came into view and watched him for a moment over the gun, a curious look on his face. "The fuck you trying to do, homie, smoke us out?" he called.

Bryant looked to his right and saw Spinks closing in against the wall. Barley was sluicing out and the dusty cloud continued to rise and spread. Bryant slunk down into a crouch and covered his head. He wanted Snake to fire soon or else the cloud would disperse too much—he just hoped he'd miss.

The mountain of grain spilling on the ground was nearing Snake's feet and he began to cough from the dust. "Fuck this," he said. Through the cloud from his crouch, Bryant could see his finger tighten on the trigger.

41

The crisp crack of gunshot: *bang*!

In the same moment, one-two, the heavy concussion of instant combustion: *Ka-FOOM*!

Gunshot flare ignited the grain dust, which instantly erupted. A yellow conflagration mushroomed into the warehouse. The force of the blowout blasted Bryant farther into the corner, shoving him from a crouch to his butt. He felt the heat ripple off his arms over his head. The force of the explosion compressed his chest and sucked air from his lungs.

Even with his eyes squeezed shut, light inundated Bryant's eyes, followed by total darkness. The flash shattered the thick windows above the doors of the factory on all sides and night flooded the space before the tinkling glass from the hanging spotlights hit the cement floor. For a moment, Bryant sat still, taking stock and working oxygen back between his ribs.

He didn't think he was injured—most of the force of the blast pushed outward into the open space of the factory, so somehow the corner constrained the impact on his body. His clothes were hot, though—flames opened wide holes in his shirt over his shoulder and sides. He still couldn't see but could sense that his eyes weren't injured—they simply had nothing to grasp in the darkness.

He heard the bodies of Spinks and Snake on both

sides of him—one moaning, one rolling over. The only sound was patter of beer still falling from the bullet hole in the storage tank into a wide puddle. Bryant thought he could stand, and remembered this was his chance to act. He scrambled to his feet and into a tottering run. Though he couldn't see anything in the pitchy dark, much less Rafa or Siego, he stumbled in the direction of the furnace.

Suddenly, the glare of a flashlight beam shone on him unsteadily—he stopped. In the silence, he heard the mechanical click of the hammer of a gun.

It was difficult to see through the flashlight beam, but when it dipped below his eyes, he could tell Siego was still holding Rafa—one hand was clamped over Rafa's neck and chest, grasping the flashlight pointed at Bryant. Each time Rafa jerked his body in protest the light wavered in a different direction. The other hand, though, was steady and firm—Siego pressed the muzzle of a black, square gun into Rafa's head just above his right ear. The pressure tilted Rafa's head to the side uncomfortably.

"Okay, okay," Bryant said. He took a step backward.

He heard coughing behind him, and the shuffling movements of Spinks and Snake coming to their senses.

"Get up," Siego called to them. "Get the fuck up!"

Bryant heard their staggering footsteps as they approached him from behind, followed by the rotten-egg stench of burned hair.

"The problem with you idiots is that all you can think of is physical strength," Siego continued, spitting with contempt. "Coercion—know that that means, shitheads? Coercion is stronger than a body—

even yours, Spinks. But it takes brains because you gotta know what someone wants. And then you twist it to your purpose.

"That's how you get someone to pick tomatoes in the blazing heat for pennies. That's how you get all the field pussy your dick can handle. That's how you get a man to crawl into a furnace."

One of them wrenched Bryant's hands behind his back and kicked the backs of his legs. His knees smashed into the floor.

"So, listen, man. You're going to climb into this, this . . . motherfucking disappearing machine—or I'm putting a hole in his head!"

A blow to the back of his neck sent Bryant crashing to the floor. One of them drove a knee into the middle of his spine, forcing the air out of his lungs. With his face to the floor, he heard the other one working the glory hole mechanism. It squelched open, and then his body was being dragged and hoisted.

Bryant wanted to call out to Rafa, to give him courage, to say something to rebut this indignity, but he couldn't breathe. He saw Siego bend his head to Rafa's ear—he was speaking to Rafa, but used it as a farewell taunt to Bryant as well.

"Now watch, kid. We're gonna roast your friend here," he said in a teacherly voice. "No, no—don't fight it. There's nothing you can do about it, and it's not your fault, okay? He made his own choice.

"But after—and this will only take a moment because it gets *really* fuckin' hot *really* fuckin' fast, you'll see—after, you'll get a choice. You can tell us where you put the ledger, or you can follow him in there. It's up to you, okay?"

Then Bryant's body was shoved through the hole and he tumbled into the furnace like laundry down a chute, his shoulder smashing into the floor and rest of his body crumpling into a limp heap. The iron window he'd just passed through slammed shut and sounded like a prison door as its clasps clamped closed. He knew they had figured out how to ignite and fire this furnace —in a moment, flaming gas would pour down from the vents in the ceiling and his body would melt in pain.

At that moment, a sadness swept over him—not because of his impending demise, but because he'd failed to help Rafa find any justice. It felt like he'd done just the opposite, in fact. He knelt and reached out to the casket in the dark—he could still feel traces of warmth on its sides from the test ignition.

Soon, Stella, he thought. *Soon.*

Father Howard's words came to his mind: "There will be a way." Bryant knew there was no longer a way for him, but maybe he could make a way for Rafa. If he could hold off his own death for a couple of moments, maybe they'd have to wait to throw in Rafa. Maybe help was coming. Maybe a few seconds would mean the difference. Maybe.

He reached up to the casket and grasped the pall-bearer bars and pulled himself up.

A hissing noise accelerated from a whisper to a rush as gas spewed into the furnace from the ceiling.

He pressed his fingers into the seam along the edge of the casket and lifted the lid. The complaint of decay still reached for his nose, but the sulfurous smell of gas bulldozed right over it. He lifted his legs and hips into the casket and rolled in next to Estelline's body. He could feel her bones next to him and beneath him, and they easily gave way as he wiggled himself lower into the lining next to her. It felt like sharing a kid's bed with a skeleton.

He heard the clicking of the ignitor and reached up to grab what he could of the satin liner of the open lid of the casket. He began to pull down when the gas caught flame—the roar slammed the lid closed. It remained dark inside the casket, but sounded like he was trapped in a cardboard box beneath a waterfall.

How long could he last in here? He knew glass melted at about the same temperature as steel—about 2,500 degrees—which is what comprised the hull of the casket. Already he could feel the sides starting to heat up.

Now already they were burning hot. A red-orange glow began to radiate around him. The rosy light revealed tendrils of smoke beginning to fill the box. He could hear sizzling.

Oh God, he thought in panic. *I'm going to roast in here!*

***

The casket continued to shake, the furnace blasting it like a jet engine. Bryant could feel his pores open up, searching for cool air. It was getting difficult to breathe—the smoke inside was turning black now and obscuring even the radiant glow of the superheated steel.

He put his head down on the pillow next to Stella's head and closed his eyes, waiting for it to be over. He just hoped he passed out from heat or lack of oxygen before his skin started to blister and melt.

Even though the horror was sending stars through his mind, he was ready for this. He didn't seek it or want it, but he was ready for it.

He was in a boat without oars, drifting ever more quickly toward a precipice. It was too late to do anything else now but hold on tight and die.

He reached out and placed his left hand on the folded bones of her hands, and their wedding bands made a clinking noise when they met.

Then, a sound from outside the casket: three clear knocks.

He opened his eyes, but they began to burn.

A thought jumped to mind: *Did they throw in Rafa already? Was he burning alive?*

Bryant knew that as soon as he opened the lid, it would be all over—the heat would overpower him and when the supercharged air met the fuel inside the casket, it would explode in an instant blaze.

It came again—three distinct knocks, purposeful and patient, and unmistakably coming from outside the casket. And then a voice—calling above the noise of the flaming vents. It was a woman's voice, hailing his name. It sounded muffled from inside the casket, but he could hear his name clearly.

Was he dead?

He pressed his hand up against the lid. The satin liner was scorching brown and black, and where he pressed it against the casket's hull, it flared into flame. He felt no burn, though. *I must be in shock,* he thought.

The lid cracked open and bright, golden light overran his eyes. Hot tendrils of fire inundated the cramped space inside and he saw his clothes ignite.

I'm beyond pain, he thought. *This is what happens when your skin burns off. You can't feel your nerves.*

He widened the lid further open, and the whole of the casket around him turned into a nest of licking flame.

He looked up to see a young woman peering in, reaching a hand to him through the fire. She was silhouetted against the orange and amber flames emanating from the ceiling vents, but the flickering light illuminated her face from alternating angles. She was beautiful, with long hair parted in the middle and tressed back by two braids on each side of her head. Strands of her hair strayed leisurely in the turbulence —Bryant wondered why she was not burning up. She smiled softly at him—it was as though she was waking him from a nap.

Only they were in a furnace quickly approaching 2,000 degrees. The roaring fire hadn't ceased. He knew he should be dead—his body should be a blistering, charred corpse next to Stella's bones.

Maybe I am *dead,* he thought.

He looked at her outstretched arm and followed it back to her face. Her features danced—at one moment she seemed a young girl; at another, a mature woman. Her body was naked, but unharmed. Shadows caressed the front of her figure as light licked around the curves of her shoulders and waist. She calmly reached for his hand and grabbed it.

If he was dead, he still had a body—her touch was firm and strong.

She looked at him and said, "*Keek-ta-yo*."

42

Rafa watched in horror as the two brutes tossed Bryant in the furnace as though they were tossing a trash bag into a garbage truck. Then the big one slammed shut the mechanism over the window and he was gone.

He wanted to shout to Bryant, to call him back. He tried to scream again, but his throat was a trumpet with no mouthpiece—he could only force out a hoarse bellow. The sting in his raw vocal chords reached into his chest.

Then they turned on the gas and he could smell the noxious fumes in the moment before they ignited. Rays of golden yellow exploded out small seams and cracks from all around the furnace and radiated flickering shafts of light like a jack-o'-lantern in the pitchy midnight all around them. The man holding him stepped back from the heat.

Rafa knew there was no one now. He was alone in this darkness. The sole light by which he could see was from the flame of suffering, and it only illuminated sorrow. He couldn't see a way through the glowing death that stood before him—nothing to do now but go through it bravely.

Maybe Papa felt the same way at the end, he thought. And if that were the case, then he wasn't alone after all. He seized the idea like a crutch and straightened a little.

Poor Mama, he thought. His brothers and sisters would get by, but he worried about Mama.

Rafa refused the fear banging on his consciousness—he simply turned it away. Then he heard something calm and cool beneath the roaring flame—something incongruously human in that hell.

It sounded like a conversation.

Had a radio flipped on somewhere?

Maybe, this close to death, people heard things, he thought. Maybe Papa was calling to him.

But that's Bryant, he thought. *I can hear him. Who is he talking to?*

***

Bryant sat up. In disbelief, he watched his clothes disintegrate as flames flickered around him. His skin remained unharmed—he felt no pain. In fact, the flaming chamber felt no hotter than his truck cab after it sat in the afternoon sun. The air he breathed felt like cigarette smoke passing into and out of his throat and lungs.

He grabbed the hand of the luminous figure before him and climbed out of the casket. The leather of his work boots peeled away from his feet in charred strips and the rubber soles turned into a boiling puddle. The vent above him blasted hot air at him, but it felt like standing below a blow-dryer. He stepped forward and soon every thread of clothing had burned away.

"What is this?" he asked. "Am I dead?"

"You think of death as one, last thing—a pit we tumble into. But it's not a leap. It's friendly as a bee," she said. "If it will put your mind at ease, you're not asleep."

Her glowing fawn-hued skin reflected as much light as it absorbed. She was taking him in with loving, piteous eyes—eyes that looked just like Estelline's when she saw he had spilled something on his shirt: warm blue-green, round, and intelligent.

"Are you an angel?"

She shook her head no and spoke slowly: "Now time's long-turning wheel is spent and slows. It finally starts to roll on back, and we are made anew—angelic—only more. It's good news I bring: the end of ending."

He remembered the anxiety when Stella started bleeding. They were so worried about the baby. Then she was rushed away. Then she was gone. Her absence created such a hole that he didn't have the capacity to explore the smaller hole within it of losing a child he'd never met.

"Tally?"

The name came out of his mouth without the approval of a thought process—it was an intuited question that dropped like a stone from his head into his heart, the splash sending ripples of wonder through everything he knew.

He didn't understand how, but he recognized her. He'd never even seen her, but he knew her. He knew her the way he knew he'd hit the ball squarely in the baseball game last week—that satisfying, rich feeling of *rightness*.

"Tally? Can it be . . . can it be *you*?"

It seemed other-worldly, but here she was: his own daughter—glorious. Stella's features came clear in her face: the penetrating eyes, the ski slope of the nose. And he also saw his *unjee's* cheeks, wide as a prairie, as well as her strong, angled arms.

"How . . . how are you here?"

An encyclopedic smile. "They called me up. I'm in the vanguard—I am up to hit with runners left on base. The ball's in play—it's time to run, so fly! Then wave her home—she'll heal in your embrace."

She pointed toward the casket behind him and he turned. The steel shell was slumping away and beginning to form a bright orange magmatic pool in the cradle over which it had been propped. Stella's white gown had long burned off, as had the soft stuffing and lining below her body. As the coffin melted, her skin and bones softly rested, floating, on the volcanic puddle in the stone manger. The heat burst into flames around her head, but didn't burn her hair—in fact, it cleaned it and bestowed a full luster.

When a chunk of casket near her feet broke off and fell into the puddle, the wave caused her head to tilt up as though she were trying to look at something behind her. She could have been napping on a pool float. The black and grey mold on her skin burned away, changing its consistency from mottled autumn leaves to pale spring buds.

He understood now the changes to his body—the strength, the perception. He was blooming, growing toward abundance—not changing into something different, but becoming somehow *more* himself, fuller and ample. And the same force changing his body was what had transformed Tally—he was just a few steps behind. She was watching him as he watched Estelline, and said, "You've longed for hope like this. It's here. It's true. The buried seed awakes; all things are new."

He looked back at Tally and opened his mouth

to . . . he didn't know what. He wanted to say something to make it feel real. She was stepping away.

"It's here," she said. "It's true."

And then she disappeared.

***

Carlos saw the confusion in Spinks and Victor before he heard it. He cocked his head—was that the sound of voices coming from inside the furnace?

He thrust his head at Spinks to open the window into the furnace and watched as he picked up a dirty rag on the workbench and maneuvered the iron latch. The mechanism swung open and a jet blast of dry heat belched into the darkness: a tethered, angry lion. All four of them raised their hands to hide their faces.

Carlos squinted his eyes to see if anything remained of Bryant, but it was like looking into the sun.

Still—those voices!

He passed the boy to Victor, who grabbed him with his tattooed arm, then looked around for some way to shield the light and heat. A welding mask lay on the workbench by the door—Carlos grabbed it and held it over his face and approached the volcanic aperture.

The visor blocked out everything but the small sun of fire in the furnace. He angled around to peer inside, then stopped suddenly. It didn't make sense—two figures stood inside, visible as soft silhouettes against the muted light. A man and a woman—was that the guy? And who the fuck was the woman?

She appeared tall—fit and capable as an elite athlete. There was something terrifying in the way they were unfazed by the heat. He saw in her body coiled power harnessed to patience: she was standing with the guy the way he saw mothers stand with sons outside the mobile clinic in Wilmot.

He didn't want them—especially her—to look at him, but he couldn't turn away. It was beautiful in a perverse way—it was like watching an animal give birth. He hated that kind of self-possession—the kind that is beyond intimidation, that won't cower because it's rapt with something invisible.

A deep terror began dripping, then trickling down the back of his spine. The ground was shifting below his feet—what could he trust? The fabric of the universe he knew and could manipulate was tearing in half.

Fuck this, Carlos thought. *I won't be bullied!*

He reached out and slammed the door shut, scalding his palm. He turned to Victor and pulled out his gun, raising it to the kid's head. Victor released the kid and stepped aside. The boy stood there looking at him with confidence, the little shit. Like he was daring him to do it.

Suddenly, the sound of a diesel engine rumbled outside—Victor and Spinks looked up. *BEEP BEEP BEEP* —it sounded like a garbage truck backing up, and then came the pealing squeak of bus doors opening. They all stood very still, trying to discern the source of the sound, looking at the bay doors.

The furnace shouted like a jet engine, and the pool of beer beneath the ruptured storage tank was tinkling down a drain in the middle of the floor. Then: three loud bangs rattled the door to its hinges, as though a giant fist was hammering the iron—as though God himself were knocking on the doors of hell.

43

Carlos rushed to the factory bay doors to throw the locking latch over the lever. Just as it slid into place the handle jerked up and caught.

His mind began to race, thinking of other exits to this building. That cripple got into the building from somewhere in the back. Then he heard a voice on the outside of the door: "One, two . . . THREE!"

The doors give a tremendous screech and begin to warp. The edge of a crowbar and tire iron appeared along the seam between the two swinging doors. The iron straps comprising the locks and levers on the door buckled, then snapped off—a nut whizzed by his head, sounding like a fastball.

Carlos' knees felt loose and he stepped away in fear, seeking more darkness. He backed into the front corner of the building, near the furnace controls, but quickly ran out of space. Victor and Spinks moved away in the other direction, toward the back of the building, where the explosion happened earlier.

A thin, frail man, well into his sixties, stepped into the light. It was the brother with the mustache from the tutoring center—Carlos remembered people calling him Martin.

What the hell is going on here?

"Fulgence, Ed—careful there," Martin said, nodding toward Spinks and Victor. Two other old men had followed him in. One walked with a slight hunch and wore brown polyester pants, the sharp crease down the legs resting on black Velcro shoes. The other was paunchy, wearing a frumpy old navy nylon jacket and dusty Notre Dame cap. The three of them looked like a huddle of retired farmers who met at McDonald's for coffee every morning at six.

Rafa wrestled free from the startled Victor and ran to the brother from the tutoring center, who embraced him. The fat one casually called outside, "They're in here." Other men began warily walking in —maybe a dozen. They could have been a busload of grandpas from a retirement home casino trip.

The man holding Rafa passed the boy to someone else and stepped quickly to Carlos—he'd forgotten he was holding a gun. The man reached down and twisted it from his burned palm. Carlos jumped, startled. Then he clamped a heavy hand over Carlos' shoulder and turned him toward the furnace control panel. "Hows-about we shut this thing down."

Carlos gave the man his unquestioning obedience, swung open the cover, and immediately pressed the wide red emergency shutoff button. The rushing sound from inside the furnace began winding down and the orange glow dimmed.

Then the brother swung Carlos around and marched him to the other side of the furnace. "You'll want to see this. It'll give you a good idea of how things are gonna go from here on out," he said.

***

The potbellied man with the Notre Dame hat

walked slowly toward Victor, hand outstretched. "Hand it over, son," he said. "My name is Brother Ed and you have nothing to be afraid of."

Victor trembled, his gun raised. "Leave me alone, you old bastard!" Carlos recognized the edge in his voice and knew he was about to pull the trigger. He slowly leaned away so to be out of the line of fire, but the brother's hand held painfully tight on his shoulder.

There was a loud clang as the gun blasted, but the old man was no longer where Victor was aiming. In a flash, he'd ducked and charged Victor, leaping into a textbook figure-4 slide. He slammed into Victor's shins before he could even lower the weapon and fire again. Victor tumbled over the top of the man, who dug his lead heel into the floor and popped up behind him.

Standing over Victor now, he immediately reached down and grabbed the gun from Victor's hand. He jerked the slide across the top until it came off and tossed the two pieces away.

Victor looked at him like he was facing a monster. Then the man seized Victor's ear and began to drag him toward Carlos, chuckling to himself. Victor was breathing hard, giving off staccato shouts of pain.

Meanwhile, Fulgence—the thin, partly-bent man with the polyester pants and Velcro shoes—was circling Spinks, his hands up as though he intended to box him. Spinks looked at him with a look that communicated both amusement and contempt.

"Easy does it there, young man," Fulgence said, like he was taming a wild mustang. "Easy—we're not here to hurt you, just to make things right."

Spinks could have sneezed and knocked this guy over. Carlos anticipated a small measure of satisfaction knowing that whatever happens—arrests or public shaming or joblessness—at least one of these do-gooders was going to pay.

Spinks gave a yell of rage and swung with all his might—a right-handed roundhouse that would have stoved in the storage tank that was still leaking beer behind him. But Fulgence ducked six inches to the side, fluid and quick as kangaroo, and his arm caught nothing but air. Spinks half stumbled to regain his balance.

Carlos felt a glimmer of doubt flash across his mind. Maybe there was more to these old men than he could see.

"You're lookin' at the flyweight champ from '62, so if you wanna dance, you'd better put'cher hands up," Fulgence said. Besides the instantaneous shift of weight and quick duck, he hadn't moved. The situation seemed to bear the same odds, but Carlos noted Spinks gathering himself into a balanced posture, turning slightly to decrease his target area.

Spinks bobbed lightly on his feet and loosened his shoulders. He stepped to his right and Fulgence pivoted to stay square. Then Spinks struck—extending a vicious left jab in a straight line toward Fulgence's cheekbone.

Fulgence stepped forward into the punch and slightly to the right. Spinks' arm reached past his left cheek, touching nothing. Then Spinks twisted and turned all of his weight into a crushing right hand blow aimed right at Fulgence's ear.

Fulgence ducked slightly with ease and a patient agility. Again Spinks' elbow snapped as his arm distended violently but met nothing.

Before he could retract his arm, Spinks' realized

he was overextended and well out of position. A flash of fear and embarrassment registered in his eyes right before Fulgence's clenched right hand buried into his nose.

Carlos heard the smack of the fist meeting face, and below that the snap of Spinks' nose breaking. Spinks' head sprung back and as his legs gave way, blood began to drain over his lips. Carlos' mouth dropped in time with Spinks' body.

Fulgence grabbed Spinks by the ankle and dragged him to the light and the furnace like he was pulling an ice chest across a beach.

"Well, glad we cleared that up," Martin said. "You can see that things are changing, and—"

He stopped talking. The rest of the old men who had entered with him were turning toward the boy and forming a circle around him. Carlos heard the kid cough and saw him bury his chin into his chest as he pawed at his shoulder, pitching backward into the man behind him. Blood was darkening his shirt.

Victor's bullet had struck the boy.

Something that felt like laughter sparked in Carlos' chest. He knew suffering came to those who do good—it was a fundamental law of nature. He'd built a life around ensuring he was always on one side of that equation, and people who suffered were on the other. Then came those people in the furnace and for a moment, he wondered if maybe he'd balanced the equation incorrectly. But sure enough, there it was. Constant and implacable as death itself.

See, he thought with a smile darkening his face. *Everything always sums to zero.*

***

Rafa had trouble controlling his breathing. Everything turned upside down so quickly. Transfixed, he watched the brothers move in, and then the bullet struck his chest, right in the spot he covered with his hand during the pledge of allegiance in the mornings at school. It jerked his body like Miggy slugging him when they fought.

The fear he felt now was different than when those a-holes knocked him off his bike in the ditch, or even when he thought they would throw him in the furnace only a few minutes ago. It was dread. The thought of dying here and now, just when things had broken open, when a way had cleared—the panicked mortification was an icy claw gripping his heart, trying to strangle it.

Hands around him gently laid him on the cold concrete floor. He tried to reach the hole to somehow pull the bullet out, to wipe the wound away, but someone was holding his hand. His dampening shirt stuck to his belly. Now that he was on the floor, he could feel blood dripping down his ribcage and running along his back and waist.

Then Martin was kneeling over him. He held Rafa's face in his hand and drew it upward—all Rafa could see now was Martin's eyes.

"Don't fear, Rafa," he said. "This won't end in death. Breathe—concentrate on breathing."

When Rafa thought about the air going into and out of his lungs, he slowed down. Clarity began to return.

"Good," Martin said. "Just breathe. Does it hurt?"

For all the terror trampling through him, he didn't actually feel pain. There was a warm feeling in his chest where the wound was, but . . . it didn't hurt.

He shook his head no.

"See—nothing to fear," Martin said. "All we have to do is get that bullet out. This will feel strange."

And before Rafa could register complaint, Martin extended his finger and plunged it into Rafa's chest. *Oh God!* Rafa thought, squinting his eyes to anticipate the pain—*Oh my God, that's gonna . . . hurt?*

His eyes opened—it was uncomfortable, but it didn't hurt. In fact...

He huffed air in an amazed chuckle.

It . . . *tickled.* Somehow.

He began to laugh and tug away from Martin—good God, it tickled!

"Hold him down," Martin said quickly to the other brothers, his voice rising at the end as his mouth broke into a smile. Two other brothers joined the one holding him—hands pinned his legs and right shoulder to the floor.

Rafa was convulsing in laughter now as Martin probed the wound. Martin leaned forward to wipe his finger around inside Rafa's chest, like he was fishing change from the seams of a couch. Tears formed at Rafa's eyes and he looked at the brothers holding him and they began to laugh, too.

"Stop, stop, stop!" Rafa tried to say—the air from his throat sounding like *stah, stah stah.* It was too much—the tickling. He gave himself over to it, remembering wrestling with Papa on the living room floor with his brothers and sister, and Papa holding each down in turn and tickling them under their arms. The joy of being so small in the hands of someone so big, so safe, and so . . . fun.

Rafa inhaled deeply and screamed a hard laugh. Something in his throat let go—like melting icicles giving way from a roofline—and the air passing through his mouth grabbed hold of his vocal chords and rang forth in a peal of laughter that sounded like a trumpet blast.

"Got it!" yelled Martin, holding up a stub of lead. "You're gonna be okay, kid!"

***

After parking the bus, Bishop Newell had hung back by the door to the factory to see how things unfolded. He'd prayed for this for a long time without knowing what it would look like—the scattering of the proud, the fall of the mighty, the raising of the lowly.

Even this bit with the kid—laughter and joy falling over them all like rain—it was so unexpected, yet so familiar.

The brothers and the boy were still catching their breath, coughing and holding their bellies and wiping their eyes, when he stepped in.

"Well, Martin, I'm glad we've been training," he said. "This is going to be fun to share with the rest of the city."

Martin took a deep breath to collect himself. He looked around, and seeing the three armed men who'd been holding Rafa, seemed to remember the danger. "What should we do with them?" he asked.

"The furnace seems to work," said one of the

brothers.

Newell knew instinctively that rendering judgment was out of their hands just as surely as bringing their own salvation had been.

"That won't be necessary," he said. "But we should do something to mark them so everyone knows who they are."

He walked over to the boy, who was sitting cross legged now. His hand was over his chest, and the bleeding had seemed to stop. Newell bent over and wiped his hand across the puddle of blood on the floor next to the kid.

The brothers holding the three men lined them up, and Newell approached each, smearing blood across their foreheads like he was anointing them. The deep red stained each man's brow, dripping in places—down one man's nose and around another's cheekbone. They looked like they were painted for war.

"You can let them go," Newell said. "They're harmless now."

The brothers released their grips and the largest of the men reached to his head to wipe away the blood, but it had dried already. He wiped harder, checking his hand to see if it was coming off, but his skin seemed stained.

The three men hurried out the door into the darkness.

"Let's open this contraption," Newell said, turning to the furnace.

44

Bryant greeted Vivian at the front door of his home before she could knock. Martin was still walking up the steps carrying the box of supplies she'd left in the back seat in her distraction. Vivian couldn't tell if the flush in Bryant's cheeks was from enthusiasm or just part of who he was now—both times she'd seen him, she was surprised at how . . . *healthy* he looked—after all he'd been through.

"Come in, come in," he said, standing aside while holding the door open. "She just started breathing. It's amazing—come see!"

Vivian stepped into the house; Martin followed and placed the box on the end table by the couch. Bryant led them to the back bedroom, and as Vivian stepped through the hallway, she remembered the last time she walked that path. The grief from that day was gone, but not the strange feeling of it all being unreal.

"Come in—come see her," Bryant cooed as he stepped into the room. "She's beautiful."

Vivian had been wondering about this moment for the last two days—ever since she heard Estelline was returning. Would she look like a zombie? An angel? Would she have that pallid wooden look from when they dressed her at the funeral home?

She entered the room to see Bryant on the far side of their bed. Estelline's body lay still on the mattress, a white sheet under a plaid blanket draped perfectly over the form of her figure. Vivian stepped closer and peered into her face.

It was Estelline, no doubt—even more so than she could have remembered. She looked like she'd spent a week in bed with a fever that had just broken—pale and thin in the face and deep around the eyes, but content and restful. Vivian looked over her body and could see the faintest rise and fall over Estelline's stomach, as though she was trying to hide her breathing.

"Bryant, I . . . I don't know what to say. How is this possible?" Vivian said. "I mean, I believe the words you said, but even seeing her now—seeing you—I don't understand."

"She looks great, Bryant," Martin said. "She's recovered a lot in just a few days. You'll have her back in no time.

"It is quite a shock, though, isn't it?" he added, nodding toward Vivian.

"It's okay, Vivian," Bryant said. "I don't really get it, either. But we'll figure it out. You brought your lab equipment, right?"

"In the box Martin carried in."

"One thing I've learned—and Martin has helped me see this—is that having her here looks momentous and dramatic, but it's not that different from what we've been experiencing all along," Bryant said. "The brothers with the pregnancy hormone, the stories about Martin here, what happened to me at the lake—we've been seeing it develop all along. It's all part of a whole."

She reached out and touched Estelline's hand—it wasn't warm, but it wasn't cold, either. It felt pliable and supple, the way the leaves of a plant feel in sunlight.

"Dollars to donuts, Viv—you take a blood sample from Stella, I bet it matches up with where the brothers were about a year ago."

Following and documenting Estelline's recovery would not only make sense of all their research, it would also clear a path so others would know what to expect and how to respond. Vivian knew that this information could ground policy and protocols. Bryant was right—she had a feeling these dots connected.

"The world won't believe what's happening, and they certainly won't understand it," Martin said, "but Estelline's not the only one coming back. And if you can describe it as a pattern, that's information we can use. Maybe we can get a timeline going so we know when to expect someone and make sure their family is around to welcome them back."

"How are the other brothers?" Bryant asked.

"Doing great—in fact, what happened at the factory sent us to our cemetery and we brought up Brother Gatien's casket. He passed on Epiphany of last year and he looked just like Estelline does here.

"And two other brothers are already planning a trip to El Salvador to accompany three families who just recently lost loved ones. They want to go back to see if this is happening there, to gather with their extended family. We've always called ourselves 'men with hope to bring,' but danged if it isn't taking on new meaning as we walk with people."

It all seemed to make sense, but Vivian didn't quite trust it yet. It felt like a new diet fad or TV series everyone was gushing about—she believed everyone to be genuine, but couldn't set aside her skepticism.

So she decided to do what she's always done: pick up the pieces, gather the data, look for patterns. She admitted that it would be exciting to be at the front of this. If it spreads, it'll be the only question worth asking for the foreseeable future. The truth will out, she knew. It always does.

***

In the last hundred yards of his morning walk, Father Howard Brown picked up his pace to a jog and came to a huffing halt in front of the steps to St. Patrick's Church. He put his hands on his knees and hung his head until his panting subsided.

He gazed at the heavy oak doors to the church as he straightened his back. It had never really occurred to him that there were three sets of double doors across the front of the church, but only the middle set was ever used. Come to think of it, they only ever used one side of the central pair—the five other doors were always locked.

He walked up the steps slowly, lugged open the door, and entered the church. The vestibule was dark—the only light came from the sunlight streaming into the body of the building and leaking back under the choir loft toward the entrance. As his eyes adjusted, he began to see the space in a new way.

Because the side doors were not being used, the space behind them inside the vestibule had been filled in with seldom-used items: dusty pamphlets, lost-and-found items, boxes of fake evergreens used during the Christmas season.

This stuff had to go, Howard concluded. A quick

browse through the Christmas boxes confirmed the impulse—it was either junk that hadn't been used in years or it was cheap décor that had outlived its lifespan. He began hauling boxes to the large trash bin behind the church. The women of the Altar Society will probably throw a fit, but it was time for something new.

He was walking back from the trash bin for another load when he ran into Bishop Newell waiting for him in front of the church.

"You look good, Howard—lost weight?"

"Bishop—hey there. Thought you were in Rome."

"Just a quick trip back to gather some things. Looks like I'll be there a while."

"Must mean you're doing some good," Howard said.

"We're ahead of the curve here in Andover, so our experience is proving helpful, especially the data we have on the brothers.

"I don't think I'm coming back," Newell continued after a moment. "You might be administrator here for the foreseeable future. I'm here to see how you're doing with it all."

"Honestly, I feel good—I'm probably healthier than I've been in a long time," Howard replied.

The mention of the administrator role confirmed the queasiness he was feeling from the outing, so he decided to change the subject. "The folks over at St. Joseph started something that other parishes are starting to pick up—it's a good idea," he said. "Know how a team of old ladies would make lunch for families after funerals—the ham sandwiches and potato salad and coffee cake? Well, they are doing the same thing when someone returns now—after they get back on their feet, the family gathers all kinds of kin in the parish hall to catch up. It's a homecoming of sorts—the receptions go on into the night. They're even looking at an arrangement with that Black Fox fella to provide beer.

"So it's all new, but we're figuring it out," Howard continued.

"That's good to hear, Howard. Thanks for organizing things. I knew you had good instincts," Newell said. He took a half step closer for the personal inquiry: "And, the drinking?"

"Sober for three weeks now," Howard replied. "Meetings help. The people have zero tolerance for any kind of bullshit, which I like. Looking back, I can see that I've been right with the Lord, but it was well past time to get right with myself. I'm coming face-to-face with some unpleasant realities about my father and self-image, but I'm working on it and it feels like I'm finally getting somewhere.

"Like the apostle said, 'When I was a child, I reasoned as a child. When I became a man, I put side childish things.'"

Newell finished the line for him: "For when the perfect comes, the partial will pass away."

***

Isabel DuPree double checked her directions as she drove past the *tienda* in Wilmot. Just seeing the orange tables through the store window was enough to bring back the wormy feeling she had when she talked with Siego that day. She remembered that look he gave her as she was pulling out—like she was a cockroach just out of reach.

She turned left and headed back out of town toward the Villahermosa residence and put those thoughts of Siego behind her. That's all he was now—a bad memory.

The cinderblock home was only a few minutes down the road, and when she pulled in and turned off the car, she could hear children in the backyard playing. She saw a white whiffle ball speed past the far corner of the house, and heard someone call, "Foul!"

Aurora warmly welcomed her inside and offered her some coffee, which she accepted. They exchanged pleasantries as she prepared the brew, the grounds cutting through the scent of spices and corn emanating from the small kitchen.

Isabel had prepared a protocol in Spanish for Aurora, and laid everything out on the table once they had settled past the small talk. Aurora looked concerned but attentive—a well-worn single vertical furrow of concentration showing in the middle of her brow.

"So you know the reason I'm here—to discuss the process for Raymundo's return. It is a very exciting time, so we want to make sure that it goes smoothly, and that your family knows what to expect.

"The best guess we have for his return is September 15—you can see when he died here," she pointed to a paper with a green bar across it hash-marked into a timeline. "This is about where we pinpoint the changes"—she pointed to a mark to the right—"so then you can just count backward to see when he'll be back.

"This packet here shows you some basic tips for taking care of the body as it reconstitutes, but the basics are just to keep him warm. It seems to help if you can rub the body with lotion or oil—it's good for the skin and circulation. And then you can just expect functions to return gradually—first breathing, the consciousness. He'll need lots of sleep, but he'll get stronger."

Isabel looked at Aurora, but her concentration hadn't broken yet. She was tracking the information very carefully, and Isabel could see that she was losing the forest for the trees.

"Aurora, this means you can recover his body," Isabel said, reaching out to touch her on the arm. "We have teams in place at the cemeteries to help—you can go get Raymundo now. He can come home."

The furrow in Aurora's brow widened and disappeared into horizontal lines as though her eyebrows were sending quivering ripples above her face. The smile she exuded ignited something in Isabel—sharing this part with a family always did that. Isabel's eyes welled with tears and her voice cracked when she said, "It's good news, isn't it?"

***

When she felt the smile from her dream break across her face, Estelline realized she was waking. She began clawing her way back to the surface of consciousness, struggling to open her eyes. Why was she so tired?

Bryant was there, already awake.

"Stella, honey—hi," he whispered. She thought it must be really early for her to feel so groggy, but he sounded like he'd been up for an hour already. It reminded her of when he'd prepared her breakfast in bed for Mother's Day the week after they learned she was pregnant.

"Bfff . . . Bly . . ." Why couldn't she talk? She was really out of it. "B—I dreamed," she managed. "I dreamed . . . Tally was with me. I met her—our baby. But she was a girl."

Her eyes came open and found focus on Bryant's face. He was leaning over her, close, and he was crying—why? Tears were streaming down his cheeks and dripping onto the blanket, but he was . . . happy.

"I know, Stella, I know," he said. "She's right here. We've been waiting for you."

ACKNOWLEDGEMENTS

I come from farming areas in South Dakota that carry the names of Bryant and Estelline and Mayfield (in fact, most of the names from this story come from towns in my home state), so I know that it takes many hands to tend a field. Many people have cultivated my imagination, from planting seeds, to watering soil, to tending weeds. Here at the harvest, so many of them come to mind with gratitude.

The earliest and most consistent gardeners in my life are my parents, Rollie and Peg Noem, with their unflagging encouragement and love. The three things that make this story tick—faith, baseball, beer—I learned from them, in that order. My sisters, Molly and Emily, have supplied good fertilizer, and I say that with a big brother's wink. Extended family—Stoughs and Fultons and Herreras—have kept me going with their interest and support.

I'm a product of good educators, going back to the Benedictine Sisters who taught me at St. Joseph School in Pierre, South Dakota. Ms. Edgington of Custer saw a spark in me at an early age. I'm grateful for the good people—classmates, colleagues, friends—at the University of Portland and the University of Notre Dame for their excellence and faithfulness. Another organization that inspired me: the Coalition of Immokalee Workers in Florida. I covered their struggle for justice in my days as a reporter and I laud their advocacy—those workers and families shaped a big part of this story.

My life has been profoundly shaped by the priests and brothers of the Congregation of Holy Cross—they have educated and formed me as teachers, pastors, servants, and friends. Father Stephen Koeth planted a small seed long ago when he saw a writer in me before I did, and Father Frank Murphy has helped me see the need to keep going. The good Fathers Jim Gallagher, Greg Haake, Pete McCormick, and Nate Wills have all brought me hope in this endeavor as honest, thoughtful first readers. I'm really lucky to have these guys in my corner.

A number of other early readers contributed mightily to this story through their candor and confidence in me: Steve and Maureen Blaha (who helped me see with the eyes and heart of a nurse), Kristina Houck, Ken Hallenius, and Holy Cross Fathers Kevin Grove, Gerry Olinger, and Terry Ehrman (who let me read his doctoral thesis on the resurrection of the body). Mike Hebbeler read a first swing at the founding of the Andover Flambeaus and waved me to second. I tip my hat to the whole Sappy Moffitt Baseball League—in particular the Liners and league champion Porters. Marty Moran loaned me considerable technical advice and encouragement. I'm grateful for the work of Stephen Barany in sharing his design expertise. And thanks to the first section of ENGL 40850 that met in the fall of 2015, where I workshopped the first third of this story: Mary Humphrey, Gerard Ledley, Gabriela Leskur, and Maura Monahan. Valerie Sayers's guidance and advice has been indispensable.

Finally, this work is only possible because of my family: Oscar, Simon, Lucy, who taught me to love more deeply than I could have imagined; and my dear one, Stacey, where everything begins and ends and begins again.

ABOUT THE AUTHOR

Josh Noem

Josh serves as Senior Editor of Grotto Network. He grew up in Custer State Park in the Black Hills of South Dakota.

He earned a bachelor's degree in the great books from the University of Notre Dame and returned for a master's in theology after volunteering at an alcohol treatment center in Alaska, working as a technician in a nuclear power plant, joining the United Steelworkers union, fighting wildfire with the Forest Service, and editing a Catholic newspaper in Florida. He was awarded the Eileen Egan Journalism award from Catholic Relief Services for reporting on healthcare in Haiti.

He lives in South Bend, Indiana, with his family, and plays second base for the Lowell Porters in the Sappy Moffitt Baseball League. You can connect with him on Twitter @gardenoem. This is his first novel.

Made in the USA
Monee, IL
20 July 2020

36795662R00204